Return to the
Italian Quarter

Domenica de Rosa started her career working at the *Bookseller*, and went on to work in children's publishing, in publicity and in editorial. Under the name Elly Griffiths she is the author of the acclaimed and bestselling Dr Ruth Galloway series of mysteries, and the Stephens and Mephisto mysteries. Domenica is half Italian and loves the Tuscan coast, although she mainly settles for Brighton, where she lives with her husband, their twins and their cat.

Also by Domenica de Rosa

One Summer in Tuscany
(previously published as *Summer School*)

The Eternal City

Secret of the Villa Serena
(previously published as *Villa Serena*)

As Elly Griffiths

THE DR RUTH GALLOWAY MYSTERIES

The Crossing Places
The Janus Stone
The House at Sea's End
A Room Full of Bones
Dying Fall
The Outcast Dead
The Ghost Fields
The Woman in Blue
The Chalk Pit

THE STEPHENS AND MEPHISTO MYSTERIES

The Zig Zag Girl
Smoke and Mirrors
The Blood Card

Domenica De Rosa

Return to the Italian Quarter

Quercus

First published in Great Britain in 2004 by
Headline Review as *The Italian Quarter*

This paperback edition published in 2018 by

Quercus Editions Ltd
Carmelite House
50 Victoria Embankment
London EC4Y 0DZ

An Hachette UK company

A CIP catalogue record for this book is available
from the British Library

PB ISBN 978 1 78648 434 5

10 9 8 7 6 5 4 3 2

Typeset by CC Book Production

Printed and bound in Great Britain by Clays Ltd, Elcograf S.p.A

In memory of my beloved father, Felice de Rosa

' … my Italy

My own hills! Are you 'ware of me, my hills,

How I burn towards you? Do you feel tonight

The urgency and yearning of my soul,

As sleeping mothers feel the suckling babe

And smile?'

Elizabeth Barrett Browning, 'Aurora Leigh'

OH! OH! ANTONIO

In quaint native dress an Italian maid
Was seeping distress as the streets she strayed
Searching in every part for her bold sweetheart
And his ice-cream cart.
Her English was bad
It cannot be denied
And so to herself
In Italian she cried.
Oh! Oh! Antonio, he's gone away
Left me alone-ee-o, all on my own-ee-o
I want to meet him with his new sweetheart
Then up will go Antonio and his ice-cream cart.

Music Hall song, 1908

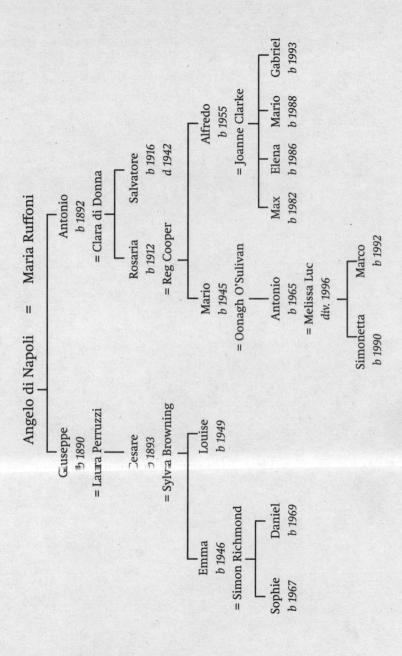

Angelo di Napoli = Maria Ruffoni

Giuseppe
b 1890
= Laura Perruzzi

Cesare
b 1893
= Sylvia Browning

Antonio
b 1892
= Clara di Donna

Rosaria
b 1912
= Reg Cooper

Salvatore
b 1916
d 1942

Mario
b 1945
= Oonagh O'Sulivan

Alfredo
b 1955
= Joanne Clarke

Antonio
b 1965
= Melissa Luc
div. 1996

Max
b 1982

Elena
b 1986

Mario
b 1988

Gabriel
b 1993

Simonetta
b 1990

Marco
b 1992

Emma
b 1946
= Simon Richmond

Louise
b 1949

Sophie
b 1967

Daniel
b 1969

PROLOGUE

Naples, 1897

The photographer looked doubtfully at the two boys. Obviously their mother thought them delightful in their stiff white sailor suits but, then, every mother thought that; it was the first thing you learnt in this job. The second thing you learnt was not to argue.

'Beautiful children, Signora.'

The faded woman beside him seemed to be trying to smile. 'Yes. They are good boys. Giuseppe and Antonio.'

'Fine names.' When in doubt, try flattery.

'Thank you.'

She seemed about to weep – better change the subject. 'Now, I have a selection of backgrounds to choose from. Niagara Falls, the Taj Mahal, all-purpose indoor scene.'

'I want it here.'

'Here?'

'Yes, here. This is where they come from, after all.'

The photographer could have said something profound but he looked about him and said nothing. A Naples backstreet, houses crammed together so tightly that no light shone between them, washing zigzagging crazily overhead, the smell of fish and cooking and the sea. 'Here?'

'Yes, here, by this doorway.'

Afterwards the seven-year-old Giuseppe could never remember if he had imagined the whole thing. The photographer with his cloak like a conjurer, the white suits, himself standing for what seemed like hours with his arm round five-year-old Antonio. And the man in the dog cart, with his gloves and the carnation in his buttonhole. Had he imagined him too? One thing was certain: there was nothing imaginary about his father's rage when he came home and discovered the photograph. In vain did his mother protest tearfully that it had cost nothing. His father swore and raged even more, adding that it was not even a good photograph – which was true. Giuseppe looked grim and unhappy, Antonio positively foolish. The only clear thing in the photograph was the background: the crumbling doorway and the bright Neapolitan sky.

PART ONE

CHAPTER ONE

August, 1983

Like his namesake, Uncle Fausto is associated in my mind with a cloud of smoke. When he first appeared in my life, surrounded by flames, he seemed almost diabolic. To my grandfather, years earlier, he had appeared more in the guise of a guardian angel.

It was at a barbecue. Or, rather, it would have been a barbecue if Cesare, my grandfather, had not thought the concept vulgar or, worse, Australian. As it was, he had had a brick structure built in his large garden, as far removed from the three-legged suburban variety as possible. The look was *al fresco* rather than barbecue (my younger brother Daniel once lived an alternative existence as a gangster called Al Fresco), with cutlets cooking over wood fires, stuffed tomatoes, green olive oil brought over specially from Lucca, wine cooling in earthenware buckets. There was even a vase of flowers on the table. Of course, it was my grandmother, Sylvia, who actually did the cooking, stuffing and pouring of olive oil and wine, but the directive came from the top. From Caesar himself.

My job was to lay the table, which I loved doing in my grandmother's house. My brother Daniel and my cousin Antonio had carried it down to the sunken garden that morning, and it was bigger than anything in our house. It seated twenty with ease and the white embroidered cloth was more like the covering for an altar than anything suited to domestic use. Our house, on a tidy ranch-style development in Surrey, was full of neat, bright, wipe-clean surfaces; my grandparents' house had dark furniture that loomed at you alarmingly in the dark. It had heavy velvet curtains and shady corners where you could curl up and read. The sole aim of our house was to be able to see through from one room into another – 'open plan', my mother called it, 'Scandinavian'. Grandmother's house was full of light and shade, like a church. The separate rooms had their own mysteries and identities and nowhere was there anything that could possibly have been called Scandinavian.

As I placed the raffia mats between the bumpy circles of embroidery, I imagined that I was an altar boy lighting the candles at the beginning of mass. I placed the heavy silver cutlery in the centre of the table and covered it with a linen napkin (Cesare was paranoid about flies). I thought about the statues in church on Good Friday when they are covered with purple drapes and how, after you have kissed the cross, the altar boy wipes the place clean with an ecclesiastical napkin. Girls were allowed to be altar servers but I had never fancied it. Aged fourteen, Daniel was already a terrifyingly reverent altar boy.

So, this is the scene. The table, glittering in the heat, yet to disintegrate into the familiar chaos of a family meal: spilt wine, espresso in tiny brittle cups, bread snatched up from the ground because it is unlucky to drop it. Cesare's Alsatian panting in the shade of the oak tree. A baby crawling happily across the grass. Cesare sitting in 'his' chair, brought from the house: he would not, for a moment, consider sitting in an inferior garden version. Antonio filling Cesare's glass with the face of an acolyte. Alfredo, Antonio's uncle – his is the baby – looking nervously at the Alsatian. Joanne, Alfredo's wife, wondering if she dares ask for lemonade rather than wine. She does so a few minutes later and is ignored. Louisa, my aunt, lighting a cigarette and inhaling deeply. Daniel, in an Italian football shirt, eating olives and spitting out the pips. Simon, my father, wishing he wouldn't but afraid to speak out in front of Cesare, whose often-stated view is that Daniel can do anything he wants.

The occasion is Cesare's seventieth birthday; the day is 15 August. It is the Feast of the Assumption and Daniel and my mother have already been to mass. Cesare, of course, is a Leo; in fact, had he not been born in August he would probably have moved his birthday, refusing to submit to the indignity of a goat, scorpion, crab or (especially) a virgin. It is mid-afternoon, the time Cesare considers proper for lunch even though Joanne is quite faint with hunger, and the day is at its hottest.

Sylvia carries the meat, wrapped in sage leaves secured by cocktail sticks, to the table. She is small with curly dark hair, picturesquely streaked with grey. At fifty-seven, she is thirteen years younger than Cesare and can still be called a pretty woman. She handles the meat with practised ease; over the years she has become as good an Italian cook as Cesare's dear departed and practically sainted mother. The pasta will be cooked indoors (until it is Al Dente, Al Fresco's younger brother) but outdoor cooking of the meat is deemed necessary. We all sit up hungrily. Joanne scoops up her baby and gives him a breadstick to chew. Antonio pauses in his endless monologue about Ferraris. Emma, my mother, starts doing some ostentatious plate arranging. Sylvia goes to light the fire.

'Don't do that,' comes Cesare's shout. 'One of the *men* will do it.' He gives the noun a faintly malicious emphasis. 'Alfredo?' he suggests.

Alfredo gets up and nervously approaches the sacred flame. His first two matches go out, Daniel sniggers, Louisa proffers her lighter. Alfredo approaches again. The wood refuses to light. Cesare makes some comment in Italian, which no one understands, though Daniel pretends to. Joanne looks embarrassed; her baby begins to cry with alarming suddenness. Antonio looks like a particularly smug statue.

'Here, Fredo!' Daniel shouts. 'I'll get it going.'

My mother shouts at him, too late, to be careful. Daniel

picks up the paraffin (meant for emergencies only) and pours it liberally on to the wood. At the same time, Louisa's lighter flares into life. The fire goes up in a solid sheet of blue flame. Joanne screams. The baby wails. The dog howls. Everyone shouts at once. Cesare throws his wine on to the blaze, part in libation, part in a singularly unsuccessful attempt to extinguish the inferno. Antonio picks up Sylvia's beautiful blue vase and throws both flowers and water on to the fire.

By the time the flames have subsided, Uncle Fausto is standing in our midst.

He looked like any properly brought-up devil. His dark suit and stiff white collar were somehow macabre against the bright green afternoon. It was as if a funeral director had appeared suddenly on Brighton beach, startling the sunbathing crowds with his black gloves and top hat.

Cesare certainly stared at him as if he were the devil himself, as if he were about to drag Don Juan back into hell. There was a moment's total silence and then Uncle Fausto threw himself into Cesare's arms.

'*Fratello mio.*'

'Faustino.'

The two men embraced, parted, embraced again and then proceeded to *speak to each other in Italian*. Do the italics surprise you? Does it surprise you that, amid the wine and the olives and the Italian football shirt, no one present spoke Italian?

It surprises me a little now, when I think of it. Cesare, of course, speaks perfect English and he never talked to his daughters, Emma and Louisa, in Italian. Why not? Then I thought it was to keep Italian special and magical, a secret that he would let us catch glimpses of but never share. We could all say odd words but none of us could string a sentence together. Now, I think it was because he did not want to be challenged as the family's leading Italian. To be fair, our parents gave Daniel and me a chance to learn the language and I couldn't be bothered. Daniel went to a few lessons, I think, and learnt some Neapolitan swear words from Cesare but that was the limit of it. Funnily enough, Antonio spoke the most Italian and he must have learnt it from his grandmother, the dreaded anti-Italian Aunt Rosaria, as his father, Mario, speaks no Italian at all.

'Emma,' said Cesare, 'get a chair for your uncle Fausto.'

Even my pleasure at hearing my mother spoken to like

a child (or a servant) did not distract me from the question looming larger and larger in my head. In the end, only Daniel was brave enough to voice it: 'Is he *really* our uncle?'

Cesare looked at Fausto, who laughed delightedly. 'My grandson,' he explained. Fausto looked at Daniel admiringly. 'No, Daniele,' Cesare continued, 'I just call him my brother out of affection. He is no relation to you.'

'Unfortunately,' said Fausto, with a polite smile around the table. Emma arrived with the chair and Sylvia started serving the pasta, giving Fausto a particularly generous helping. In the background, the meat began to crackle on the flames.

'What a fine family you have, Cesare,' said Fausto, helping himself to Parmesan. Unlike Cesare, he had a distinct Italian accent. 'Myself, I have only one son and he is a disappointment to me.' He sighed.

'Come, Fausto,' said Cesare, brightening at this news, 'children are never a disappointment.' This was news to Emma and Louisa, who exchanged glances. 'What is he called, this son of yours? Is he married?'

'Roberto.' Fausto sighed. 'Robertino. No, he is not married. He is a womaniser.' He made it sound like a profession, like teacher or fireman.

Cesare laughed heartily. 'So were we in the old days, *amico mio!*'

Daniel could bear it no longer. 'When were the old days? How did you two meet?'

Fausto reached out to pat him on the head, then smiled widely. 'Why, we met in prison, Daniele.'

CHAPTER 2

June, 1998

The answerphone light is flashing when I get in from school. I dump my briefcase on the hall table, letting the two folders I am holding under my arm fall to the floor. Why do teachers always have so much to carry? If I have a vision of a glamorous job, it is one that you can do carrying only a mobile phone and a designer handbag. I dump my (non-designer) handbag too, letting purse, phone and Tampax join the pile on the floor, and bend to stroke my cat, Tybalt, who is purring crazily round my ankles.

I have lived in this flat now for five years and I have finally got it how I like it. I'm slightly ashamed to admit that how I like it is very, very tidy. I have always thought of myself as a wild, creative, zany, 'let's do the show right here' sort of girl, so it is rather a disappointment to learn that I'm the sort of person who colour codes their milk bottles and keeps spaghetti in a special jar marked 'pasta'. Now I pick up the files and arrange them neatly on my desk (I'm not going to open them, I'm not that bad), put everything back into my handbag, hang up my coat (on a hanger, not by the collar), feed the cat and wash up the fork, before I check my messages.

Five messages. One from an ex-boyfriend, Rick, who is getting married. Please, God, don't let him want me to be best woman or anything that shows the world how maturely we've handled our break-up. Actually, it was quite amicable and I like his fiancée very much, but not enough to turn up at church in a hat and read from Omar Khayyám. Two messages from my mother, 'Hallo, Sophie. It's Mum.' I can almost hear her putting quotation marks around the hated M-word. She wishes Daniel and I would call her Mummy, like characters from *The Archers*, or even Ma, anything but Mum. Hard luck, Mum. One message from Jane, my head of department, asking me to bring in my lesson plan for *Macbeth* tomorrow (damn, I'll have to open those files, after all).

One message left.

'Sophie. It's Antonio. Can you ring me?'

Antonio. My cousin, or second cousin to be precise. He is two years older than me. When we were younger, we used to be pushed together at family gatherings – 'Antonio, take Sophie to see your spacehopper/model railway/new motorbike.' Only Cesare, believing as he does that when any man and woman are in a proximity of less than ten yards they will immediately have sex, discouraged this closeness. 'It's unhealthy,' he would say, vaguely but none the less dogmatically. 'They're cousins, after all.' Well, Cesare needn't have worried. I didn't have much time for Antonio in those days. He seemed like an unattractively keen Cesare clone. He supported Juventus when all his schoolfriends liked Man U. He wore a large gold cross round his neck and went on Catholic youth rallies. He claimed that his favourite music was Italian opera at the same time that I had a crush on Adam Ant (Cesare: 'The man is clearly sick, wearing all that make-up. Luckily we don't have that kind of thing in Italy'). Added to this, he was physically unattractive, with a large nose, greasy skin and frizzy hair. Really, it would have taken all the spacehoppers in the world for me even to kiss him.

Things changed a bit when he went to University College, London: he didn't live at home but in an impressively dingy flat-share. He and his flatmates threw famously wild parties, the kind that went on for days with neighbours coming in to complain and being found days later, sleeping in the bath. By the time I was at King's College, London, after coming back from Italy, Antonio was a postgraduate with long hair and frightening opinions on experimental plays.

I went to a couple of his parties and had to admit that the new student Antonio, with his frizzy hair grown into a Medusa-like mane and his laid-back (almost certainly drug-induced) manner, was a distinct improvement. But we were never really close. For a start, Antonio always had a disconcertingly pretty girlfriend in attendance, usually blonde and perfect in contrast to his general grunginess. For another thing, we hadn't much in common apart from our family – and who wanted to talk about *them* all the time? We were both reading English but Antonio seemed to inhabit a different literary world. I acted in prim Oscar Wilde revivals, he improvised a show about masturbation at the Edinburgh Festival. My favourite writer was Charles Dickens, his was e. e. cummings. Hopeless.

And so it continued. After university, I trained as a teacher. Antonio ditched his PhD and disappeared on the hippie trail to Goa, came back, cleaned himself up, cut his hair and got a job at the BBC. This was an exceptionally annoying period in his life: not only did he have a good job ('He's at the BBC,' Aunt Rosaria would say, in a loud whisper. 'At *Wood Lane.*' As if the address made it even more impressive) but he got married, to an irritatingly pretty girl called Melissa, whose feet always seemed to be in ballet positions. His wedding day was a real low point for me. I didn't have a boyfriend at the time so I had to take my friend Marcus, whom everybody (except Cesare) knew was gay. When Melissa came prancing down the aisle, looking stunning in an off-the-shoulder dress, I felt tears of envy coming to my eyes. I was furious with myself – I was meant to be a feminist, for God's sake, but that didn't make it any better. Next to me, Marcus was sobbing happily into his silk handkerchief.

Now things are a bit different. Antonio is a freelance journalist and he has just started to become rather famous. I'm always hearing him on the radio, the sort of programme in which everyone sits around being clever about politics. I think it's his name that attracts people. An oxymoron of a name:

Antonio Cooper. Aunt Rosaria married an Englishman called Cooper (though always known to Cesare as 'the bastard') but gave both her sons Italian names. Her eldest son, Mario, despite marrying an Irish woman, carried on the tradition and called his son Antonio. I don't know why he doesn't just call himself Tony. But, famous or not, Antonio is also *divorced*. He and Melissa had two children and got divorced seven years later. It is said to have broken Aunt Rosaria's heart and I imagine it like the heart on the statues of the Sacred Heart at school: held aloft outside her body, split in two.

So, what with one thing and another, it is years since Antonio has called me at home. In fact, I am slightly irritated by his assumption that I have his number. Looking through my Filofax, I see that I have three addresses for him. The first sounds studenty, Flat 1B somewhere in Brixton. The second unmistakably married, 2 Vicarage Gardens, Hertfordshire. The third is noncommittal, 12 Raleigh Gardens, Chiswick.

The Chiswick address has a phone number so I ring.

'Sophie,' he says immediately, as if he's been waiting for me to call. Weird.

'Antonio. You left a message. What is it? Are they short of panellists on *Question Time*?'

He laughs, but then immediately switches into serious mode, as if the radio programme had moved from jokes about this week's headlines to serious topical issues. 'Can I see you?'

'See me?' I echo stupidly. 'Why?'

'It's . . . well, it's hard to explain . . . It's about Cesare.'

'*Cesare*?'

'Can I come round?'

'When?'

'This evening. Is that all right?'

Standing at the window, I watch Antonio arrive. He parks his car (a Lancia, I notice) under the tree and gets out. Looking down, I see that his hair is going grey and this gives me a real jolt. Antonio is, after all, only a couple of years older than me. Perhaps in an attempt to distract from the grey hair, he is wearing a leather jacket and jeans. He points at his car with one of those executive I'm-too-important-to-waste-time-locking-my-car gadgets and strides purposefully towards the entrance to the flats.

Close up, he doesn't look too bad. His hair is still predominantly black and the wild curls of his younger self have been tamed with a short haircut. He looks tanned and prosperous, checking an expensive-looking watch as if my time is already running out. 'Nice flat,' he says, insincerely.

'Great,' I say. 'Hope you locked your car.'

He looks worried momentarily (those gadgets are all very well, Antonio, but it's not as reassuring as turning the key yourself), then decides it was a joke and smiles.

I offer him coffee but decide against making the real thing as Antonio will no doubt appear some day soon in a Sunday magazine feature entitled 'Me and My Cappuccino'. We chat for a bit and Tybalt tries to sit on Antonio's lap (good mark) but he pushes him off (bad mark). Finally, I say: 'So, what's this about Cesare?'

At nearly eighty-five, Cesare is alive and well and living in a townhouse in Canterbury. He and Sylvia sold the country place about five years ago and, although Cesare enjoyed the lord-of-the-manor pose, this really suits him better. He can stroll out in the morning for a newspaper and a cup of coffee and watch the world revolve around him. He loves to walk in the grounds of the cathedral and tell people that 'it was ours once', meaning that in the happy days of archbishops murdered at the foot of the altar, it was a Catholic church.

The city walls remind him of an idealised Rome with no Vespas or one-way systems or young Italians in tweed jackets pretending not to understand him.

'I know this journalist,' says Antonio, 'called Guido della Francesca.'

'Blimey.'

Antonio smiles briefly. 'He's not what you'd imagine. Anyway, he's writing a book about Italian prisoners of war during the Second World War and he's going to interview Cesare.'

'Why?'

'Well, you know Cesare was a prisoner of war.'

'Yes.' That's about all I do know, though. For someone whose favourite subject is himself, Cesare is remarkably secretive about his war experiences. We know some of the pre-war stuff. Cesare was a racing driver and seemed to have lived a classic 1930s existence: chasing women, racing cars and generally behaving badly. I have a wonderful photograph of him lounging against one of those little rocket-shaped cars, wearing a silk scarf and a remarkably smug expression. But after the war had started, nothing.

'Well, apparently his Home Office files have just been released.'

'There are Home Office files *on Cesare*?'

'So Guido says. And, according to him, they make pretty interesting reading.' He pauses and sips his coffee with an expression of distaste.

'In what way?'

'Well, they're all about how he was, and I quote, a "leading and fervent Fascist".'

I can't think of anything to say so we sit in silence for a moment, listening to the summer roar of traffic outside. In the distance a police siren sounds.

'Are you sure?' I ask at last.

'Guido is. He had the cheek to ring me for a quote. I said that, to my knowledge, my great-uncle is the only person in Canterbury to have *Marxism Today* delivered.'

I am beginning to see why Antonio is so upset. It's not just the family honour he is worried about but his own reputation as Radio 4's favourite cuddly lefty. 'My uncle the Fascist by *Westminster Blue's* Antonio Cooper'.

'Was he a Fascist?' I ask.

Antonio shrugs. 'How should I know? All that Communist stuff now could be one of his jokes. What I'm worried about is what will happen when he meets Guido. God knows what he'll say to him. That's why I think you should be there.'

'Me? Why me?'

'Because, knowing Cesare, he'll insist that the interview is in Italian and you speak Italian.'

Yes, I now speak pretty fluent Italian. But that's another story.

'How can I be there? I can't just ring and invite myself.'

'Yes, you can. You know how Cesare likes an audience. And, if you don't, how will I . . . *we* know if he's telling the truth?'

'How do we know anyway? We don't know what went on all those years ago.'

'No,' Antonio agrees gloomily. 'And, apart from Cesare, there's only one person who does.'

I nod. 'Uncle Fausto.'

Two more things happened the summer that Uncle Fausto appeared. The first was that I lost my virginity, to a boy called Martin who doesn't otherwise come into the story. The second was that I asked to see a copy of Cesare's birth certificate. I think it was for a school project. We were doing the Second World War for history A level (the examiners seemed fascinated by extreme politics – the choice was either Fascism in Europe or Communism in China). I wanted to write a biography of Cesare: born Naples 1913, prisoner of war 1940-45, etc. I thought he would be pleased.

I brought the subject up during one of our regular Sunday lunches with my grandparents. The pattern of these was always the same. We would set off from Surrey full of excitement, my mother might bring a pudding she had made, never wine because Cesare declared that only English people brought wine to parties. We would arrive and Cesare would make a great fuss of me and Daniel. We would go for a walk with him and he would ask us about school, always taking our side against the teachers: 'Man's a fool. If you don't feel like doing PE, don't do it.' Then we would sit down to an elaborate lunch, prepared by Sylvia. When I was a small child, these lunches seemed to go on for ever. I would think enviously of my schoolfriends, sitting down to fish and chips (even, sometimes, things in *tins*), free to go out to play by one o'clock. One o'clock saw Cesare just hitting his stride. England, the English, the shame of the Italian football team who had let him down personally by drawing with Scotland, the failure of young Italians to keep up the *bella figura*, the wickedness of his cousin Rosaria, the evil of Margaret Thatcher, the necessity for frustrated priests to have sex with nuns ('only attractive ones', as if this made it better). On and on and on. My father would gaze into his wine and say nothing. My mother would sometimes try to argue with Cesare, which only made things worse. Daniel and I would stare out of the window and long to turn on the television.

After lunch, Cesare would sleep in his chair. Sylvia and my mother would wash up and my dad would read the paper, longing for home and his comfortable *Telegraph*. Daniel and I would play bad-tempered games of Snap, or I would ignore him and read one of Cesare's gory murder mysteries. Then Sylvia would serve tea, refused with a shudder by Cesare, and we would be free to go, Cesare standing at the gate to give that strange backwards-facing Italian wave.

Anyway, that particular Sunday, I chose the singularly inopportune moment of Sunday lunch to bring up my request for Cesare's birth certificate.

Cesare looked up slowly from his gnocchi. 'What?' The very quietness of his voice should have warned me to stop but I was in love with the idea of myself as the keen history student, chronicler of the family's past.

'Your birth certificate. For a project. On the Second ... World ...'

Too late I saw his expression. The emperor was about to give me a spectacular thumbs down. 'Never. Ever. Been asked such a presumptuous thing. My birth certificate. *My* birth certificate. For a project showing about a war that *my* people lost. Never would have thought that a grandchild of mine ...'

Wrong-footed, I tried to argue, then burst into tears and rushed out of the room. Daniel knocked over his glass of wine (we always had wine, even as children) and my father, uncharacteristically, shouted at him. I ran out into the garden, to the grassy spot where we had had the barbecue and vowed never to speak to any of my family again. Much later, Cesare came and found me and said he was sorry. He gave me one of his lovely lemon-scented hugs and I forgave him. It was only years later that I wondered: why was he so angry about a birth certificate?

After that, I went off Italy for a bit. We went to Greece for our next family holiday and the blue sky and white stone seemed simpler and more attractive than previous Italian experiences (off-season hell in Sorrento with an empty swimming pool and shivering trips to Pompeii). But blood will out, I suppose, and when it came to my gap year, there was only one choice that appealed. The land of my grandfathers.

My parents were surprisingly encouraging. They were particularly pleased with me at the time because I had been offered a place at Oxford. I was quite pleased with myself and tried not to think about how I had hated the place passionately when I went up for interview.

Cesare said, 'An au pair. How demeaning.'

Daniel said, 'How boring. Why not go to America?' He called himself Dan now and wore a New York Yankees baseball cap.

I travelled across Europe in an uncomfortable state of cockiness and fear. I shared my carriage with a nun and three soldiers; all four held eye contact all the way across France. My knowledge of Italian, limited to virtuoso pronunciation of gnocchi and tagliatelle in restaurants, had hardly prepared me for the chaotic sounds around me. Advertisements and street signs reared up in a haze of unfamiliar typefaces, like ransom notes; station announcements passed in a blur of vowels. When the nun spoke to me to offer me a sugared almond, I stared at her in wild incomprehension.

I was met at Rome by my 'host family', the Gallis. With the three hyperactive children in the back of the car, they drove me through the ugly suburbs of Rome to their huge, modern flat near Cinecittà. The rooms were full of old-fashioned darkwood furniture and modern electrical appliances. The sitting room was dominated by a massive television screen. My bedroom had a high, hard bed, steel shutters and an oil painting of an old crone selling flowers. It felt very odd and not at all what I had expected.

The family were quite nice, really. The father, Paolo, was an accountant, who set off every day in his air-conditioned Alfa for his office in the centre of Rome. The mother, Antonella, was frighteningly glamorous, incredibly slim with streaked hair and chunky jewellery. The children were uncontrollable but sweet and affectionate. Paolo and Antonella had a lot of friends with young families and at weekends they would all go to Ostia or Frascati. On my days off I would go to my Italian lessons and occasionally for a meal with some other au pairs, but I felt strangely isolated. It was as if the real Rome, with its arches and fountains and dusty glamour, was always just out of reach. It wasn't only that I couldn't understand the language. I felt as if I needed someone to unlock the door for me, to connect me to the stones and pavements. I think that was why I got in contact with Uncle Fausto.

I had only seen Uncle Fausto once since his Assumption Day appearance, two years earlier. He had been in London for (unspecified) business and had taken the family out to dinner. It was a terrifyingly smart restaurant and Uncle Fausto mysteriously ordered food that did not appear on the menu. He did not consult us about the choice but spoke directly, in expressionless Italian, to the head waiter. The food was wonderful and Uncle Fausto mesmerisingly charming. He spoke to Daniel about football and to me about universities – I was just about to apply to Oxford. 'Bologna is the oldest university in the world,' he said sweepingly, 'but Pisa is the best.' I had absorbed enough of the Oxbridge propaganda to protest but Fausto continued undeterred. He gave me his number in Rome and told me to get in touch if I ever came to visit.

Unlike the Gallis, Fausto lived in the very centre of Rome – Viale Vaticano. His windows overlooked the walls of the Vatican. From his balcony, you could actually see the Pope's apple trees. Fausto's attitude to his next-door neighbour was rather ambivalent. On one hand, he used to bow his head piously at the words 'Holy Father', but on the other he told patently untrue stories about the Pope's mistresses and drug dealing. That the Pope was Polish he took as a national affront: 'Aren't there enough holy people in Italy?'

Fausto had suggested I arrive at midday and I was rather hoping for another sumptuous restaurant meal. It was November, but warm enough to walk around in shirtsleeves – although the Italians were swathed in floor-length furs – and I bounded up the steep hill in high spirits. Fausto's apartment (Italians did not seem to live in houses) was in a handsome building of sepia paint and crumbling brick. The main door was propped open by a motorbike so I walked straight in. As I climbed the wide stone stairs I felt as if I was climbing higher and higher into the seven hills of Rome. Through occasional small windows I could see trees and houses and ancient ruins spread out like a picnic.

Fausto's apartment door was also open. I called, 'Hallo!' my English voice sounding nervous and out of place. There was no answer so I walked in and was blinded by the light streaming from open balcony doors. A man, not Fausto, was standing looking out over the Vatican gardens. Suddenly, I had an absurd compulsion to turn and run, back to the Gallis' modern apartment with its screaming children and giant television set. But it was too late. The man turned round. He was about forty, dressed in black and holding a glass of wine. Pointing his cigarette at the Vatican, he said in English, 'How can one man have so much? Is this fair? And why isn't it me? One puff of smoke, black or white, and you are next to God himself. How is this fair?' Suddenly I thought of Uncle Fausto and the smoke clearing at the barbecue to reveal him, smile first, like the Cheshire Cat.

I shrugged. 'Any adult male Catholic can become Pope.'

CHAPTER 3

Antonio is right. There is no problem with getting an invitation to attend Cesare's interview with Guido della Francesca. When I ask if I can come to lunch one day, Cesare answers immediately, 'Come next Sunday. I'm being interviewed by this chap. Says he's Italian so it might be nice to have someone there who speaks a bit of the language.' 'A bit of the language' is how Cesare customarily refers to my near fluency in his native tongue.

I drive to Canterbury on a beautiful summer day. The town is full of tourists with fluorescent backpacks but Cesare's house is an oasis of quiet good taste. Where the country house was full of faded sofas and vases of flowers dropping their petals on to window ledges, the townhouse is a place of cool, smooth surfaces. The floors are polished wood, white bookshelves display Cesare's eclectic collection of Italian poetry and American detective stories and at the back is a small courtyard where Sylvia has painted a trompe l'œil urn in a white archway.

When I arrive, Cesare is sitting in the courtyard with Guido della Francesca. As Antonio predicted, Guido is not what I imagined. For one thing he is red-haired, an honest-to-goodness carrot red. His skin has the pallor associated with his colouring and, as protection from the sun, he wears a white baseball cap. It's hard to think of a less Italian-looking person. Cesare, on the other hand, is wearing a jaunty panama with what looks like an old Harrovian band. Actually, he did go to an English public school, but not Harrow.

'Guido della Francesca.' Cesare does the introductions suavely without getting up from his chair. 'My granddaughter Sophie. She speaks a bit of Italian.'

Sylvia brings glasses of wine but declines to stay for the interview. 'I've heard it before,' she says, winking at me.

'Well, then, we'll talk Italian,' says Cesare smoothly. 'Is that OK with you, Mr della Francesca?' Guido nods.

Cesare's dog, Rollo, arrives and parks himself on Cesare's lap. While his relationship with the Alsatians that preceded

Rollo was always a rather brutal master-and-servant one, Cesare is remarkably soft on this rough-haired mongrel adopted by Sylvia from the Canine Defence League. He strokes him now, looking like one of the villains in a James Bond film.

Guido gets out a tape recorder and puts it, rather nervously, on the wrought-iron table. But he begins confidently enough: 'Mr di Napoli, you were arrested as an enemy alien in 1940. Is that correct?'

'Yes. In July 1940. As soon as Italy entered the war. Part of the ... er ... collar-the-lot mentality.' Cesare is enjoying himself.

'You were put on the *Arandora Star*, bound for Canada. When the ship sank ...'

'She was hit. By the Germans. My allies. Because the British neglected to put a red cross on the side.' Cesare has a real soft spot for the Germans to whom he always refers as 'my allies'. He always supports them in sport, especially if they play England.

'Many Italians were killed on the *Arandora Star*.'

'Yes.' Cesare leans forward. 'Because they were put in the lowest cabins. Below sea level. Many were old men who should never have been interned. They had no chance at all.'

'How did you escape?'

I look up. Though I know, of course, about the *Arandora Star*, Cesare is always strangely reticent on the details; all we usually get is some guff about seagulls. Sure enough: 'Ten hours floating in a freezing sea. All I could hear were the seagulls. To this day I hate the cry of seagulls.'

'Who rescued you?'

'Canadians,' says Cesare briefly. 'Fine people, the Canadians. The French ones anyway.'

'So you were sent to the Isle of Man?'

'Terrible place.'

'Were conditions bad?'

'No, not really,' Cesare has to concede. 'We had some of the top chefs at our camp. Chaps from the Savoy and the Ritz. So food was pretty good. It was the boredom mostly. We were young men.'

'How did you pass the time?'

'Played cards. Read books. Someone even made a radio.'

'You made a radio?'

'Yes. Some of the chaps were very mechanically minded.

We used to crowd together in my room to listen to it. We even heard Mussolini speak once.'

The name hovers uncertainly in the air for a minute or two. Cesare takes a complacent sip of wine; I look at my feet. Then Guido says, 'Your Home Office records say that you were a great admirer of Mussolini.'

For a while Cesare says nothing, he seems absorbed in watching Rollo play with a grey felt mouse that squeaks horribly. Then he says, 'Don't believe everything you read.' Ear-splitting squeaks.

'You didn't admire Mussolini? A lot of London Italians did. After all, he did a lot for them. Clubs, Italian lessons, trips to Italy—'

Cesare breaks in furiously, 'I never took any of those things. Never. My cousins, yes. My cousins Rosaria and Salvatore, they went on one of those trips to Italy. But not me.' Squeak, squeak, squeak.

'Why not?'

Cesare smiles one of his best Roman emperor smiles. 'I am not a London Italian. I'm an Italian Italian.'

Guido smiles back. 'So am I.'

Cesare looks at him doubtfully. 'Do you have an Italian

passport?' He grades Italians according to some mystical scoresheet of his own. Top marks for an Italian passport. The next best thing is describing yourself as an Italian and not Anglo-Italian or, worse, British. Points are deducted for supporting the England football team or anglicising your name. Aunt Rosaria is well into negative numbers.

'Yes,' says Guido proudly. 'I am an Italian citizen.'

'How do you vote?'

I feel I should protest but Guido answers, apparently unperturbed, 'Communist.'

Cesare grins. 'Me too.'

Now Guido does look surprised. 'You're wondering why an ex-Fascist should vote Communist?' asks Cesare. 'You shouldn't be surprised. Left and right, they're the same, really.'

I interrupt, 'You can't say that. Fascism is about violent suppression, anti-Semitism—'

Cesare stops me. 'You're talking about Nazis not Fascists.'

'Is there a difference?'

'Yes. Mussolini was a Fascist. He wasn't anti-Semitic. He wasn't a Nazi.'

I shrug. 'As you say, they're the same, really.'

During this exchange, Guido has been watching me closely with an expression that seems midway between amusement and distaste. It's very disconcerting. Suddenly, the courtyard seems too small. The urn on the wall seems to be bearing down on me. I get up and grab the mouse from Rollo, who grunts in surprise.

Cesare is watching Guido look at me. 'My granddaughter lived in Italy for a time,' he says.

'Oh, really?' says Guido. 'Where?'

'Rome,' I say.

'Ah, Rome,' says Cesare. 'Although I'm a Neapolitan I see Rome as my true home. I think that must be so of all Italians. Don't you think so, Mr della Francesca?' He is playing again but now I'm not sure exactly what the game is.

'Maybe.'

'Perhaps because it is the centre of our religion,' muses Cesare. 'Perhaps it is the spiritual home of all Catholics, however lapsed.'

'Maybe,' says Guido again. 'Maybe. But actually I'm Jewish.'

Rome. Robertino stepped off the balcony and into the shadows. In the long, narrow sitting room a table had been

laid. I felt a momentary pang of disappointment for my sumptuous restaurant lunch but the table, with its heavy silver
and glass, looked pretty promising. Fausto was nowhere to be
seen (in fact, he turned out to have been collecting the pasta
from the restaurant next door) and Robertino poured me a
drink. It was intensely red, like a drink offered by a witch in
a fairy story. I felt a sort of dizzying lurch, as if the table and
the balcony and the Pope's apple trees had suddenly been
turned upside down, and I think it was then that I knew I
was doomed. I knew that I would not return to England. I
knew that I would never go to Oxford. I knew that I would
fall in love with Robertino.

Robertino. The name was a childhood nickname meaning
'Little Roberto'. Fausto, although otherwise brisk and businesslike in his dealings with his son, called him Tino. Neither
name seemed particularly appropriate for the burly man in
the black shirt who stood blocking out my light. He was not
handsome. His hair was receding at the temples into two
Satanic points and his waist was already thickening, but as I
stood sipping my witch's drink and feeling the ground swoop
and sway beneath my feet, I knew that I was utterly lost.

My memories of the rest of that day are rather confused.

We ate a long, delicious meal at the table in front of the balcony. Contrary to popular belief, love did not make me lose my appetite; rather, it sharpened all my senses so that the ravioli and the veal and the bitter almond biscuits burst in my mouth like little explosions of delight. Irritatingly, although he and Robertino seemed to drink quite a lot, Fausto only filled my glass once. But I didn't really mind. I drank fizzy mineral water and watched Robertino as he talked. I don't remember what he said, only that he talked the whole time. As he spoke, his hands punctuated the air with wonderful burlesque gestures. Occasionally he and Fausto would have what sounded like a violent argument. I just sat smiling into my glass and saying nothing. It is the only time that I have ever felt completely passive.

We stayed at the table until night fell outside. Viale Vaticano was filled with the twinkling brake lights of Vespas and the hoarse shouts of Romans at play. Robertino drank back a tiny cup of bitter coffee in one gulp, spread out his hands and said, 'So, Sophie. I take you home. No?'

Instead he drove me to a place called Zodiac Hill where you can see the whole of Rome spread out below you, kissed me with professional thoroughness and drove me back to his apartment in Trastevere. There he took me to bed. I don't much like talking about sex but I will just say that making love to Robertino was a revelation, like hearing a tune played by an orchestra when you had only previously heard the piano accompaniment. It was as if, for the second time that day, I had found the whole of Rome spread out before me.

I never went back to the Gallis. My suitcase and backpack are probably still there. Robertino bought me a whole new wardrobe and cut my hair himself, sitting on the edge of the bath. He loved clothes and fabric and colours. In England, any man so interested in fashion would have been considered somewhat suspect but Robertino was so overwhelmingly masculine that he could get away with mornings spent shopping for velvet scarves and knowing the name of every footwear designer in existence.

Everyone was furious, of course. My mother came charging over from England to rant about Oxford and throwing my life away on a man old enough to be . . . etc., etc. I spent a terrible day with her, traipsing round Roman tourist attractions and arguing bitterly. In the Vatican she said that she had always wanted me to go to Oxford and that I was breaking her heart. In the Pantheon she said that Robertino would tire of me within a year. Sitting exhausted on the Spanish Steps she said that any woman who slept with a man before marriage was a tart. Returning on the bus she cried and said that she had lost a daughter. Back at the apartment, Robertino cooked us spaghetti carbonara and later drove my mother back to her hotel (she refused to sleep under our sinful roof). When he got home, he spread out his hands saying, 'Beautiful woman. But so unfulfilled.' He was at his most irritatingly Italian.

With Robertino, I felt what I had never felt before: English. All my life the spectre of Italy loomed large in the corporeal form of Cesare. I knew that I was not like other kids at school. I knew how to pronounce tagliatelli and that Michelangelo was just his Christian name. Sometimes, when everyone was bonded together in jingoistic togetherness over a football match, I used to wish that I could support England like everyone else. But I also felt a sort of melancholy pride in my otherness. I might look and sound English but I knew I was different.

Robertino used to boast about his 'English girlfriend'. He loved my name, Sophie Richmond, saying that it had a perfect English sound. 'Richmond. That's a park, no? Deer and hunting and English homosexuals in the bushes.' Even when my Italian got to be quite good, he always used to make fun of my accent, pronouncing it *'Tipicamente inglese'* in what he imagined was a typical English voice.

Who was I, then? The outsider Italian who could never quite fit in with the strait-laced English? The lost little English girl in Rome who put milk in her tea and liked bacon for breakfast? I don't think I cared. I was a different person anyway when I was with Robertino, careering wildly around Trastevere in his open-topped Alfa Romeo or drinking coffee in secret, dark cafés or making love in his high, carved bed while all the cats in Rome sang on the rooftops.

Of course, Robertino did tire of me. It took a bit longer than a year, though. It was about two years before he started to go away on unspecified 'business' and strange women started to leave messages on our answerphone. But it was a full three years later when he sat down next to me one morning and said, 'Sophie, you're too young, too beautiful, too sweet.'

It rained all the way back to England: great, grey tears sluiced down the sky while I stared, dry-eyed, out of the plane window. Back home, no one said I told you so. I got a place at London University, then took a teaching qualification. I had several boyfriends and even moved in with one, Rick, for a while. Two years later, when I heard that Robertino had got married, I felt as if I had physically to hold on to my heart to stop it from breaking.

CHAPTER 4

'So he hasn't actually denied being a Fascist?' Antonio stares moodily at a plaster angel and lights another cigarette.

'Well, he hasn't admitted it either.' I lean forward and light my own. It is probably the only thing that Antonio and I have in common: we both smoke in a world of non-smokers. At school, I have to go outside the grounds to have a fag. I sometimes wish I could join the kids behind the bike sheds.

We're in a graveyard adjoining the hospital where Aunt Rosaria is having a hip replaced. Why are graveyards so often near hospitals? It seems tactless, to say the least. It's a beautiful day though, hot and cloudless. Young couples lie sunbathing on the ground, their wide-spread limbs juxtaposed with the crazy angles of the tombstones. It looks like a medieval painting of the dead awakening.

'Was Guido satisfied?' asks Antonio.

'I don't think so. He wants to see Cesare again.' It was hard to know whether Guido was satisfied or not. Cesare seemed subdued after Guido's Jewish bombshell and answered his remaining questions more or less straightforwardly. After about an hour, Sylvia served lunch. Guido ate heartily (I couldn't help noticing that the medallions of pork caused him no problems) and maintained a flow of light conversation that only Sylvia could match. He left late in the afternoon after arranging another interview. I was not invited.

'Can you be there?'

'I don't think so. I don't think Guido took to me.'

Antonio laughs, throwing a match into the shrubbery. I'm rather annoyed that he doesn't dispute this.

'How well do you know Guido?' I ask.

'Not very. He's quite well respected in the business. He's written a couple of books about the Italian diaspora.'

'The Italian *diaspora*?' I laugh incredulously. 'Since when has Italy had a diaspora?'

Antonio looks annoyed. 'Whatever you like to call it. The Italians in exile.'

Exile. Diaspora. It's beginning to sound like the Old

Testament. We're only talking about twentieth-century Europe, not crossing the Red Sea.

'Cesare's not in exile,' I say. 'He chose to come here.'

'His parents did. You know what they say? First-generation immigrants cling to the old traditions, the second generation tries too hard to assimilate, the third generation – that's us – has to get it in perspective.'

'You can hardly accuse Cesare of assimilating.'

'Rosaria did.'

'How is she?' I ask, after a pause.

'Amazing, really. After all, she's nearly ninety. She's got them all running around in there. My grandson the radio star.'

Aunt Rosaria. For Cesare, her name alone was shorthand for everything he hated about the English, Italians who became English and bossy women in general. 'Oh, yes,' he would sneer, when one of us would venture that, perhaps, Bella Lasagne in the *Fireman Sam* cartoons was not the worst slur on Italy since 'Oh! Oh! Antonio', 'that's just what your aunt Rosaria would think.' And then we would know that we had got it awfully, unforgivably wrong.

I knew that Cesare and Rosaria had been quite close as

children. They were first cousins – Rosaria was the daughter of Cesare's uncle Antonio. For a while, the two families had lived together due, I think, to the ill health of Antonio's wife, Clara. Rosaria, Cesare and Salvatore, Rosaria's younger brother, spent a lot of time together, playing together in the Clerkenwell streets. I remember Aunt Rosaria telling me that Cesare had a sort of go-kart with metal wheels that used to strike sparks off the cobbles. He used to ride this contraption down Saffron Hill, hanging on to the back of carts and generally being a menace to society. She also told me that Cesare had once stopped a runaway horse, although I don't think this can have been true.

However, during the war, Rosaria and Cesare quarrelled. I never knew exactly what had happened but there was always the implication, from Cesare at least, that Rosaria had done something which could never be forgiven. Towards the end of the war, she married a man called Reg, whom Cesare loathed. When Cesare and Sylvia married, I think Sylvia made some attempt to heal the rift but one visit to Rosaria and the bastard was enough. Cesare stormed out, swearing he would never speak to Rosaria again. And he never has.

Yet despite this, we children still saw Rosaria and her

family. I think this was partly because Sylvia steadfastly refused to quarrel with them and partly because Cesare felt that, even if he hated them, family was still family. I remember my mother taking us round to Aunt Rosaria's stuffy little house in North London. The rooms were full of ornaments, holy pictures and photographs (mostly of Antonio, her favourite grandson). My greatest treat was to be allowed to play with her collection of china animals: a cat, a koala bear and several dogs (Aunt Rosaria loved dogs and for years owned a bad-tempered pug named Rudy, after Rudolph Valentino).

Cesare, for whom female beauty is incredibly important, never mentioned Aunt Rosaria without some slight on her appearance – 'looks like a horse, looks like an *ugly* horse'. And maybe as a child she was plain, but as an old lady Aunt Rosaria was magnificent. She had very black hair (possibly dyed but maybe not – Cesare is still black-haired) piled up into a towering beehive. She always wore lots of jewellery: her hands were positively encrusted with gems, like the dragon in *The Hobbit*. Even the flowered apron she wore for housework was secured by a vast emerald brooch. My mother once said that having a lot of jewellery was lower class (easy to pawn if times get hard) yet to me Aunt Rosaria seemed rich and powerful. When I went for walks with her (funnily enough, usually to this very cemetery, to put flowers on her parents' graves) even fighting dogs would flee from her raised walking stick and booming Londoner's voice.

Aunt Rosaria liked me. As I have said, Antonio was her favourite, but I came a close second. I would make her laugh, imitating schoolteachers and telling her the latest off-colour jokes (like Cesare, Aunt Rosaria had no time for anyone in authority). My mother would be shocked and tell me to have more respect, but Aunt Rosaria just laughed her smoker's laugh, which ended in a violent cough. 'Leave her alone, Emma. Bleeding teachers. What do they know?'

'Antonio! Sophie!' Someone calls our names and we both jump.

It's Joanne, the wife of Rosaria's younger son, Alfredo. She is walking towards us through the graves, accompanied by a tall young man: Max, the baby who screamed through Cesare's birthday party fifteen years ago. Joanne and Alfredo went on to have three more children. Max has grown up rather handsome, with Italian olive skin and Joanne's blonde hair.

'Hi.' Antonio gets up to kiss her. 'Hallo, Max.'

'Hallo, Tony.'

Tony! I steal a glance at Antonio to see how he likes the abbreviation but he seems not to have noticed.

'We've been to see Nonna,' says Joanne, sitting down next to us. It's odd how Joanne, who is English, uses the Italian word for 'grandmother' while neither Antonio nor I can get our tongues round it. She even calls Rosaria, her mother-in-law, 'Mamma'. Cesare has been Cesare to me for as long as I remember, perhaps because the name sounds so much like a title. Daniel sometimes calls him 'Nonno' but, then, he always was a creep. Sylvia hates 'Nonna' – she thinks it's too much like the distinctly lower-class 'Nana'.

'I'm just going to see her,' I say. I feel the need to explain away being found with Antonio. 'I just met Antonio here. Having a cigarette.' I wave mine as evidence. Joanne coughs. She always was too sensitive for our family.

'Keep in touch, Sophie,' says Antonio, meaningfully.

'Yes, do,' Joanne echoes vaguely. 'You must come to lunch or something.' Max stares at the ground. He looks as if he could do with a cigarette.

Aunt Rosaria certainly could. She has smoked twenty a day

for the last seventy years. She asks me for one as soon as she sees me but I cravenly pretend I've run out. I sit beside her and try to change the subject. 'Nice hospital,' I say, trying to ingratiate myself with the hovering nurses.

'Bleeding awful place,' says Aunt Rosaria, who has no such qualms. Unlike Cesare she speaks with an unrefined London accent. Cesare's mother, Laura, being rich, sent him to a posh school; Rosaria and her brother Salvatore went to the local council school although Rosaria, I think, got a place at the grammar school. 'The doctors are all black and the nurses are all . . . you know.'

'What?' I say, to embarrass her.

'Lezzies.' No such luck. 'Rings in their noses. You haven't got a ring in your nose, have you?'

'No.'

'Good. Pretty girl like you. Why aren't you married?'

Hey-ho. Here we go again. Because no one has asked me? Because the man I love is in Italy and married to someone else? Because underneath this summer dress I'm really covered in tightly curling black fur? 'I prefer being single. You can please yourself.'

Unexpectedly, Aunt Rosaria laughs. 'Quite right. Sometimes

I wish I'd never married. The heartache children cause you!'

'What about your husband?' For a moment I can't remember his name. I almost refer to him as 'the bastard'.

'Reg? He was all right. No trouble, really. Cesare always hated him.'

'Why?' This, I must admit, is partly why I've come. It has occurred to me that Aunt Rosaria is the person who has known Cesare longest. She might be able to tell me about his wartime allegiances.

'Because he was English. After the war Cesare hated everyone English. He never forgave me for changing my name.'

'When you got married?'

'No, before that. During the war. I changed it from di Napoli to Denning.'

'Denning!' I laugh, but Aunt Rosaria looks irritated.

'Lots of people did it. Including the Queen. It wasn't much fun having an Italian name during the war. It was OK for Cesare. He was locked up with a lot of other Italians. I lost my job at the factory because I was Italian. Funny, the only firm that would employ me was Jewish . . .'

Rosaria stops to cough and I pass her a box of tissues and think of Guido della Francesca. *Actually, I'm Jewish.*

'It was worse for Salvatore,' she says at last. 'He was in the army.'

'The British army?'

'You didn't know? Yes, Salvatore joined up. Cesare never forgave him.'

'Were Salvatore and he close?'

Rosaria pauses for a moment and her habitual expression of extreme belligerence softens. 'Yes, very. When we first came to England we lived with Auntie Laura and Uncle Giuseppe. Auntie Laura looked after us when my mother got ill. She was very kind, Auntie Laura. Salvatore went everywhere with Cesare. They couldn't be bothered with me, of course, but they were like brothers. Cesare always stood up for Salvatore, I'll say that for him. Salvatore was gentle, you see. Not like Cesare.'

'Salvatore died in the war, didn't he?'

Rosaria is silent for a moment, looking down at her hands, ringless for once, clasped together on the brown hospital blanket. 'Yes, in Italy, you know. My mother never got over it.'

'Where is he buried?'

Rosaria looks up. 'At Caserta. Funny thing, it's only a few miles from where our father was born.'

'Have you been to see the grave?'

She sighs. 'No. But I hear they keep it nice. Very tidy.' This would mean a lot to Aunt Rosaria: she's always been a great one for tidy graves.

'Cesare must have been upset when he died.'

The softness vanishes. 'Cesare! He wrote to say he was sorry but he didn't want anything to do with us when he came out. Thought himself too good for us. Always did. Just because his mother came from Florence. Sent him to some poncy public school, she did, and he came back looking down his nose at us. I'll tell you a story about your grandfather, shall I?'

'Yes,' I say, dispiritedly. Try stopping her.

'I was walking down the street with him one day and it started to rain. Really pissing down. He had an umbrella but he wouldn't put it over me. Know why? He'd just paid a shilling to have it furled.'

I laugh. 'He paid to have his umbrella furled?'

'Oh, yes,' says Rosaria darkly. 'You don't know the half of it.'

59

She stops to drink some water. Now is my chance. 'Was he a Fascist?' I ask abruptly.

'Pardon?'

'Cesare. During the war. Was he a Fascist?'

'Oh, yes,' says Aunt Rosaria. 'I thought you knew.'

Driving home, I'm dimly aware that the streets are rather quiet for a Saturday. When I get in, I switch on the television and see that it's full of men in lurid summer suits, grass, flags, people with their faces painted in national colours. In other words, the World Cup. I push Tybalt off my lap and go and pour myself a beer. I have a weird relationship with football. All through my childhood, it played a central role in the How Italian Are You? game. Cesare, of course, is a passionate Italy supporter. But more than he wants Italy to win, he wants England to lose. He's capable of saying, quite seriously, that 1966 was the worst year of his life. Yet he never seems particularly pleased when Italy win. I remember watching the 1982 World Cup final at Cesare's house. When Italy won, the expression on his face was more like that of a condemned man who has suddenly been granted a reprieve. He sank back in his chair, pale and silent, as Daniel and Antonio danced a war dance around him.

Football matches became a deadly battleground. We wanted Cesare to be happy – family life was simply so much better when he was happy – so we wanted Italy to win. Against us were the press ('You're Pasta Your Best, Gazza Tells Italians'), the crowds ('Briton Dead' ran the headlines the day after thirty-nine Italians had been killed at the Heisel stadium), the Italian team, who never seemed to try quite hard enough, and finally fate, which was not likely to allow us anything that we wanted that much.

When I told all this to Rick, years later, he said, 'What was the fuss about? The Italians always win.' I was struck dumb by this. I had been so used to seeing the Italians as the underdogs, the whole world against us, that I had missed this quite simple fact. Italy did win a lot; much more than England. Italy had won the World Cup three times against England's once. Quite often England did not even qualify, yet to me they still seemed like the all-conquering master race of Cesare's imagination.

On the face of it, Robertino's attitude to football was more straightforward. He believed that the Italian team was the best in the world. Not having access to English newspapers, he did not know of their conviction that England were actually the best (foreigners being disqualified for excessive use of sneaky, unmacho techniques like skill). That established, he was not very interested in the game. We did once go to the Stadio Olimpico to watch Roma play. We sat among women in squashy fur coats and men in waxed jackets and drank brandy from a flask. Robertino insisted that we left before the end, saying he was bored.

Thinking of Robertino makes me restless. I get up, meaning to phone a friend and arrange to go out for the evening, and my doorbell rings. I press the entryphone and hear, 'Sophie? This is Guido della Francesca.' As I let him in, I wonder if he ever abbreviates his name.

Guido seems even less at ease than he did at Cesare's house. He prowls the room until I tell him, rather sharply, to sit down. Tybalt immediately jumps on to his lap. 'What's his name?' he asks.

'What?' I'm in the kitchen, getting us a drink.

'The cat. What's he called?'

'Tybalt.'

'Oh. King of Cats.'

I say nothing but I'm impressed. Hardly anyone has worked out the significance of Tybalt's name – 'a sad little English graduate's joke', as one ex-boyfriend called it. I begin to wonder about Guido. I suspect that he's a sad little English graduate, too. Why is he here?

When I hand him his beer (he requests a glass, which Daniel tells me is deeply uncool), he says, 'I saw your grandfather today.'

'Oh. I didn't realise it was today.' It strikes me as an almost dangerous coincidence that Antonio and I were sitting in the graveyard discussing Guido at around the same time that he was interviewing Cesare.

'Yes. I took him out to lunch.'

'I'm sure he enjoyed that.' Cesare loves being taken out to lunch – he's a fiendishly difficult guest.

'Yes,' Guido says glumly.

We sit in silence for a moment. I'm too busy wondering why on earth he's here to be able to frame even the simplest of questions. Guido is staring at the silent TV screen.

Finally he says, 'Italy are playing.'

For a second, I don't know what he means. Then I see that the little figures on the grass are wearing blue shirts and rather well-cut white shorts. 'Do you want to watch?'

'No, no.' He obviously does so I turn up the sound and we watch the match. It's every bit as boring and stressful as I remember. Italy seem immeasurably skilful without ever looking as if they are going to win. The opposing side are clearly homicidal lunatics for whom the referee has an incomprehensible soft spot. By the time Italy have scraped a win, the sky over the birch tree is deep blue and Tybalt has shed half his coat on Guido's beige chinos.

'We'll never get beyond the quarter-finals at this rate,' says Guido, with pleasurable gloom, 'and we've got to play France. They're the favourites.'

'Maybe it's all fixed,' I say. 'Like 1966.'

'Oh, that was fixed all right,' says Guido immediately. He accepts another beer.

'How did you get my address?' I ask.

'From Antonio.'

Well, thank you, Antonio: all through our conversation about how Guido didn't much like me, he somehow forgot to mention that he had asked him for my address.

'Why?' I say.

In answer, Guido reaches into his battered backpack and pulls out a tape recorder. I turn down the television (Glenn Hoddle's jaws, furiously chewing gum, fill the screen) and he presses the Play button. Immediately Cesare's voice (speaking English this time and sounding very upper class) fills the room.

Cesare: 'I'm glad you asked me that. I was sent back to England because I was considered extremely dangerous. Doesn't it say so in your Home Office report? [Guido mutters unintelligibly.] I was considered desperate and dangerous. They sent me back under armed guard. With my friend Bruno Baldasare. I wish you could have seen us! We looked the part. We were both wearing leather trenchcoats . . .'

Guido: 'What had you done?'

Cesare: 'Started a riot, old boy. Yes, that's right. A riot. Bet you'd never heard about that before.'

Guido: 'No.'

Cesare: 'More wine? No? I'm not driving so I will. Yes, that's right. There was a riot at the Isle of Man camp and Bruno and I were arrested as the leaders and taken to Chelsea Barracks.'

Guido: 'What was the riot about?'

Cesare: 'What is this wine? New Zealand? Oh, well . . .'

Guido: 'What was it about?'

Cesare: 'Oh, this and that. You can't keep men cooped up for all that time without something boiling over. This wine isn't bad at all, you know. They're learning.'

Guido switches off the tape recorder. 'Well. What do you think?' He looks at me.

'He doesn't like New Zealand wine much.'

Guido doesn't laugh. He shakes his head impatiently, like a dog – a red setter – trying to get water out of its ears. 'Did you think he was avoiding the question?'

'Yes,' I admit. 'But he's like that. He hardly ever gives a straight answer. Did you ask him again?'

'Oh, yes,' says Guido, rather bitterly. 'I kept coming back to the riot but he kept heading me off. Very charming and everything, but he never told me what the riot was about. So I wondered if you knew. Antonio said you were very close to your grandfather.'

'Did he?' I'm beginning to get rather irritated with Guido, Antonio and the journalistic profession in general. 'Well, leaving aside the question as to whether or not I want to do your research for you, Cesare has never mentioned any riot to me.'

Guido fixes me with an intense stare. His eyes are not the watery blue that I associate with red hair but a rather deep green. 'And don't you think that's strange?'

'No,' I say crossly. 'Why are you so interested in this riot anyway?'

'Because I think it was an anti-Jewish riot,' says Guido, quietly. 'I think it's proof of the anti-Semitism of Italian prisoners of war.'

'Rubbish!' I say. 'Cesare's not anti-Semitic.' I'm aware that I'm blustering. That I'm protesting too much. The truth is that I don't know what Cesare believed in the war. But I don't want him to be anti-Semitic. I can, just about, take the admiration for Mussolini (or, at least, put it down to youthful indiscretion) but outright anti-Semitism? No. That's the one thing I can't forgive.

'I'll ask him,' I say, too loudly. 'I'll ask him what the riot was about.'

'Thank you,' says Guido, though I haven't promised to tell him what I find out. 'I'd better go now.'

As we stand by the door, there's an awkward silence between us. I am embarrassed and furious with him for coming to my flat, making me watch some awful football

67

match and forcing me to think terrible things about Cesare. I'm also furious with Antonio for giving him my address and for involving me in this ridiculous business in the first place. I don't want to know what my grandfather did in the war. I have a sudden unwelcome vision of Nazi war criminals who have turned, over the years, into sweet little old men. Somebody's grandfather. Don't involve me, I shout silently. It's not my fault.

Guido is staring at the floor. Tybalt is still purring sycophantically round his ankles. Suddenly he says, 'Will you come out to dinner with me?'

CHAPTER 5

Guido takes me to a nearby Indian restaurant. We go in his car, which I realise is a tactical error but I'm not sure how to get out of it. Let me drive my own car so I won't have to ask you in at the end of the evening and wonder if you want to sleep with me? It seems rather pathetic still to have these worries at the age of thirty-one. Surely by now I should have achieved a sort of inner serenity, the kind that goes with wearing beautifully cut linen clothes and not having a TV.

At least it gives me a chance to assess his car. Having had the superiority of Italian cars rammed down my throat all my life, I now automatically distrust anyone who drives one. The other night Antonio's posh grey Lancia depressed me almost as much as his grey hairs. Especially as he had

an Italian flag stuck to the back window. Guido drives a VW
Golf, once white but now formidably dirty. Inside it is full
of books, apple cores and empty tape boxes. There is also a
dog lead, the kind that extends for miles. 'I hope you have a
dog,' I say, pulling it out from under me. 'Otherwise this is
a bit hard to explain.'

'An Alsatian,' he says. For some reason, this strikes me as
ominous.

The restaurant is crowded and we're wedged into a tiny
table near the kitchens. I suddenly feel rather awkward to
be sitting so near Guido. I can see the faint freckles over the
bridge of his nose and realise that his eyelashes are black,
rather than red.

'Do you like Indian food?' I ask brightly.

'Yes,' says Guido, 'though I don't know much about it. I
read somewhere that what we think of as Indian food all
comes from one region. It's like Italian food. What English
people think of as Italian food – pizzas, pasta, tomato sauce
– all comes from the south. Most Italian restaurants simply
offer Neapolitan food.'

'What part of Italy are you from?'

'Venice.'

'Hence the red hair,' I say. For some reason this makes him blush. 'Titian and all that,' I add.

'Have you ever been to Venice?' he asks.

Once, with Robertino. It rained and he refused to go in a gondola. We sat in a bar all day, drinking red wine from the tap and reading the *Gazetta della Sport*.

'No,' I say.

'It's an amazing place. You can wander round in circles for ever. I've been there so many times but I still get lost. You suddenly find yourself in a square that you've never seen before in your life.'

'Like *Alice in Wonderland*,' I say.

He looks up at me and grins. 'Exactly like that. You can actually imagine things getting larger and smaller all the time. Or finding a magic door leading to a miniature garden. You need to eat a magic cake to shrink yourself before you can get in.'

'Eat me, eat me,' I say. He looks very different when he smiles.

'Venice also has the largest Jewish quarter in Italy,' says Guido.

'Funny expression, isn't it?' I say, tearing off a piece of naan bread. 'Quarter. I'm a quarter Italian.'

'Really?' He seems surprised. 'Is that all? I'm completely Italian.'

'Where were you born?'

'London.' He sees me looking at him. 'It doesn't make you a donkey if you're born in a stable.' That was always Daniel's response to my taunt that he wasn't really Italian because he was born in Maidstone general hospital. My answer was always: 'It makes you an English donkey if you're born in an English stable.'

'Why does it matter what you are?' I ask. I mean it lightly but he seems to take it very seriously, pausing a long time before answering.

'It matters to me,' he says at last. 'There's a theory that we all want to be part of a narrative. Maybe I want to be part of the Italian narrative.'

'And the Jewish narrative?'

He smiles. 'Well, in a way that's the best narrative of all. With the best sources. It must be why some people want to be Jewish. Even though the recent history has been so tragic, it's linear, it's all part of the story.'

'I think nationality matters most in England,' I say. 'If Cesare says he's Italian, people say, "Oh, but you live here, you speak English," et cetera. If he says he's English, people say, "Cesare di Napoli! Who are you trying to kid?" and they despise him for wanting to belong.'

'People in England are judged by how they speak. Your grandfather sounds like a posh Englishman and that's how people treat him. It would be different if he went around saying, "Whatsa the matter? You no like my ice cream?"'

I laugh. '"Oh! Oh! Antonio" with his ice-cream cart. That song used to drive Antonio mad when he was younger.'

For some reason, the mention of Antonio seems to depress him.

Our food arrives with much juggling to fit all the little silver bowls on to our table. My curry is sizzling away at my elbow. I spoon a huge amount on to my plate. I'm absolutely starving.

'Have you got a boyfriend?' Guido asks suddenly.

I swallow a piece of chilli and have to gulp down some water. 'No,' I gasp. 'I was seeing someone for a while but we split up last year.' This is true: I'd been seeing a fellow teacher called Tom for about a year. He was nice, we had a lot in common, but when he got a job in Newcastle we both leapt on the chance to separate with undisguised relief. I don't tell any of this to Guido.

'What about you?' I ask.

'I'm divorced,' he says. 'Married straight after university but just sort of drifted apart. She's a doctor.'

'Have you got any children?'

'No. Thank goodness – I mean,' he adds quickly, 'because the divorce would have been traumatic for them, not because I don't want any.' For some reason, he's blushing again. Over coffee and shiny Indian sweets like jewellery he tells me that he would like to go back to live in Venice.

'I can't imagine living there,' I say. 'It doesn't seem like the sort of place where anyone lives ordinary lives. You know, going to the bank or the fish-and-chip shop.'

'Collecting the dry-cleaning.'

'Going to the dentist.'

'Taking the dog for a walk.'

'Good point. Can your dog swim?'

'Yes,' he says, 'but he needs to work on his social skills.' He leans back to ask the waiter for the bill.

'I'll pay,' I say quickly.

'No.' He looks shocked.

'Half each.'

'No,' he says again. 'I asked you.' He fishes for his credit card, looking very serious. Suddenly the ease that we have built up over dinner has vanished.

Outside it is nearly midnight but still warm. There are tables on the pavement as if this were Rome and not Streatham. Above a nearby Italian restaurant, the Italian tricolour and the Union Jack hang limply.

'I'll get a taxi,' I say. 'There's a rank just here.'

'Oh, no,' says Guido, 'I'll drive you home. I insist.'

Outside the flat, I ask him if he wants to come in for coffee. He says no thanks, he'd better not. Is he sure? I say.

He looks at me for what seems the first time this evening. 'You're very beautiful,' he says.

'I'm thirty-one,' I say. I believe one statement contradicts the other.

'I know,' he says. 'Antonio told me.' Bloody Antonio.

A crowd of drunks passes the car, their voices raised in a raucous football song.

'I want to sleep with you,' Guido says, 'I've thought about nothing else since I first saw you.'

'You'd better come in, then,' I say.

Oh dear.

*

It wasn't like this with Robertino. Or was it? It's hard to remember now. Sometimes everything that happened with Robertino seems like a dream from which I'll wake up and find myself in the Gallis' apartment, watching their huge TV and learning my transitive verbs.

Certainly Robertino would never have said, 'I want to sleep with you.' He would have thought it too crass and too obvious to need stating. All through that long meal in Fausto's flat, I could feel him burning through my skin. Just watching his hands peeling a peach, heavy workman's hands with incongruously manicured nails, made me feel dizzy and faint. The air between us, filtering through the half-closed blinds, seemed heavy with longing.

Robertino used to laugh at men, particularly English men, who asked, 'Do you like me?' 'What a question!' he would say smugly. 'If you have to ask, your cause is lost.' He never asked: he didn't have to.

I remember one day when we had driven to the sea at Ostia Lido. It was early in the season and no one was swimming (Italians believe it is mortally dangerous to swim in the sea before the first of August). But it was a swelteringly hot day and I took off my jeans and T-shirt (my student's clothes, Robertino called them) and stepped into the sea in my bra and pants. The water felt cool and almost solid, like green jelly. I floated on my back and felt the sun on my face. Robertino, in his blue shirt and well-cut chinos, lay on the beach and watched me.

Suddenly I was aware of a disturbance in the water and twisted round to see Robertino striding towards me, fully dressed. The waters seemed to part before him – he looked like a well-dressed Moses crossing the Red Sea. Then he was swimming, great untidy strokes like a bear. He grabbed me and I went under. I came up, spluttering, to find Robertino tearing off my pants with deadly intent. We fell on each other greedily, half swimming, half standing in the water. Halfway through, a party of schoolchildren tramped across the beach, giggling and pointing, but we took no notice.

Afterwards, Robertino dried me with his cashmere jumper. We lay steaming on the now deserted beach. 'Water sports,' said Robertino, 'have their compensations.'

He didn't ask. He didn't have to.

NAPLES, 1906

Giuseppe ran crazily down the street towards the docks. He knew that he should not be away from the workshop. His master would be angry, perhaps even beat him, but the chance of food was too great an opportunity to miss. For several minutes, Giuseppe had stood in the workshop doorway, half blinded by the midday sun outside, and considered his options. Upstairs his master was sleeping, shutters closed against the heat, the wine he had drunk with his breakfast helping to make his snores regular and deep. All the shops in the street would be closed for siesta but Montagna, the cobbler, had insisted that Giuseppe keep the shop open: 'Do I pay your wages so that you sleep? If no one comes, you can sweep up, cut the leather, pay me back for my many kindnesses. Basta! Not another word.'

Paying Montagna back for his kindness, reflected Giuseppe, as he dodged into the shadows to avoid being seen, would involve taking *the leather-cutting knife and stabbing him as he slept. Montagna was supposed to be teaching his apprentice the shoemaking trade; instead he had a slave.*

Giuseppe had been educated by the nuns in the orphanage. In effect, this meant that he had had one of the best educations in Naples. His written and spoken Italian were good, he could read Latin and recite from the Bible. The nuns insisted that every orphan play an instrument and learn a trade. Giuseppe had learnt the mandolin and loved its sweet, haunting voice. With his trade he had not been so lucky: he had been apprenticed to Montagna.

Giuseppe knew that he and his brother, Antonio, were not typical orphans. For a start, when they had entered the orphanage, at the ages of eight and six respectively, they had not been orphans. Their father, Angelo, was still alive.

Angelo di Napoli was well known in Naples as a drunkard and a bully. For Giuseppe, he was now little more than a memory of blinding violent rages, of his mother sobbing on the floor as she shielded her head from his blows, of the neighbouring women comforting her and calling on his namesake Santo Giuseppe, patron saint of husbands, to protect her. When his mother died, his father had taken one horrified look at her frozen body and run out of the house, his apron over his head, howling like a baby.

For a day, eight-year-old Giuseppe and six-year-old Antonio had been alone with their mother's cold body. Antonio kept touching her hair. 'Mamma? Mamma? Wake up. Mamma? I'm hungry.'

Eventually, Giuseppe could bear it no more. 'She's dead, Tadone. Now, run and get Father Pietro.' But when his brother had gone, Giuseppe could not resist touching his mother's hand, even laying it on his own head in a last caress. 'It's all right, Giuseppe,' he said to himself. 'It's all right. Mamma's here.'

When the priest came, he lit candles by the body, called in the neighbouring women to pray and took the boys to the orphanage. The next day Angelo had appeared with a small bag containing their belongings. He had stood for a long time, staring at his sons, his large hands hanging uselessly at his sides. Then he had raised one in a curiously jaunty gesture of farewell. 'See you soon,' he had said. Giuseppe never saw him again.

Angelo died two years later, destitute and drunk. Giuseppe assumed that it was this that made people whisper behind their hands when they saw him and that made the nuns particularly kind to him and to Antonio. His mother had been a saint and his father a drunkard. No wonder people stared as he swept up silently at the back of Montagna's shop, his dark, intelligent eyes downcast so that his master would not accuse him of 'frightening the customers'.

Giuseppe had liked the orphanage. The nuns were kind and it was a relief to be away from Angelo. Anyway, as long as they were together, the brothers did not much mind where they were. At night, in the darkness, they held hands across the space between their beds. They swore they would never be parted.

But when Giuseppe was sixteen, the nuns gave him a silver St Christopher medal, said they would pray for him and apprenticed him to Montagna. Then the terrible time began. Beaten, half starved, Giuseppe slept on a pile of rags at the back of the shop. Despite the heat of the days, the nights were very cold and Giuseppe shook so much in his sleep that, when he woke, his body was covered in bruises.

He wanted to run away but where could he go? He had no money: Montagna's 'training' was in lieu of wages. Besides, he could not leave Antonio, who still had two years to go at the orphanage. (Giuseppe was allowed to visit him on Sundays, the only happy hours in the week.) So he survived somehow, his meagre rations supplemented by occasional scavenging of fish heads from the docks.

Now Giuseppe ran down to the quayside. A fishing boat was in and the seagulls were swarming round the nets, their raucous voices loud in the midday silence. One of the sailors was throwing crusts for them. Giuseppe's stomach contracted. Bread! It was sixteen hours since he'd eaten and the thought of eating made him feel sick and dizzy. *The sailor, who must have had a good voyage, threw the heel of a loaf on to the quay. Giuseppe sprang for it, hunger making him faster even than the gulls. But he slipped on fish guts and fell, hitting his head on the stone. A seagull grabbed the bread with a triumphant cry and wheeled off into the air.*

Giuseppe wept. He couldn't help it. He knew he was sixteen and almost a man but he lay on the ground and cried as the seagulls swirled happily around him.

'Boy,' said a voice, 'why are you crying?'

Giuseppe looked up. He saw a dog cart with its wheels painted gaily in scarlet and black. He raised his head higher and saw a man sitting in it, the reins held in his elegantly gloved hands. There was only one person in Naples who always wore gloves.

Don Vittorio. Everyone in Naples knew the Don. He was the man you went to if your business was doing badly, if your wife had left you or your son was mixing with the wrong company. Don Vittorio could help you, by lending you money, dragging back your wife by her hair and knocking some sense into your son. His justice was harsh but swift. Now he sat there, in his gloves and panama hat, staring down at Giuseppe. 'Why are you crying?'

'I'm hungry,' was all Giuseppe could think to say.

'But your master, Montagna, doesn't he feed you?'

Mutely, Giuseppe shook his head.

'Come.' Don Vittorio held out his hand. 'Come, Giuseppe. Get into the cart.'

And Giuseppe went, without even wondering how Don Vittorio knew his name.

At Montagna's shop, Don Vittorio asked Giuseppe to hold his horse. Then he knocked loudly on Montagna's door, and wiped his gloves carefully afterwards. The door opened and Don Vittorio entered the shop. After a remarkably short time, he emerged and beckoned to Giuseppe. 'Here, Giuseppe,' a coin was pressed into his hand, 'don't be frightened. It will be all right now.'

And it was. Whatever had passed between the two men in those few minutes, Montagna now treated Giuseppe with a slightly scared respect. Giuseppe ate with the family and slept in a proper bed with sheet and blankets. During the day, Montagna diligently taught the boy his trade. Giuseppe still hated him but he had to admit that the man knew his job. Then, on his eighteenth birthday, Giuseppe received an envelope from Don Vittorio. It contained enough money to set him up in business on his own. He was free.

For a long time, Giuseppe stood there, holding the envelope. On it, Don Vittorio had written just two words: 'Remember me.'

CHAPTER 6

I wake in the morning in true French-farce style – seeing the face next to me on the pillow and double-taking theatrically. Some of the less-reconstructed men at university used to grade women as one bag, two bags and a coyote. One bag when she was so ugly that you had to put a bag over her head, two bags when you put a bag over your own head, and a coyote when you were so horrified to wake up next to her that you chewed your own arm off to escape. Despicable sexist stuff, but I find myself looking longingly at my own arm.

Not that Guido is ugly. His body was a nice surprise, lean and fit, and his love-making was both tender and inventive. I think I've even got used to the red hair, or perhaps it looks more muted in the mornings. It's just that I don't want to be the person who went to bed with someone she hardly knows just because he told her how many Italian restaurants there are in Glasgow. And that you're beautiful, I remind myself, as I get up carefully. Guido murmurs in his sleep. He's lying neatly at the side of the bed. Unlike Robertino, who used to sprawl everywhere and occasionally (significantly?) pushed me out. I tell myself not to think about Robertino, as I have had to do in many similar situations.

When I came back to England, after Italy, after Robertino, it was some time before I could bring myself to sleep with anyone. Eventually, when it happened, it had more to do with logistics, embarrassment and London transport than anything else. I had been to a concert with a college friend called Stuart. At the time, I was sharing a flat with two girlfriends and, as it was only a short distance from the National Theatre, we walked. It was a warm July night and London was really doing its stuff – the Thames wide and inky, Waterloo Bridge like a string of fairy lights, every passing taxi seeming full of promise. On the bridge we stopped and kissed. It seemed the most natural thing in the world. Or, rather, it seemed better than natural, like a film with a trendy retro soundtrack, 'Waterloo Sunset' perhaps. We kissed for a long time and then walked on, hand in hand.

But the kiss was definitely where it should have ended. Dim the lights, Kinks fade to close and roll the credits. (Cesare always insists on watching films to the bitter end so that he can see if there was anyone Italian in it. 'Look! The chief grip's Armando Pescatore!') But what happened was that when we got back to my flat, Stuart tried to ring for a minicab and couldn't get one. By now the Tube was closed and, faced with the prospect of Stuart walking back to Finsbury Park, of course I had to offer to let him stay the night. If it hadn't been for that kiss, he could have spent it chastely on the sofa, cup of tea in the morning, perhaps a piece of toast and off to lectures together. But after that movie-star kiss, we both felt we couldn't back out. I said, 'You could stay here . . .' and he grabbed me with a kind of nervous desperation.

It was the awkwardness, I think. Like Guido, Stuart was OK in bed (Guido actually more than OK) but it just felt so *awkward*, seeing him there so close to me. Sleeping was terrible: I lay awake all night trying not to touch him by accident – full penetrative sex OK, accidental arm-touching absolutely not. With Guido, it just feels so strange, seeing his face on the pillow. So embarrassing. His red hair on my navy blue Habitat pillowcase. His chinos flung over my chair. Somehow seeing our clothes jumbled together seems worse than the thought that their owners have had sex.

I want coffee and a bath, in that order. In the kitchen Tybalt, who has now developed such a passion for Guido that we had to shut him out of the bedroom, leaps on me with angry purrs. I feed him and make the coffee, trying not to think about any of it. After I split up with Tom, I decided to be celibate. I did up the flat, went to the theatre with girlfriends and tried to teach myself the piano. That was nearly a year ago and my life has become, if not ecstatically happy, at least something that looks a nice shape from outside. Why did I throw it all away to sleep with this red-haired journalist who wants to prove that my grandfather was a racist? I suppose a Freudian would say that I have a grudge against Cesare and that is why I was attracted to Guido, who wanted to expose him as I had never dared to. But I'm not particularly attracted to Guido or I don't think I am. Why go to bed with him, then? my inner voice asks immediately.

And why does it matter if my grandfather was a Fascist?

I saw a headline in the paper the other day: 'Was Tintin a Fascist?' Poor Tintin, with his quiff and his plus fours and his penchant for sailors. He probably *was* a Fascist, if judged by today's standards. Probably everyone was. Certainly some of the remarks of wartime politicians leave a nasty taste in the mouth now. Anti-Semitism was rife among the English upper classes. Why shouldn't Cesare have picked it up along with the accent?

In the bath I decide that I'm making too much of my night with Guido. I'm thirty-one (how *could* Antonio have told Guido?), these things happen. It's quite ordinary, rather amusing and a little exciting. I'm a worldly mature single woman. Why shouldn't I go to bed with a man if I feel like it? Gradually, the bath and the coffee do their work and I start to feel a bit more like a worldly mature woman. I am in control of my life, I tell myself.

I decide to make Guido some coffee. After all, I do *like* him. I creep through the sitting room into the kitchen. Coming back with the coffee, I see Guido's backpack open on the floor with his tape recorder on top of it. Should I get hold of it and erase the tape? Surely that's what any good spy would do, sleep with the enemy, then destroy the evidence. But, leaving aside the fact that I've no idea how to erase a tape, I'm not sure that I want to. I want Cesare's story to survive, I just don't want it to belong to Guido.

When I heard Cesare's voice on the tape yesterday, I felt a crazy possessiveness. If Cesare was going to tell his war story to anyone, I wanted it to be me. Suddenly I make up my mind. I will go to see Cesare. I will ask him about the riot and whether it was anti-Semitic. I will ask him about the war and clear things up for once and for all. And it will give me an excuse to get Guido out of the flat.

I put the coffee down on the bedside table and shake Guido's shoulder, not too gently. 'Guido. Wake up. I've got to go and see my grandfather.'

After yesterday's sun, it's a dull grey summer's day. The traffic is heavy on the motorway and I nearly turn back, but then I think of Guido and all those unanswered questions. Of Antonio and his fear that Cesare's past will affect his career. Of Aunt Rosaria and her face when she talked about Salvatore. Of Joanne and Max sitting in the graveyard talking about 'Nonna'. Of Fausto and his appearance in the garden, dark against the sun: 'Why, we met in prison.' I think of myself and Guido making love on my blue sheets and I find myself pressing my foot down on the accelerator.

I park outside the city walls and walk to Cesare's house. The door is open so I go straight in, calling for Sylvia. The front door opens straight into the sitting room and I see Cesare immediately. He is sitting in the courtyard staring at the trompe l'œil urn. As I reach the patio door he turns and, with a shock, I see that he's suddenly looking old. He looks smaller too and the hand stroking Rollo is shaking. He holds out his other hand to me in a curiously pathetic gesture. 'Fausto is dead,' he says.

And, God help me, I think not, Poor Cesare (all his friends are dead now), or even, Poor Fausto, but, I will see Robertino again.

CHAPTER 7

It does not need Cesare's unnecessarily graphic description to explain why, in hot countries, people are buried quickly. Fausto died on Saturday night and will be buried on Tuesday. Antonio and I fly out for the funeral on Tuesday morning.

My own motivation in flying to Italy at such short notice and considerable personal inconvenience (term is not quite over) is embarrassingly clear to me. What is less clear is Antonio's reason for jumping on a plane at Cesare's peremptory request that he join me in 'representing the family'. I would like to ask him but he's at his most distant and professional. He pulls strings (and waves his press pass) to get us upgraded to first class, then sits with his radio headset on, drinking complimentary brandy. After his third glass, I pull the headset away from his ear. 'Who's going to drive when we get to Rome?' We've decided to rent a car at the airport.

'You are,' he says nastily. 'After all, you're the one who knows the place so well.' Then he snaps the earphones back against his head.

At Ciampino, the heat hits us like a blow. It is, in fact, the hottest summer in Italy for many years. My suitcase is the last to come off the carousel and Antonio, who only has one small, expensive-looking piece of hand baggage, grinds his teeth. Melting, we stand in line to hire a car and wait while the man chats me up in a charming but mechanical way. Antonio sways a bit but I'm not sure if this is boredom or the brandy.

We drive straight to the church, which is on the outskirts of Rome, near Frascati. I've been here before as Fausto had a summer house nearby, but I'm finding it difficult to get used to driving in Italy again. As I edge along the slow lane, drivers hoot and swerve around me. Antonio falls asleep, which strikes me as deeply unhelpful. I'm beginning to panic that when Robertino sees me, for the first time in eight years, I'll be sweaty and red-faced. My cotton dress, bought the day before, is creased and travel-stained. Sweat is running between my legs and the hot Rome air has blown my hair into wild curls. Suddenly I see a likely signpost and swerve frantically off the motorway. Derisive chorus of hooting.

In contrast to the hell of the airport and motorway, the church is peace itself in a placid town square, surrounded by dark trees and shuttered windows. Antonio and I, he rubbing his eyes and I trying desperately to smooth my dress, climb the shallow stone steps. Inside it is very dark and smells of flower stalks. I begin to shake. Antonio takes my arm. 'For God's sake,' he says.

The coffin, with one bunch of white lilies on it, lies by the altar steps. The church seems full of women in black. I feel absurd in my cream dress ('He wouldn't want you to wear black,' decreed Cesare), an English rose that has been left out in the rain. We sit as far back as we dare. Where is he? I make myself look left and right. Perhaps he's overcome with grief. Perhaps he and his wife are lying on a Sicilian beach, not giving a damn. I'm shaking so much that I have to drop my head to stop myself fainting.

'Sophie.' Antonio nudges me. 'Is that Robertino?'

I look up. A grey-haired man, accompanied by a thin woman and two dark children (children!) passes so close beside me that I could have reached out and touched him. The thought makes my head swim and I'm only dimly aware of what follows: the organ playing, Antonio having to take my arm to help me to my feet, the priest with his voice rising and falling operatically. I stare at the back of Robertino's head. The slightly sunburned neck, the beautifully cut hair (but completely grey now – oh, Robertino!), the white collar of his shirt against his dark suit. At one point, he puts his hand to his hair and I see the gold gleam of his wedding ring. How could he be married? How could she stand next to him, so blasé about him that she doesn't even need to touch him? How could he make love to her, give her children? Antonio holds my arm tightly. Behind us, an elderly, beautifully dressed Frenchwoman is sobbing unrestrainedly.

It's very quick. Surely English funerals (even Catholic ones) are longer? The undertakers have emerged like Mafia hitmen from the four corners of the church. The coffin is carried out. Robertino follows, his hand on the shoulder of his elder son (they have two boys, does he really want a daughter?). This time, his eyes meet mine and he smiles. A sweet, rather quizzical smile. Then he walks past me.

We drive back into Rome for the burial. Trust Fausto to be

buried in the very centre of Rome: he always claimed to have been the third child suckled by the wolf. The cemetery is full of looming family mausoleums, like little Gothic houses, and modern gravestones, many of which have photographs of the inhabitants on them. I wonder how they choose them? Do you have one of yourself old or one where you're in your prime? I bet Fausto will have chosen one where he is young and handsome. For almost the first time I think of Fausto, with his designer suits and scurrilous jokes about the Pope, lying in his coffin and I find that I'm crying. Then, Robertino throws soil into the grave and it's all over. I turn and walk quickly away. I don't even look to see if Antonio is following.

'Sophie?' His voice, of course, is unchanged.

'Robertino.'

'It was good of you to come,' he says, in English.

'I wanted to,' I reply, in Italian. 'Fausto was always very kind to me.'

'He loved you.'

For a moment, we gaze at each other. He looks tired and there's a mark on his chin where he cut himself shaving. Perhaps he needs to wear glasses.

'Goodbye, Robertino,' I say.

He smiles again. 'Sophie Richmond,' he says.

Back at the car, I scrabble madly at the lock before realising that I'm trying to open it with my house keys.

'Here. Let me.' It's Antonio. He extricates the correct key and unlocks the door. 'I'll drive,' he says. 'I've sobered up now.'

Even his presence can't stop me crying hysterically. It's as if all the tears I wanted to shed for Robertino eight years ago are coming out now and I'm powerless to stop them. Their taste reminds me of childhood. Once we're clear of the cemetery, Antonio stops the car. He lights a cigarette and offers me one. I shake my head, still crying.

'Look,' he says, 'this is ridiculous.'

'I know,' I say, hiccuping.

'For God's sake. Haven't you got a handkerchief?'

I say no and he hands me his. It's typically expensive and smells of aftershave.

'Look,' he says again. 'So you saw your ex-boyfriend. So what? It's been a long time now. You've got to move on.'

'I know.'

'It's not such a big thing,' he says, in a slightly softer voice.

'I know,' I say again, sniffing unattractively.

'Listen,' he says, with a return of his aggressive manner, 'I saw Melissa at the weekend. She wants to take the kids and go and live in America. Imagine that. My kids living on the other side of the world. That's something to cry about.'

'Oh, Antonio,' I say, feeling humbled, 'I'm so sorry. Is that why you wanted to come to Rome? To get away from it all?'

'I suppose so,' says Antonio. He starts the car again. 'I just needed time to think. And it's not easy with you crying all the time.'

I'm beginning to be irritated by him again. 'I'm sorry if I'm ruining your holiday,' I say haughtily. 'It's not easy for me. Fausto dying. Seeing Robertino again.'

'He's too old for you anyway,' says Antonio, putting the car into gear. 'I don't know what you ever saw in him.'

'No, I suppose you wouldn't,' I say.

We drive to the hotel, which I chose because I remembered it as fairly quiet for central Rome. Although it's late afternoon, it's still very hot and I haven't eaten since the meal I didn't eat on the plane. Hunger makes me feel slightly better.

'Do you want something to eat?' Antonio asks, as we check in. 'Or are you going to cry all evening?'

'I'm not going to cry,' I say, with dignity.

'Well, let's meet in an hour, then.'

In my room, I look at myself in the mirror. My face is dirty with sweat and tears, my hair is standing up wildly and my dress is crumpled beyond rescue. Even Guido would find it hard to think me beautiful at this moment. I decide not to think about Guido or Robertino or anything. I go into the wonderful marble bathroom and have a cold shower. Then I pull the curtains, throw myself on the bed and sleep.

The phone wakes me. 'It's eight o'clock,' says Antonio's impatient voice. 'I'm starving.'

I dress quickly in a shirt and cotton trousers, pull a comb through my still-wet hair and decide not to bother with make-up. Antonio is only my cousin, after all. He is pacing up and down in the lobby. He has changed his shirt and his hair is slicked back with water. He looks both younger and less familiar.

We eat at a restaurant near the Piazza Navona. It's the sort of place that Fausto would have condemned as for tourists only. There are tables outside and a depressed-looking gypsy serenades us on his violin. However, the food is good and it's rather pleasant to sit here and watch life pass us by. Crowds of Germans with backpacks and sunburn, a flock of nuns hurrying past in the twilight, Arabs selling handbags and statues of the Vatican, Italian businessmen talking on their mobile phones, hot-eyed young men on Vespas calling out to self-possessed girls eating ice cream on the piazza. I have missed Rome.

Over dinner, Antonio tells me about his children. 'Marco's OK about it. He's too young to understand, really. But Simonetta finds it really difficult. She can't understand why I'm not there all the time. When she does see me she's either all over me, crying that she wants to come home with me, or she's really cool and distant. It sometimes takes me ages to win her round.'

It strikes me that Simonetta is the one woman who has Antonio exactly where she wants him. 'Italian names,' I say idly. 'Simonetta and Marco.'

'Why not?' says Antonio, irritated. 'We've both got Italian names.'

'Robertino used to say that I had a typically English name,' I say sadly. 'Sophie Richmond. It reminded him of English homosexuals in the park.'

Antonio looks at me over his coffee cup. 'Are you still in love with him?' he asks.

'No,' I say. It feels as if I'm discovering this for the first time. 'I think that's what's making me so sad. All these years I've thought I was in love with him. And it hurt so much to see him again, but when he spoke to me, he was just another middle-aged Italian man.'

Antonio says nothing for a minute, then shocks me by asking: 'Are you sleeping with Guido della Francesca?'

Surprise, outrage and anger are so confused inside me that I'm quite interested to hear how my voice will come out and what I'll say. 'What the fuck gives you the right to ask that?' Not bad.

He shrugs, turning away to light a cigarette. Then he says, rather belligerently, 'I know he fancies you. He rang me up to ask for your address. Then you said that you'd seen him on Saturday night.'

'Seeing him doesn't mean I'm sleeping with him.'

'But you are, aren't you?'

I fully intended not to tell him, but the question is so expressionless and matter of fact that I find myself nodding.

Then I make it worse by adding, 'But it was only once. It didn't mean anything.'

Antonio lowers his eyes disdainfully. 'I don't want to know the details,' he says.

Suddenly anger is uppermost. 'Why do you want to know at all? What the fuck has it got to do with you?' Antonio says nothing and, almost with relief, I let anger take over. 'Well, fuck you,' I say, getting up, knocking over my chair and trying to storm my way through the crowded tables. He doesn't follow me.

The anger lasts through the Piazza Navona and a good part of the way back to the hotel. Then I start to slow down. I don't want to go back to the hotel. Bed, table, television, marble bathroom. It's dark now but the streets are still crowded with people. As I stand, indecisive, they turn me this way and that. Eventually, for want of anything better to do, I follow the largest crowd and find myself at the foot of Viale Vaticano.

As I look up at the familiar, steep hill, I think of Fausto and his next-door neighbour. He was always rudely surprised by the present Pope's continuing survival. 'If he's so keen on meeting God, he ought to hurry up about it.' How mortified he would be to know that the Pope had outlived him. I don't want to climb the hill and look up to the balcony where I first saw Robertino so I follow the crowds into the Piazza San Pietro. Cesare used to go on about Mussolini speaking to the crowds from a balcony – suddenly it seems rather sinister that when I first saw Robertino he was wearing a black shirt.

I had assumed that everything would be shut by now (it's about ten o'clock) but it must be a special occasion of some kind because people are streaming into the basilica. Eventually I follow them.

I haven't been into the Vatican for years. Robertino used to boast that he had never been inside ('All that Bernini. Too depressing.') although I don't know if that was true. I visited it as a child with my parents, my mother pretending to be in spiritual ecstasy over the *pietà*, and, later, with a group of other au pairs when I was working for the Gallis. Then it seemed to me rather soulless, with cameras whirring in the dark and people checking that you didn't go in wearing shorts. Now, with a choir singing and priests at the altar, cloudy with incense, it really does seem like a magical place and I remember Fausto telling me that the basilica was built on the site of an older, pagan temple.

The inside is so huge that the crowds are swallowed immediately. The people form a sort of huddle near the front, like sheep on a cold night. The mournful intonations of the mass are lost too, in a kind of international monotone. I've no idea what language the priest is speaking.

I walk slowly round the edge of the church, past ornate little confessional boxes with notices saying which language is spoken inside. I wonder if it's any different making your confession in another language. Perhaps in Italian your sins sound tragic and decadent, like Grand Opera. In German they would sound businesslike and impressively polysyllabic. Would you get a lighter penance from an Italian, a Frenchman or an African?

I sit on a spindly gilt chair at the back of the congregation. Twice in one day, when I haven't been to church for years. My mother used to try to make me go at Christmas, or for what she referred to as 'my Easter duty', but even she has given up. Although, intellectually, I don't believe that sex before marriage is wrong, I think that somewhere I must have begun to believe I lost my immortal soul when I first slept with Robertino. I'm sitting near a twisted-candy pillar covered with swarming gold bees. Fausto once told me that the bees were the family symbol of Pope Urban VIII's mistress. Nearby, a bronze baby's face peers out at me with slightly sinister bonhomie. One of Pope Urban's by-blows? Fausto would have known – it was the kind of detail he loved.

I get up and walk out of the church. In the candlelight the *pietà* looks magical enough almost to justify my mother's hysterics all those years ago. That night over our Indian meal, Guido had said that one of the things he liked about being Italian was the link to that long line of painters, sculptors and musicians who had given so much to the world. Now, leaving this amazing building, lights reflecting on bronze and marble, I don't feel that this is true. I don't feel any special link to Michelangelo just because he came from the same peninsula as my grandfather. I don't feel any special kinship with the modern Italians riding Vespas and gesticulating into their mobile phones. I don't feel any special kinship for English humanity en masse either. Does anybody? *Are* there people who really feel that they belong in a particular place?

When I get back to the hotel, Antonio is sitting in the bar, drinking brandy. It occurs to me that he drinks rather a lot. In the background, a group of Italians are watching highlights of the World Cup on television. Antonio looks up at me and I go over to where he's sitting.

'Sorry,' I say.

'That's OK,' he says ungraciously. Then, 'I'm sorry too. I was out of order. It was none of my business.'

Suddenly I feel very tired. 'That's OK,' I say. 'I owe you for the meal.'

Antonio shrugs. 'Don't worry. I'll put it on expenses.'

The group around the television suddenly shout at a disputed penalty.

'Are Italy playing?' I ask.

'No,' says Antonio. 'That's tomorrow.'

'I think I'll go to bed.'

'Stay. Have a drink.'

'Maybe just a coffee,' I say virtuously.

'Bloody schoolteacher. Have a brandy.'

'Oh, all right, then.'

When he comes back with my drink (and another for him), Antonio says, 'What do you want to do tomorrow?' Our flight isn't until the afternoon.

'I thought I'd go to Caserta.'

'Why?'

I'm aware that this will sound rather odd, so I take a great gulp of brandy first. 'I want to see Salvatore's grave,' I say.

CHAPTER 8

I'm surprised when Antonio offers to accompany me to Caserta. After all, last night he described the idea as morbid and mad. He even – cheek, considering that it was him who started it all – accused me of becoming obsessed with 'all this family business'. He declared that *he* was going to sightsee tomorrow or sit in a bar having a drink and a cigarette, *not* set off down the motorway on the hottest day for fifty years while I demonstrated my total lack of driving skills to an irritated audience of impatient Italian motorists. Our plane was leaving at 3 p.m. and he did not want to be stuck in a traffic jam at Ciampino at two. He had seen all the graveyards he wanted to for one trip and, frankly, my idea showed that I'd got this whole war thing completely out of proportion. Cesare's cousin was not Cesare and looking at his grave would not tell us whether Cesare had been a Fascist. It was simply that I'd become morbid and overemotional. It would be a better idea if I spent the morning seeking the services of a good psychiatrist.

So when I find Antonio waiting for me in the car park the next morning, grim-faced in designer sunglasses, I'm tempted to say something about rapid-onset schizophrenia. But as I open my mouth to speak, he forestalls me: 'For God's sake, let's go quickly before I change my mind.'

Bearing in mind Antonio's crack about my driving, I don't accept his offer to drive. However, my Italian driving has come back to me and I cut merrily in and out of the lanes on the way to the motorway. It is, indeed, stiflingly hot, even with the windows and sunroof open. At least today I'm wearing shorts and not a dress. Antonio's also in shorts, which is, frankly, rather a shock. Every time I change gear (gradually getting used to using my right hand), I catch a glimpse of extremely hairy leg. I don't remember him being so hairy but, then, I suppose I haven't seen him in shorts since childhood. His map reading, though, is excellent and we're on the motorway very quickly.

We reach Naples mid-morning and decide to stop for

coffee. A mistake: I'm no match for the circle of hell that is Piazza Garibaldi – ten lanes of traffic all seemingly jammed and fast-moving at the same time. Eventually Antonio has to get out in the middle of the road and ask the way. As his Italian isn't as good as mine, I'm rather pessimistic about this but he makes himself understood, throwing himself back into the car to a chorus of hooting and pointing at the left-hand lane, '*Diritto! Diritto!*'

We have coffee at a busy café with a view over the piazza, which looks like an illustration in a child's book of *Different Kinds of Traffic*. Around the outside cars, taxis, motorbikes and buses fight for space and, in the centre, there are signs for trains and the *metropolitano*. The Neapolitans stroll in the midst of all this: noisy, aggressive and good-humoured. For a while Antonio and I smoke in silence. Then I say, 'It doesn't feel very familiar, does it? After all, this is where we come from.'

'On one side maybe. I don't feel much of a pull to Norfolk where my grandfather came from. Or Ireland.'

I'd forgotten that his mother was Irish. 'But Italy's different, isn't it?' I say. 'We had it rammed down our throats by Cesare all through our childhoods.'

Domenica de Rosa

'Cesare's idea of Italy. After all, when was he last here?'

I have to think. Cesare and Sylvia used to go to Forte dei Marmi every year for two weeks but it has been several years since their last visit. And, even so, what do two weeks in a holiday resort tell you about a country? I realise I've probably spent more time as an adult in Italy than Cesare has.

'That's probably why he has such strong feelings,' I say. 'It's the ex-pat syndrome. Look at all those blue-rinses in South Africa and Australia voting for Thatcher. A strong leader always looks more attractive from a distance.'

'And the war,' says Antonio, stubbing out his cigarette. 'That probably crystallised his feelings about Italy. Made him choose a side and stick to it.'

I look at him. His head is bent and I can see his thick black hair with its threads of grey. Suddenly I have a wild desire to touch it.

Antonio looks up. 'Come on,' he says, 'Salvatore's waiting.'

We get lost again in Caserta. Antonio's guidebook describes the town as 'the Versailles of Italy', boasting a fantastic palace and water gardens. However, this is not at all obvious from the ugly, industrialised suburbs. We drive past the same windowless factory three times before Antonio jumps out again to ask the way of a passing motorist in one of those three-wheeled Ape vans. For a while, I watch his efforts at communication, then get out to help him. The Ape motorist grins, compliments me on my Italian and my legs, and tells us the way. Antonio doesn't seem particularly grateful.

All in all, our easier mood in Naples has disintegrated again. The midday sun is fierce and, as we get out of the car at the Campo Santo Inglese, I feel faint and light-headed. For a moment everything is surreal and technicoloured. When, at the ornate gates, I see a workman on a ladder, I have the ridiculous idea that he's painting the roses like some weird *Alice in Wonderland* gardener. Antonio stops to buy some flowers from the stand outside the main cemetery. 'That's a nice idea,' I say, when he catches up with me.

He shrugs. 'If we're going to do this lunatic thing, we might as well do it properly. Are you OK? You look very pale.'

'I'm fine,' I say.

The graveyard is beautifully tidy, with smooth green lawns and neat rows of white headstones, completely unlike the baroque dottiness of Fausto's Roman cemetery. The sky is so blue and the grass so bright green that I feel dizzy again and, for a moment, the little white graves spin in front of my eyes like a crazy smile. Antonio is already off searching for Salvatore.

It takes us some time to find him but eventually Antonio waves and points. I walk over to him.

The grave is exactly the same as all the rest. 'Salvatore di Napoli, 1916-1942'.

I had forgotten that he was a di Napoli. The last of the di Napolis, as Cesare has no sons. He was only twenty-six, younger than me, buried under the same blue sky that saw his father's birth. Antonio kneels to put the flowers on the grass and I feel tears starting. Then, suddenly, Antonio says, 'Look, Sophie!'

I follow his pointing finger. On the next-door grave I see, with horror, my own name. I blink and it comes into focus. 'Stanley Richmond, 1915-1942'.

'How weird,' I say to Antonio, my voice shaking.

What happens next is extraordinary. I turn to Antonio to touch his arm, just a casual cousinly gesture in recognition of the strange coincidence of the names, but instead I'm in his arms. There, in the deserted English graveyard, amid the tidy lines of the headstones, we cling to each other and kiss and kiss; not in a gentle, cousinly way, but so passionately that it has us gasping and panting for breath. And again I have the strange feeling that we're standing quite still, alone at the centre of the earth, while the graves and the grass and the painted roses spin past us.

Antonio and I get into the car and drive back to Rome. Neither of us speaks. I drive and this time the traffic seems to part before me, like one of those motor-racing games you find in arcades. When we reach Rome the streets are empty and the few people we see look somehow shocked and diminished. Perhaps the Pope has died at last. It's only the next day that we discover the reason. Italy had been knocked out of the World Cup, losing to France on penalties. Maybe Guido was right and the whole thing was fixed; maybe I was right and Italy are just perpetually unlucky. Either way it didn't seem to matter much.

We book into the hotel again. The receptionist looks at us curiously; Antonio stares back blankly, I am beyond embarrassment. In the lift, we stand on opposite sides as if stuck there by centrifugal force.

'Your place or mine?' asks Antonio.

'Mine,' I say. The keys give me an electric shock. When

we enter the room, Antonio looks at me almost quizzically, a half-smile on his face. It is I who pull him towards me, I who reach up to kiss him, burying my hands in his hair, I who grab greedily at him, as if I know that time is running out for both of us.

Much later that night, the phone rings. I rise up out of a dark pit. We're lying on the bed as if we'd fallen there from a height. Drugged with sleep, I answer the phone.

'Sophie? It's Dad.'

'Dad?'

'You'd better come home. Cesare's been taken ill.'

CHAPTER 9

We travel home, hardly speaking. I lean forward in my seat, as if this will make the plane go faster, until Antonio says I'm driving him mad. Our intimacy of last night (only last night?) seems to have vanished, but at Gatwick airport, as we're waiting for my luggage, Antonio suddenly pulls me towards him in a tight one-armed hug. 'It'll be OK,' he says.

We drive to Kent in his flash Italian car. I think I'll forgive him everything – the knee-jerk patriotism of his car choice, the holy picture on the dashboard, the fact that he made love to me all night and made me ache with desire and longing, everything – if only we get to Cesare in time.

It's almost dark now and twice we miss the turning to the hospital. Antonio grinds his teeth and the gears and I think of Caserta again. My stomach is churning with so many

Domenica de Rosa

things, panic, fear, lust, that I can hardly breathe. I'm leaning forward again. Antonio tells me to sit back, but gently.

We race into the hospital, past the reception desk and the meaningless modern art on the walls, into the lift and up to the ward, as Dad had instructed. Out of the lift, I'm running up the corridor when Antonio calls me back. He's pointing towards a waiting room. There, amid the broken armchairs and old copies of *Country Life*, are my father, gazing down at a plastic cup in his hands, my mother, head back, eyes shut, and . . . Cesare.

'Cesare!' I run forward, then stop. Cesare looks terrible. His smart pinstriped suit looks too big for him. His hands are shaking and he's looking past me, past Antonio, at nothing.

'I'm sorry,' says Dad. 'I got the message wrong. It's Sylvia.'

'Grandma?'

'She's had a stroke,' says my mother, opening her eyes. Cesare begins to cry.

We sit in the waiting room for what seems like hours. Dad goes to find a doctor and comes back with the news that there is no news. Antonio, rather irritatingly, goes off on the same errand and comes back with a doctor in tow. 'She's having a scan now. We won't know the extent of the damage until we have the results. It all depends on how quickly she gets back her faculties.'

'She didn't know me,' Cesare says brokenly. 'When I called her name, she didn't know me.'

Mum pats his arm ineffectually.

'We won't know until after the scan,' repeats the doctor, but kindly. She's a tiny Chinese woman, who looks about twelve. 'It depends which side of the brain was affected. You can see her as soon as she's back on the ward.'

'What happened?' I ask, as soon as the child-doctor has left.

Cesare doesn't answer, so Mum says, 'She fell when she was in the garden. Daddy went to pick her up and her breathing was all funny. He called the ambulance. He was completely distraught. The neighbours saw the ambulance and called us. They must have assumed it was Daddy.'

'Bloody fools,' says Cesare, making a slight recovery.

'We came as soon as we could,' says Mum, with her unerring ability to make me feel guilty.

'Where's Daniel?' I ask, smoothly passing on the guilt.

'In America. For work. He's getting the first plane back. Louisa's touring but I left a message with her agent.'

'She didn't know me,' Cesare says again. 'She couldn't say my name. Just like Joyce. She could never say my name.'

'Who?' I ask.

'He's rambling,' says Mum briskly.

'Don't talk about him as if he's not there,' I snap. Perhaps fortunately, a nurse comes in and says we can see Sylvia. We troop off after her but, somewhere in the back of my mind, I store away that detail. Who was Cesare talking about? Who was the woman who could never say his name?

Sylvia looks very small in the high hospital bed. I think of how much I love her, with her wonderful meals, her endless kindness and her quiet irony. I can't imagine any of us carrying on without her.

'Mummy?' says my mother, in a loud voice. 'Can you hear me?'

Sylvia's eyes look past her, searching anxiously, until she sees Cesare. 'Cesare,' she says clearly. 'Darling. Are you all right?'

Later we have a whispered conference in the waiting room, which now seems like a second home. Rome, Antonio, even school and my flat, it all seems a million miles away.

'Someone should go home with him,' hisses my mother.

Cesare is still sitting by Sylvia's bed. She's asleep but he refuses to leave her. I'm in the waiting room with my parents. Antonio is outside having a cigarette. I think how long it is since I've been alone with my parents. Not long enough, in any event.

'We can go back with him, Emma,' says Dad.

'But for how long?' My mother's voice starts to rise in its familiar air-raid siren of hysteria. 'You've got work. I've got *appointments!*'

I look out of the window. I can see Antonio smoking in the car park. It reminds me of the time I looked down on him from the window of my flat and was shocked by the grey in his hair. For some reason, he doesn't look old any more. He flings away his cigarette and gets out his mobile phone. I can still see smoke rising from the discarded fag.

'I'll go home with Cesare,' I say. 'It's the holidays soon. I'm sure they can spare me.'

I wake in the spare room of Cesare and Sylvia's house. It's very tidy and, even half asleep, I savour the order. Yellow curtains reflecting the early sunlight, blue button-back chair with a yellow cushion, pale yellow walls with a careful selection of pictures (prints of ancient Rome and watercolours of Kent), dressing table with a blue glass bowl, three books neatly arranged on the bedside table: *Leeds Castle in Colour*, *Pride and Prejudice* and a lurid thriller called *Dead Men Can't Dance*. Except for a bee buzzing somewhere in the room, the house is silent.

My whole body aches as if I've been running for miles. I feel dirty and travel-stained but also intensely alive, as if all my nerve endings are jangling. When I put my hands to my face, I can smell Antonio.

We said goodbye last night by the hospital entrance, watched by gloomy night-shift workers and A&E patients who had long since given up hope of being seen by a doctor.

'I'll call you,' said Antonio.

I nodded. He reached out, I felt his hand touch my hair and he was gone.

I bury my head in Sylvia's clean white pillowcase. Everything is terrible: Sylvia is ill, Antonio has gone and I don't know when I'll see him again, in a few minutes I have to ring Jane and tell her that I won't be coming in to school today, I have days of looking after Cesare ahead of me (and

I know how much work that will take), yet I feel wildly, unreasonably, gloriously happy.

I lie in bed listening to the bee buzzing and ask: Why am I here? Well, partly, of course, to look after Cesare and to chase that look of harassed martyrdom from my mother's face. Partly because I suppose I just wanted to escape for a while, away from the demands of Antonio, Guido, Salvatore, into the peace of the spare room. But somewhere in my mind, a little voice is saying: Now you're alone with Cesare, he might tell you his story. He might tell you the truth.

When I come downstairs, Cesare is dressed, immaculate in a cream summer suit with a blue cravat. Typically, he has done nothing towards getting breakfast and has not even made a cup of tea. I go into the kitchen.

'Tea?' I offer brightly.

Cesare shakes his head with an exaggerated shudder. 'No. Coffee. Lavazza. In the proper Italian machine.'

I'm tempted to ask him what the magic word is. 'Have you rung the hospital?' I ask instead.

'No. I was waiting for you.'

I ring. They say that Sylvia has had a good night and has got back almost all sensation on her left side. Her speech is fine and she has been asking after Cesare. 'He's fine. Give her our love and say we'll be in later.'

Cesare is standing so close to me that he can hear the nurse's voice. When I put the phone down I look at him and we both smile. 'She's going to be OK,' I say.

'Yes,' says Cesare. 'Yes, she is.'

We drink our coffee in the sunny courtyard. Rollo rushes about trying to catch butterflies.

'How was the funeral?' asks Cesare.

It seems a million years ago. I take a sip of coffee and think about it: Robertino's grey hair, his children in their matching black suits, Antonio's face when he asked about Guido, the neat rows of graves at Caserta, 'Salvatore di Napoli, 1916-1942'.

'It was OK,' I say. 'Robertino was there. He's got two children now.'

Cesare knows about me and Robertino, of course. At first he was angry and thought that Robertino's rejection of me was a slur on his family's honour. Sylvia had to stop him writing a letter to Fausto beginning, 'Your son has abused my granddaughter and I demand satisfaction . . .' Now he seems at least to have forgiven Fausto in death.

'That boy was always a disappointment to his father,' he

says. 'Poor Fausto. God rest his soul.' Elderly Italians always look slightly smug when they utter this phrase, as if they're really congratulating themselves on their own cleverness in staying alive. Cesare does so now, sipping his coffee with exaggerated delicacy. I tip my head back and close my eyes.

Did I think about Robertino when Antonio and I lay in bed listening to those same Roman sounds (traffic, church bells, cats wailing) that I had first heard with Robertino? Not at first. It was different with Antonio. Robertino swept me off my feet: I became a different person when I was with him. With Antonio it was like climbing back into myself. Kissing him, making love with him, was like completing something. It was as if all this investigation into the family had led me back to where I'd come from – into the family, into myself. I'm not sure if that's deeply perverted, and right now I don't care.

'Antonio's a good boy,' says Cesare suddenly.

I open my eyes. 'Yes,' I say cautiously.

'Did you hear that wife of his is going to take the children to America? I never liked the girl.'

'Nor did I.'

'Poor Antonio. He's not a lucky boy. But he's got a good heart, like his grandfather.'

'Uncle Antonio?'

'That's right. My father's brother. They were very close.'
Cesare heaves a sigh. 'Come on, let's go to the hospital.'

At the hospital, Cesare obviously wants to be alone with
Sylvia so I sit in the waiting room. Over the next few days I'm
to become depressingly familiar with this room and its surroundings: the coffee-vending machine, the library trolley,
the loos ('This bin is for hospital refuse only'). I sit and read
an old copy of *Cosmopolitan*. 'Six Ways to Tell if Your Lover Is
Unfaithful' – what about: 'Six Things to Do if You are Sleeping
with Your Cousin' or 'Six Ways to Tell Your Cousin that You
Want to Sleep with Him Again, as Soon as Possible'?

'Sophie?' Cesare is standing in the doorway, his jacket over
his shoulders like a movie star. 'Lunch?' Nothing – *nothing* –
will stop Cesare eating three full meals a day.

'Shall we go to the canteen?'

'Certainly not. I know a nice place very near here.'

We go to a small Italian restaurant with candles in Chianti
bottles and a mural of the Bay of Naples on the wall. We talk
about life, his and mine. The waiter, who is very camp with
pink-streaked hair, takes our order and glides away. Cesare

says, 'I've got nothing against them. It's when they corrupt young boys. That's what we thought then. I don't know now.'

'Cesare,' I say, 'what *are* you talking about?'

'Homosexuals,' he says. 'That was what the riot was about. We wanted the homosexuals moved to another camp.'

'Why didn't you tell Guido?' I ask.

Cesare looks shifty. 'Well, I didn't want to hurt his feelings. After all, he is . . . you know . . . one of those.'

I laugh. 'What made you think he was gay?'

'I just assumed . . . he had one of those handbags . . . he wasn't wearing socks . . . he seemed so well mannered. Gentle. He asked Sylvia for her Bakewell tart recipe.'

'Cesare! You thought he was gay because he was polite and didn't wear socks? You didn't want to hurt his feelings? He thought it was an anti-Semitic riot. Had you forgotten he's Jewish?'

'But it wasn't anti-Semitic,' he says, sounding shocked. 'I've got a lot of Jewish—'

'That's what they all say. I bet you've got a lot of gay friends too, if you only knew it.'

In the afternoon, we go to see Sylvia. Her face still looks a little lopsided but Cesare says he can see no difference.

'That's love,' I tell her.

'Yes,' she agrees. 'That's love.'

When we get back to the house, the phone is ringing. Heart pounding, I grab it. It's Louisa. It isn't Antonio, it's Louisa.

'How's Mum?'

'Much better. The doctors think she'll make a full recovery.'

'Thank God. Look, Sophie, I'm coming home but the first flight I can get is at the end of the week. Will you be OK looking after the old man?'

'I'll be fine,' I say.

I cook Cesare's supper and chat to him while we eat. I'll soon be the size of a house with all this food. I almost mention Guido again but think better of it. After supper, we watch a film on television ('Look, the assistant director's Italian!'), Cesare dozes and I read *Pride and Prejudice*. We go to bed early. Antonio still hasn't rung.

Remarkably quickly, we get into a routine. In the mornings, Cesare sees Sylvia on his own, then we have lunch in one of Cesare's seemingly endless supply of trattorias; in the afternoons we visit Sylvia together. I bring her glossy magazines and tempting food, we chat and Cesare stares at Sylvia, as if the intensity of his gaze will make her well again.

It's not until nearly the end of the week when, one evening, as we are eating our supper, I ask, 'Who was Joyce?'

'What?' Cesare nearly drops his glass of wine (also a daily essential).

'Joyce. When we were at the hospital that first time, you said that Sylvia couldn't say your name. Like Joyce.'

Cesare takes a long gulp of wine. He has started to eat and drink more like an old man. 'My first wife,' he says at last.

'Your *what*?'

'My first wife. I was married before your grandmother. It was before the war. She was English. Could never speak a word of Italian. Could never pronounce Cesare properly.'

'Why didn't you ever tell us?'

'I don't know. It didn't seem relevant. It was so long ago.'

'Cesare,' I say, 'that won't do. Why haven't you told us the whole story about the war? Why does Guido think you're hiding something? Tell me.'

He laughs. 'What do you want to know? We lost. England won. We hear about it every day. The Dam-bloody-busters.

Never so sodding few. Fight them on the beaches. All that rubbish.'

'I don't mean that,' I say quickly, to stop him heading off into a rant. 'I mean, what was it like for you?'

He looks at me. Without his glasses his eyes are faded and old. 'Is this about your gay friend – Guido?'

'He's not . . .' I begin ' . . . my friend,' I end lamely.

'Is this about the riot?'

'Well, partly,' I say. I had been so relieved that the riot wasn't anti-Semitic. True, the prisoners' behaviour had been bigoted and ignorant, but that is how many people were at the time. But then I think that you could use the same arguments to excuse anti-Semitism. This makes me uneasy. 'I want to know what it was like for you,' I say again. 'Being interned. Leaving your home. Leaving Joyce.'

He laughs again. 'Leaving Joyce was easy. Leaving Joyce was a relief.'

'But it must have been difficult,' I persist. 'You were . . . how old when the war started?'

'Twenty-six.'

'You were a young man. It must have been hard to go to prison.'

'Yes, it was hard,' says Cesare briefly. 'Have we got any cheese?'

The next day when I get up, Cesare is fully dressed, as usual, and waiting for me. Today, though, he is at his desk in the sitting room. Rollo is panting expectantly at his feet. When I come in, Cesare stands up. He looks different somehow. If I didn't know him better, I'd have thought he was nervous about something.

'I've got something for you,' he says. I see that he's holding a brown envelope and a small piece of silver jewellery. Please, God, I hope it's not his will. Cesare's will is notorious in the family for being about a hundred pages long and full of detailed bequests ('For Antonio, in acknowledgment of his devoted support for Juventus . . .'). Even this is not as bad as his funeral arrangements, which include instructions to scatter his ashes on the seven hills of Rome.

'What is it?' I ask.

He puts a silver medal in my hand. 'It's my father's St Christopher medal,' he says. 'I want you to have it. He brought it from Naples. I think it was given to him by the nuns at the orphanage.'

'I didn't know he was an orphan,' I say. The medal is worn with age but you can just make out the figure of St Christopher with the Christ child on his back. St Christopher, pray for me. Is he even a saint any more?

'He was sent to the orphanage with his brother.' Cesare points vaguely at the picture on the mantelpiece, which shows two small boys in sailor suits standing by a doorway. 'That's them. In Naples. My father loved that picture.' He gives me the brown envelope. 'This,' he says, 'is my birth certificate. I'm sorry I got so angry with you that time.'

I open the envelope. Name and surname: Cesare Vittorio di Napoli. Date and place of birth: 15 August 1913, London, England.

London, England.

I look up at my grandfather. 'You were born in England.'

'Yes.' Cesare laughs briefly. 'That's my secret. I was born in England. And she ... *she* ... was born in Italy.' 'She' must be Aunt Rosaria.

'Cesare,' I say, sitting down on the sofa, 'tell me about it.' So he does.

PART TWO

CHAPTER 1

It was a different world, that's what you have to remember. Times were different, people were different. London itself was different. You and Antonio, you modern Londoners, you wouldn't recognise it. No cars, cobbled streets, gaslights. And the dirt! You can't imagine the dirt and the smells and the poverty.

Our house was always spotless, though. My mother washed and cleaned all day long. All the women did. Scrubbing away at their front steps, boiling clothes in great cauldrons, their arms red to the elbows. I always thought of this when people called us 'dirty Italians'. There were English children on the streets with no shoes, nits in their hair, noses full of snot. My mother looked after their families, showed their mothers how to keep the house clean, how to avoid infection

135

and disease, but still they yelled after us: 'Dirty Italian! Ice-creamio! Eyetie!' My God. I get angry even now talking about it.

My story. Well, now you know that I was born in England. As far as I'm concerned that will never make me an Englishman. Oh, I know, being born an Englishman is winning first prize in the lottery of life and all that nonsense. Who wrote it? Some English idiot. Well, maybe he was right. Maybe it is a fine thing to be an Englishman; certainly I knew some good Englishmen during the war. One was the commandant of the prison where I was locked up, but more of that later. No, there are some good Englishmen but I'm not one of them. I never have been and never will be an Englishman. What was it that Daniel used to say that made you so angry? It doesn't make you a donkey if you're born in a stable. It doesn't make you a fine English racehorse if you're born in an English stable. I'll be an Italian donkey until I die.

I've never wanted an English passport either, though I could easily get one. I can never understand that fella who owns Harrods being so keen to get an English passport. Sod 'em, I say. The English will never respect you if you crawl to them, if you beg to belong. I've always been proud to be an Italian and I think the English liked me better for it. Even at school, the children who shouted 'Dirty Italian' at me respected me in the end. After I'd beaten them up a few times.

I was born in August 1913. My mother always said that my birth nearly killed her. I was a huge baby, over thirteen pounds, and my mother was a tiny woman, barely five foot tall. The old women used to say I was meant to be twins. Well, I certainly caused her enough trouble for ten children.

Once a month all the local women would come round to our house and make pasta. I can see them now, sitting at our kitchen table, rolling out the pasta, thin ribbons for fettuccine, little potato balls for gnocchi, the older women wearing black, the younger ones – like my mother – in brightly coloured overalls. They spoke in Italian, a mixture of dialects, with the occasional English word: 'Shepherd's Bush', 'bus stop', 'cuppa'. As they worked, they talked: how lazy their husbands were, how their children were running wild, not like the old days in Italy, how the local priest was a saint even though he was Irish. But their favourite subject was childbirth. I remember my mother telling the story of my birth over and over again: how terrible it was, how agonising, how the nurses sewed her up and the stitches burst. Then the women would all look at me as if it was my fault and I would run away to find my father.

What surprised me was the way my mother told the story, full of gestures and shouts of laughter. She would hold on to her stomach and groan and all the other women would groan too and call on Santa Maria to protect them. My mother was usually so reserved, polite always, but rather formal in her speech. And although the neighbours all loved her, my mother never forgot that she was different from them. She might live in the Italian Quarter and be married to a cobbler but she was different. She was a Tuscan.

The First World War started when I was a year old. I barely remember it although, funnily enough, I dreamt the other night that I was in the dark with giant birds flying overhead and, in the dream, I said: '*Ché cosa, Mamma?*' Now why do you think that was? *Ché cosa, Mamma?* In Italian. It's been many years since I dreamt in Italian. And my voice was a child's voice, calling for my mother. Now, what does that mean? Is it a bad omen, do you think? Does it mean that I'm not long for this world?

I do remember my mother telling me that there had been

a massive march of London Italians in favour of the war, led by two ex-Garibaldini, Stinghi and Geleso. More than eight thousand London Italians returned to Italy to fight in the war and they had a grand send-off from the Mazzini Garibaldi Club. Most of these men were attached to regiments on the Austrian front and many were awarded the Croce di Guerra for bravery. My mother's own brothers had fought in the *alpini*, the Alpine regiment. I remember them visiting and me playing with the feathers in their green hats. My father volunteered for the Italian army. Apparently he was on his way out of the recruiting office with his papers when an official ran after him with the news that the army had raised the height restrictions. At five foot one my father was too short. So, once again, the di Napolis missed out on glory.

When I was born, we were living above my father's shoe-repairing shop in Farringdon Road. This is one of the three roads – Farringdon Road, Clerkenwell Road and Rosebery Avenue – that make a sort of triangle at the heart of the Italian Quarter. There was another Italian Quarter too, in Soho. This was full of Italian waiters and chefs who worked in the high-class restaurants. The Sohoites, as they were called, looked down on the Clerkenwell Italians. Sometimes gangs from Soho would come to Clerkenwell and cause trouble in the shops and cafés, there would be street fights with knives and broken bottles, sometimes even with guns. That all stopped when Mussolini came to power.

Why did the Italians settle in Clerkenwell? My father always said it started with the chestnut-sellers from Garfagnana and Lunigiana. They came over in the last century but I remember them in my time: the red-hot braziers, the sound of the barrel organ playing, sometimes a sad monkey capering on the end of a chain. Salvatore was afraid of the monkeys – he said they looked like shrunken little men.

After the chestnut men came the ice-cream men, you'll have heard of some of them, names like Gatti and Santorelli. They sold ice cream in beautifully decorated handcarts, like little gondolas. Later on they bought cafés and milk bars. I hated the ice-cream sellers. When we walked to school, the London children used to shout 'Ice-creamios' at us and laugh. You know the song 'Oh! Oh! Antonio with his ice-cream cart'? They used to sing that whenever they saw us. I would fight them but Salvatore never did. Still, there's no doubt that some of those ice-cream sellers became very rich. The last laugh's on them, I suppose.

The chestnut men began to sell other food, like hot pota-
toes and peas. Then they bought cafés and restaurants, which
were popular with the British because they also sold alcohol.
The ice-cream barrows became shops and small businesses.
Whole families worked in the shops: grandparents, aunts,
uncles, cousins. Every so often, more cousins would come
over from Italy and the shops would open new branches.
Some of the families became very rich.

The artisans had started to come to England at the end
of the last century: mosaic and terrazzo workers, *figurinai*
making religious statues and miniatures, clock-makers and
glassblowers. I'll always remember one shop that sold artificial eyes. It terrified me, as a child, the thought of all those
eyes in rows behind the counter – I imagined them moving
of their own accord, watching me as I stood at the window.

By the time I was born, Clerkenwell had Italian shops,
cafés, tailors, hairdressers and lodging houses. There was also
an Italian school and an Italian hospital in Queen's Square.
But it's the grocery stores that I remember best: Terroni's,
Gennaro's and the others, dark, glittering places full of mysterious jars and bottles. If I close my eyes I can still smell
those shops: a mixture of sawdust, salami, pickles, coffee

and cheese. I used to go in with my mother and watch as the assistant weighed out dried mushrooms or cut thin slices of prosciutto. Then my mother would go home to cook, bottle and preserve. Remember, in those days you couldn't just go into a supermarket and buy this sort of thing. Sainsbury's Italian Week and all that patronising rubbish. Italian cooking was hard work, back then.

So, you see, I was born in England but really I lived in Italy. A rather grey Italy, but still a place where you could buy fresh pasta and porcini mushrooms in jars. You could walk the streets of Clerkenwell and never hear an English voice. You wouldn't hear much Italian either: it was a wild jumble of dialects – Neapolitan, Sicilian, Sardinian. But in our house we always spoke proper Italian. My mother insisted on it.

My father came to England in 1910. He arrived with just the clothes on his back and a few coins in his pocket, barely enough to pay for a meal. He had a cobbler's shop in Naples but he had left his brother, Antonio, in charge of it – it made barely enough to keep Antonio and his wife. Certainly, my father took none of the profits. I don't even know where he got the money for the passage.

My father had a friend, Marco Fantani, who helped him.

Marco's parents were *padroni*, people who came from the old country and set up businesses in England. They brought with them children from their home towns to work for them. Sometimes this was nothing more than slave labour: the apprentices worked long hours for little pay, slept in crowded rooms (or even under the shop counters) and were treated harshly. But it has to be said that sometimes the *padroni* gave them a real chance in life. Many went on to open their own shops and became very successful. Loyalty to your *padrone* was very important. That was why my father never spoke of why he had left the man he had been apprenticed to in Naples. You never spoke ill of your *padrone*.

Marco's parents made and sold ice cream. In the early days, Maria Fantani made it in her own kitchen; the milk was left to cool overnight, then frozen with ice and salt, bought from the 'ice men' who sold it door-to-door. They used to sell the ice cream in 'licking glasses' that had to be washed between customers. Of course, the English thought this unhygienic and it is probably where a lot of the talk about 'dirty Italians' came from. I completely refute this: no people on earth wash as much as the Italians. My God, the Romans were building public baths when the British still lived in caves. To the end of her days my mother took two baths a day. Even so, the man who introduced the wafer biscuit probably saved the Italian ice-cream industry.

Marco's parents wanted my father to work for them and for a while he did, selling ice cream from a handcart. But my father always wanted to work for himself. He didn't want another *padrone*, grateful though he was to the Fantanis. Each week he put a little money away until he had saved enough to rent a shop of his own. From there he started his cobbling business.

When I was young and stupid, I hated the fact that my father was a cobbler. I wanted to be smart, to mix with the upper classes. I didn't want to be the son of a little Neapolitan shoemaker. I'm sure my father was hurt by my attitude but he never showed it. He was a quiet man, a gentle man, he didn't let you know his feelings. But he was clever. When he died, he owned two shops and three houses. I lost all the money later, of course.

So Papa worked hard and he did well. He lived in two rooms behind the shop and he worked almost all the hours God sent. How did he pass his few spare hours? I don't know. He probably played cards with other expatriate Italians and talked about the old days in Naples. He certainly didn't waste his time learning English; to the end of their days neither of my parents spoke the language fluently.

And he didn't go to church. Like me, he wasn't a religious man. Oh, yes, he had a holy picture that he carried everywhere – I think his mother gave it to him before she died – and he had the St Christopher medal that I gave you. But I never saw him take them out and pray over them. I think they were a kind of good-luck token to him. A reminder of the old days. He didn't speak much about his childhood in Naples, only with his brother, Antonio, and then they spoke Neapolitan so I couldn't understand them.

Politics was his passion. He was a great admirer of Antonio Gramsci, the Sardinian socialist who helped organise the factory workers in Turin. When he met with his friends, played cards and drank grappa, it was politics they talked about. My mother, who disapproved of these friends, used to say they were Communists but I don't think this was true. They were old-style socialists: they believed in trade unions, redistribution of wealth and a workers' Utopia. They even published their own left-wing newspaper. It vanished when the *fasci* rose to power.

But there was one time when my father did go to church. In the summer of 1912 he went to St Peter's Italian church. This was not because of any religious event but because Caruso, the great Italian opera star, was going to sing. In those days it was quite common for visiting opera stars to go to St Peter's on Sunday and sing with the choir. As you can imagine, this caused great excitement. Most of the Italian Quarter must have been there that day. My father, who never sat down in church, would have stood at the back with the other men. Apparently, Caruso sang 'Panis Angelicus' so beautifully that my father felt the hairs rising on the back of his neck. After the service there was a reception. And there my father met my mother.

My father says my mother's first words to him were, 'Are you married, Signor di Napoli?' 'No,' he answered, 'but when you marry me I will be.' My mother said this wasn't true, I don't think she liked the idea of seeming so forward but, whatever the truth, they were married a few months after that first conversation.

This is the only photograph that I have of my mother as a young girl. Beautiful, yes, but she never thought so. 'I looked respectable,' was all she used to say. It was a big thing with my mother, being respectable. She was no typical Italian immigrant. She hadn't come to England to escape dreadful poverty, she had come as part of a European tour with some Tuscan friends. She was a Florentine, she came from a rich family of merchants who certainly expected something better for her than a penniless Neapolitan cobbler. A *short*, penniless Italian cobbler.

My mother's family, the Perruzzis, were related to the Italian royal family, the Martinis. My mother, Laura, was the youngest child and, I think, very spoilt. She used to tell me that she had her own carriage and used to drive out in the Tuscan hills, wearing a sealskin coat and muff, with her greyhound running at the wheels. She had one story that I never tired of hearing. She and her father were driving home from Montecatini when their carriage was waylaid by brigands. These men took the carriage, with my mother and her father still in it, to their headquarters. My mother described how they waited there for the bandit chief and that she imagined him like the wolf in the fairy tale, with rows of sharp teeth and a green forester's jacket. Anyway, when the bandit chief arrived he roared with fury at his men: 'How dare you kidnap this man! He is a friend to the poor.

He and his family must never be touched.' The bandit chief then personally escorted my mother and her father back on to the road to Florence.

I would beg for this story as a child. I loved the idea that my grandfather was so noble and kind, like the best sort of rich man in stories. I loved the idea of Italy as a magical place, a mysterious world where brigands lurked behind every tree and bandit chiefs turned out to be princes in disguise.

When my mother was sixteen, her mother died. I don't know what she died of but I think it was a great shock. She must have been quite young. Certainly my mother, her father and her brothers never got over it. My mother used to tell me this terrible story about seeing her mother's body in the grave. You know, there is an Italian tradition that two years after someone has died you open the grave to move them to the family vault. Grisly, I know. Please don't do this to me. I want to be scattered over the seven hills. Or the Stadio Olimpico. Anyway, when my mother went with her family to dig up her mother's body, they got a terrible shock. The body had not decayed. My grandmother had been buried in pink, which was apparently the tradition for women in the Martini family, and she lay in her pink dress, like a fairy-tale princess. Her hair, which had continued to grow after her death, billowed around her like a shroud.

My mother never got over this sight. She went into what was then called a decline but I suppose you'd call it depression. She refused to eat and sat for hours in her room, staring out of the window. Young men had started to ask her father for permission to court her but she refused even to see them. Her family became very worried. Was she going to stay in her room all her life? Eventually, in desperation, they sent her on a tour of Europe with another rich family, the Anzanis. They went first to Switzerland, then to Germany, then to France and finally to England where, after being swept away by Caruso's music, she met Giuseppe di Napoli, the little Neapolitan cobbler.

Sophie, Sophie. It's impossible for you to imagine how horrified her family were at the match. Florence and Naples were not just different parts of Italy, they were different worlds. They had different traditions, different attitudes, different languages. My mother's family, like all rich people, only really liked other rich people. God knows, they would have preferred a wealthy Englishman, German or even an Austrian; anyone rather than a despised southerner.

My mother never told me how she won her family round. Perhaps they thought that, at the grand old age of twenty, she was on the shelf and would now never marry one of those suitable Florentine suitors. Perhaps she simply wore them down – for a young, gently reared girl she had a remarkably strong personality. She wanted Giuseppe and she got him. They were married in November 1912, with the Anzani sisters and Marco Fantani as witnesses. Afterwards, my father went straight back to work. There was no wedding party and no celebration. But the occasion must have been celebrated in one way because, nine months later, I was born.

When I was only a few months old, the family went back to Italy. Why? I never really knew. My mother wanted to show me to her family, perhaps hoping that this large, bouncing boy would finally win them round. But there was also certainly a plan to settle permanently in Florence. There was talk of finding Papa a job and of bringing me up with my Perruzzi cousins. I don't know why it didn't work out but I think it had something to do with my father. He was a gentle, soft-spoken man but he could be stubborn. He didn't want to be beholden to anyone and I can just imagine how condescending the overpowering Perruzzis were to him.

Anyway, the upshot was that by the time I was a year old we were on the move again, back to England.

When I was a foolish, rebellious young man, I resented my father for denying me this chance to be a true Italian. I could have been brought up as a rich boy in Florence, rather than as a poor ice-creamio in Clerkenwell. But later I came to respect him for it. He was his own man, my father. That was why he left his *padrone* in Naples and set up on his own. That's why, when he came to England, he didn't want to be beholden to the Fantanis. He was not about to be patronised by a bunch of rich merchants from Florence. He was his own man and that, I think, was why my mother married him.

Were my parents happy together? My mother must have loved my father very much: she gave up her home, her family and her privileged way of life for him, but as a child I don't think I saw any sign of this love. People weren't so demonstrative then, none of this stupid sloppy kissing all the time. Thank God. It makes me sick to see people chewing away at each other's faces on television. My parents were always polite to each other and they seemed to be happy together. My mother made the decisions and my father backed her up. My mother wanted me to learn the violin and my father

made sure I did – my mother was tone deaf and never knew
whether I was practising or tuning up. My mother wanted
me to speak Italian and not Neapolitan so I did. My mother
dressed me in fine, beautifully made clothes, completely
inappropriate for my surroundings. Neighbours, seeing the
rows of finely sewn shirts on the line, said that it looked as
if she had a whole army of sons.

Definitely, for me, my mother was the dominant one. She
was a demure little person but she had a loud Tuscan voice
and would bellow at me if I stepped out of line. She was
always beautifully dressed, with her hair in a neat bun. She
was out of place in Clerkenwell and she knew it. For all her
genuine kindness to her neighbours, she never forgot that
she was their superior. And, I suppose, she taught me to
think that I was superior too.

My father was at once simpler and more complicated. He
was quiet and self-contained, with his work and his friends
and his endless games of *scopa*. In the evenings he liked to
sit and read the English paper. For some reason, my mother
found this annoying. I think it was because, for all her refined
schooling, she couldn't read English. 'He can't understand a
word of it, you know,' she used to hiss.

.My father was endlessly tolerant towards me. 'He'll grow out of it,' is what I remember him saying, all the time. When I fell off my scooter on Saffron Hill and needed eight stitches. When I fought with the street boys and came home with a bloody nose. When I said that I wanted to run away from home and join the circus. 'He'll grow out of it, Laura.' And my mother would snort and go off to crash plates in the kitchen.

I'm not sure how old I was when my uncle Antonio and his family came to live with us. I can't have been more than two because Salvatore wasn't born then and he arrived in 1916, when I was three. By this time, we had moved from the rooms behind the shop to a terraced house in Farringdon Road. My father had the upstairs made into a flat for Antonio, his wife Clara and Rosaria. Later on they had a place of their own.

My father was close to his brother. In fact, in some ways he was closer to him than to anyone else. He was a link to the old days in Naples. When they spoke in Neapolitan together, or sang Neapolitan songs after a glass of grappa, I could see my mother looking at them narrowly, as if she realised the brothers shared something she could never quite understand. She always made a point of moving the conversation back into Italian or ending the singing by announcing loudly that supper was ready. As I say, she was not very musical. But she was very kind to Antonio and particularly to Clara.

Clara was a pretty woman, with long dark hair that she wore wound round her head like a turban. She was gentle and kind, but not strong. One of my earliest memories is of hearing that Auntie Clara was 'unwell', she was resting and could I please not make so much noise in the yard. When Clara rested, my mother cleaned her flat as well as her own, she cooked for Antonio and looked after Rosaria. She did all this without the slightest complaint. Don't look at me like that. It's not my fault. That's what Italian women were like back then.

I was forced to spend a lot of time with Rosaria. My mother had a ghastly picture of the two of us, me wearing a revolting sailor suit and Rosaria in a frilly dress. We're holding hands but I look as if I'd rather be doing something else, playing with my hoop or my toy soldiers, running down Saffron Hill with the other boys. Rosaria always wanted me to play with her, those games girls play with dolls and prams and dressing up in their mothers' shoes. I don't know why she didn't find some other girls to play them with, but she never did. 'Play with your cousin, Cesare,' my mother was always saying. 'She's lonely. You must look after her.'

After Salvatore was born, Auntie Clara seemed to take to her bed for good. Certainly, my mother took over practically all the care of the baby. I was never quite sure, from the whisperings of the women in the kitchen, but I think that my mother couldn't have any more children after I was born. That must have been hard for her (and hard, in another way, for my father) but she never showed any outward unhappiness. She looked after me, Rosaria and now the new baby. She was also a kind of unofficial local nurse, caring for the neighbours' children when they were ill. One of my earliest memories is of her in the kitchen, frantically puffing on a cigarette. She had been nursing a child with scarlet fever and thought that the tobacco fumes would kill the germs and stop her passing on the disease to me. Perhaps it worked. Certainly I was never sick.

When Salvatore was two, Auntie Clara had a breakdown. That was how it was described to me and for a long time I imagined her with springs and cogs coming out of her insides. I couldn't understand why Uncle Antonio couldn't fix her – he always mended my toy cars when they broke.

To this day I don't know what happened to Auntie Clara. All I remember is Uncle Antonio hammering on our door one night and my parents going upstairs, me following in my pyjamas, and finding Auntie Clara crouching under a table, crying and wailing like a baby. Whenever Uncle Antonio went near her she screamed even louder. He was distraught, tears running down his face. My father put his arm round his brother: 'It's all right, Tadone. Laura will look after her.' My mother crouched under the table too and spoke to Clara in a low voice. My father ushered the rest of us out of the room. The next morning, when I came into the kitchen, my mother was there with Salvatore on her shoulder. Auntie Clara had been taken away, she told me, for a long rest. I was to be a good boy and help look after the baby and, of course, be nice to my cousin Rosaria.

I found out later that they had taken Auntie Clara away to a psychiatric hospital. She stayed there nearly five years. I remember going to see her and it seemed a nightmarish place, full of old women plucking at my jacket and asking me to give them a kiss. I begged not to go again but my mother insisted. We visited Auntie Clara every Sunday and she always seemed perfectly normal, a little quiet and subdued, but nothing like the demented old crones. The funny thing was that she still wouldn't have Antonio or my father anywhere near her, just my mother and the children. 'It's obvious,' the women in our kitchen said. 'She's gone there to get away from men.' Whatever the truth of that, the stay in the asylum seemed to do Auntie Clara no harm. In fact, she outlived the lot of them: my father, my mother and Uncle Antonio. Sylvia used to take you to see her when you were a child.

I liked Uncle Antonio. He was a loud, jolly man, noisier than my father and probably less intelligent. He was always ready to join in with our games. He built me my proudest possession, a kind of tin go-kart on wheels. I would launch myself down Saffron Hill on it, clinging on for dear life. Usually I would fall off at the bottom and come home bruised and bleeding. My mother would cry and forbid me to go on it again. My father would sigh and say, as usual, that I would grow out of it. But I never did: it was the beginning of my obsession with speed.

Uncle Antonio had one of the first cars in Clerkenwell, a Sunbeam Talbot, and he and I spent many happy hours with it, tinkering, tuning and perfecting. Despite my entreaties, my father stuck to his old horse and cart. I can still see him looking quizzically at us as we crouched by that car, covered in oil and grease. 'This is the future, Peppone,' Uncle Antonio would say. He always called my father Peppone, a childish form of Giuseppe. My father called him 'Tadone'. 'The future is going to be very dirty,' my father would say. And who's to say he was wrong?

Rosaria followed me everywhere. As soon as I was big enough, I wanted to be out, playing with the local children. Rosaria would trail behind me, like some awful mini-mother: 'Cesare, you're not to play with rough children. Cesare, you're not to ride your cart down hills. Cesare, I'll tell Auntie Laura.' I would run away from her and my mother would shout at me, 'It's not easy for her with her mother away and her baby brother taking up all my time. Be nice to her or you'll have me to answer to.'

Salvatore, though, was different. I don't know why, but there was something about him that made me want to look after him. He was very shy, scared of everything, from my mother's fat ginger cat to the *arrotini*, the knife-grinders, who came to the door with their grindstones and murderous-looking sharpeners. But he could be fun. He laughed more easily than anyone I have ever met. He would literally cry with laughter, rolling on the floor and clutching his stomach. And, of course, he laughed at my jokes the most. I was his big cousin: he looked up to me and I suppose I liked it.

Later on, when we went to school, Salvatore had a terrible time. At first, he was bullied unmercifully. I would meet him at the gates after school and he would say, 'I've got three people for you to beat up today, Cesare.' And I would fight them all in turn. By this time, the bullies didn't give me much trouble, they certainly didn't call me a 'dirty Italian' any more and, after a while, they learnt to leave Salvatore alone when I was with him.

All three of us went to the local council school. I think my father felt that the toughening up would be good for me, and my mother didn't realise what kind of school it was. As well as the Italian immigrant children, there were lots of London children from desperately poor families. Many were without shoes, and one boy in my class wore a paper suit. You can imagine what they thought of the Italian children with their starched shirts and elaborate, frilly dresses. They followed us down the street, jeering and spitting. It's ironic, really: the children jeered because we were too clean but their parents still called us dirty.

As I say, my mother always dressed me in the finest clothes. I hated it. I was one of the biggest boys in my class, unbeaten in street fights, and my mother dressed me up like Little Lord Fauntleroy. I always remember one year, for the Easter procession, she made me a satin suit, half of it was the British flag and half the Italian flag. Can you imagine? I thought of all the local boys laughing as I went past, prancing along beside the statue of the Madonna del Carmine, and I went cold all over. Besides, I think that even then I realised that the suit was a lie. I wasn't half Italian and half British. I was all Italian. I tried to refuse to wear it. My mother begged and cried and shouted but still I refused. Eventually, my father spoke: 'Cesare. Enough. Wear the suit.' So I did. I never disobeyed my father on the rare occasions that he put his foot down. But I'm sure it scarred me for life.

On my first day at school, the boy in the paper suit, who was called Nicholls, came up to me with a challenge: 'Think you're a fighter, do you?' I said nothing, weighing him up. He was a heavy boy, slightly shorter than me but with the look of a bruiser. His hair was cut very short, almost shaven, in a style my mother despised because she said it meant nits, and his bare feet were caked with dirt. Still, when he rolled up his sleeves I could hardly back down. I took off my jacket, beautifully pressed that morning, and laid into him. I had no idea what I was doing but I managed to knock him down once before he got the better of me. We were separated a few minutes later by a teacher and, from that day, Nicholls was my friend.

My mother was horrified. 'Giuseppe!' she'd say. 'Do something! He's mixing with those horrid street children. Why can't he stay at home with his cousins?' My father ignored her – after all, he had been a street child himself. Nicholls and I would hang around the streets together, swinging on to the back of trolleybuses, hurtling down the hills on my go-kart, fighting with the Irish boys from Hammersmith. Rosaria followed us around, scolding and threatening to tell, but, of course, we took no notice of her.

Once, Nicholls and I stopped a runaway horse. We were playing with our tops in the street when this huge animal, a dray horse from the local brewery, came galloping past. I heard later that it had been frightened by the band striking up to practise for the procession. It charged down the street, nostrils red, its cart bumping crazily behind it. Nicholls and

I immediately gave chase. Somehow we caught up and we hung on to the reins for what felt like hours but was probably only about ten minutes. The horse reared and stamped, its huge iron hoofs striking sparks from the cobbles. Nicholls, who had been brought up on a farm, spoke gently to it and eventually it calmed down. I just hung on, thinking how much I preferred cars. Then the brewery man appeared, panting and grateful. 'Well done, lads,' he said. 'You're proper heroes, you two.' He gave us a shilling each, which seemed like riches. My mother was furious, of course.

Perhaps it was because of Nicholls that my mother became obsessed with sending me to a private school. I remember whispered late-night discussions – my mother saying that they'd only got one son so he deserved the best, my father that I couldn't care less about school so why waste their money? Eventually my mother won, as I had known she would. I was sent to a minor public school two bus rides away from Clerkenwell.

I hated it. It was a pathetic place, obsessed with its own heritage: marble plaques with the names of old boys who had died in the war, obscure school slang, ridiculous rituals, cricket matches in the summer, rugby – a game for homosexuals in my opinion – in the winter. It was only a grubby Victorian building, surrounded by warehouses, but it thought it was the playing fields of Eton. I hated cricket, I hated the masters, I hated the other boys with their 'Jenkins Minor' and their stupidly anglicised Latin. But I learnt one thing at that school for which I was eternally grateful. I learnt how to speak English.

Oh, yes, of course I already spoke English, of a sort. My mother had been strict about me learning English properly, although we spoke Italian at home. A lot of London Italians, even those who had been born in England, spoke with a heavy Italian accent, but not me. At first I spoke street English, like Nicholls and the other council-school children. But at my new school I learnt the English of the upper classes. The King's English, they used to call it. That's typical of the British. Give them a chance to grovel to royalty and they're happy.

But, in all seriousness, this is one of the great mysteries of English life. It doesn't matter if you never pass an exam in your life, if you speak with the right accent people still treat you with respect. But my father was right, the money spent on my education was wasted. I left as soon as I could, having passed no exams and made no friends. The only thing I took away with me was an accent that, when I was arrested, made the policemen step back in surprise and call me 'sir'.

CHAPTER 2

I was only nine when Mussolini visited London. I remember furious rows between my parents. My mother would say that the fact that Mussolini was visiting the Italian Quarter meant that at last someone cared about the immigrants. 'Look at my passport, Giuseppe!' she would say. Italian passports had changed; once they said, *'emigrante'*, now the phrase was *'lavoratore italiano all'estero'*. Italian worker abroad.

My father would snort. 'What does he care about the workers? Trade unions outlawed. People forced to join the Fascist party. He's no friend of the workers.'

But, by and large, the Clerkenwell Italians agreed with my mother. Mussolini had given them back their identity. Once they had been immigrants, poor, despised in this new country, clinging desperately to the old ways. Now they were Italian again.

After Mussolini's visit to Clerkenwell, the *fasci* began to emerge. These were really just little Italian social clubs, places where Italians could go on Sundays, dressed in their best clothes, play cards and talk about the old country. But after Mussolini came to power, the Fascist Italian government poured money into these little clubs. The London *fascio* moved from dingy little rooms in Greek Street to grand premises in Charing Cross Road. I remember my mother taking me there once. When we entered the Sala dell'Impero, I could hardly believe my eyes. It was an enormous space, with marble stretching as far as the eye could see. Miles above us immense chandeliers glittered, and a gallery ran round all four sides of the room. Embossed on the marble wall were Fascist slogans, and engraved on the balcony were the words '*Credere, Obbedire, Combattare*' – Believe, Obey, Fight.

We were there to hear Gigli sing with the Sinfonica Italiana but my father refused to go, even though Gigli was his favourite opera singer. 'I won't set foot in that place,' he said stubbornly. 'Not even for Gigli.' I didn't have any views about Mussolini at the time but I could certainly feel something different in the atmosphere. There was confidence, even a sense of menace, in the air. I decided I liked it.

The *fasci* also organised holidays for children – Rosaria and Salvatore went on one. My father refused to let me go. They held Italian language classes and produced their own newspaper *L'Italia Nostra*. The message was the same: be proud to be Italian, learn about your heritage, don't feel inferior to the British. You have to remember, before this we had been oppressed, laughed at, despised. Dirty Italians. Stupid peasants with their ice cream, their chestnuts and their hurdy-gurdy music. Now we were standing tall. It was a good feeling.

When Mussolini needed money for his Abyssinian campaign, the *fasci* went into a frenzy of patriotism. At St Peter's Italian church, they held a service where women swapped their gold wedding rings for base-metal ones. The gold went to help the war in Abyssinia. It was called the *Giornata delle Fedi* – the Day of the Wedding Rings. I always remember, though, that my mother refused to give away hers. 'Patriotism is one thing,' said my father sardonically, 'but white gold from Florence is another.'

What was I doing at this time? Oh, I was far away from

Clerkenwell. I left school at sixteen. I wasn't clever like you, all I cared about was cars. On my fifteenth birthday, Uncle Antonio gave me some money and I went out and bought a Morris Cowley, built like a tank. Cars were still quite rare in Clerkenwell. There were no driving tests, I just got in and drove it away. By the time I reached Shepherd's Bush, I had hit two buses and a motorbike. When I got home my mother said, 'If you're going out in that thing again, I'm coming with you.' She put on a hat, stabbed in a hatpin, and got into the passenger seat. I drove as far as Croydon. My mother held on tightly to the sides of the seat – there were no seatbelts in those days – and said nothing. By the time we got home, I was a driver.

I suppose I was very wild at this time. There was a club called the Frattelanza Club in Clerkenwell that had a very bad name. It was full of gamblers, men who used to bet huge sums on horse racing. All illegal, of course. The gambling was organised by two families, the Sabinis and the Cortesis, and it led to terrific rivalry. Once, it was said, there was even a shoot-out between the rival gangs. I found it all tremendously exciting, like being in 1920s America. Much to my mother's horror, I took to frequenting the club.

I had also started racing cars. I sold the Morris Cowley, bought a dilapidated sports car, tuned it up and went in for races at Brooklands. I made friends with other racing-mad chaps and we spent hours tinkering with our cars and racing each other round the Brooklands track. It was a notoriously difficult track, with banked-up corners where you could get up tremendous speed. It was dangerous, though. I knew a man who drove right over the top and killed himself. I was the best cornerer in the south of England. You ask Enzo.

È vero, Sophie, it was a wonderful time. Sometimes we would drive down to Brighton in an open car – no windscreen wipers, remember, and no heating: our hands used to freeze on the wheel. We would go to Sherrie's or one of the other clubs to meet girls. There was never any shortage of girls. I don't want to go into detail but I will say just one thing. With women, being Italian is never a disadvantage.

I began to get a bad reputation. One day I took a girl called Anne – she was the daughter of my violin teacher – to Brighton. On the way back, my car ran out of petrol and we didn't get back until early the next morning. Now, in those days, this caused quite a scandal. My mother complained that the Clerkenwell women were all whispering about me and forbidding their daughters to see me. I didn't care. I didn't want to go out with their daughters anyway – I've always preferred English girls – and it didn't bother me that people crossed the street when they saw me coming. But my mother was upset and this upset my father. Then, one night, racing home at midnight, I crashed into a café window. The neighbours were up in arms, my mother was hysterical, Rosaria was disapproving. I left home.

I went to Edinburgh. Why? Well, you know my old friend Enzo? Remember going to a party for his golden wedding anniversary? You know him as a sweet little old man but, believe me, he was quite a hellraiser in his youth. We all were. Well, Enzo came from one of the rich Scottish ice-cream families. He was a mechanic at Brooklands, not a brilliant driver but he knew everything about cars. He and I were great friends, we did everything together. So, when Enzo said that he was going home to Edinburgh, I decided to go with him. We took Enzo's white MG and did the journey in two days, taking turns to drive. In Edinburgh, we stayed with Enzo's family and partied as hard as we could. When my money ran out, I got a job selling skiwear at a department store.

Does this surprise you? I knew nothing about skiing, of course, but in those days I had all the cheek in the world. I told the manager I came from a famous alpine skiing family and he believed me. The accent helped and that I'd been to the same school as his cousin. The old school tie is very long sometimes. I sold skiwear to rich Scottish women and, yes, I was pretty good at it. You can laugh, but your grandfather was a good-looking chap then.

It was in the shop that I met Rose. She had come in to buy clothes for her annual holiday in St Moritz. She was a well-brought-up girl from a rich Jewish family and she thought I was terribly exotic, possibly a bit dangerous. I'm afraid I played up to this for all I was worth. I told her stories about the Italian Quarter, about fighting in the streets with Nicholls and playing cards at the Frattelanza Club with a gun on the table. She couldn't have been more impressed if I'd been Al Capone himself. Al Capone with a public-school accent, mind you.

Only Enzo was sceptical. He said that when her parents found out I'd need an undertaker, not a ski-suit. He knew the Goldbergs. They were rich, and Rose was their only daughter. They wanted someone better for her than an Italian shop assistant. And when Rose eventually introduced me to her parents, it was a bit like the Perruzzis being confronted with the Neapolitan cobbler. An Italian, a Catholic, a *shop assistant*. Rose told me that she was forbidden to see me. She clung to me, weeping. *Va bene*, I thought, if they want a fight, they've got one. 'Don't cry,' I told Rose. 'We'll get married. That'll teach them.'

We moved into a tiny flat in Picardy Place, in the Edinburgh Italian Quarter. Rose loved it. Before meeting me, she had never even eaten spaghetti. Now she was eating in Italian restaurants every night, dark little places where the owner would sit at the table with us, picking his teeth and talking about politics. I loved introducing her to this life. For a while, we were very happy.

One night, coming home from a party with Enzo, we were set upon by Rose's two brothers and some of their friends. They outnumbered us but I hadn't been brought up in Clerkenwell for nothing. The nicely brought-up Scottish boys were no match for us. I knocked down one brother, Archie, with my first punch and the others soon ran away. Despite the popular myth, some Italians quite like a fight.

I'm not sure how long we would have stayed together but

after a few months the novelty had begun to wear off, for her as well as for me. She was very sweet but, my God, she was boring. Why did she agree with me all the time? For Rose, I think the charm of the Italian Quarter was paling. She began to ask why we couldn't go to Cannes for the summer and why I had to go to work every day in the shop. We'd been together about four months when, one night, Enzo appeared at the door. My father had been on the phone to his parents: he wanted me to call him at once. In those days, telephone calls meant bad news. I ran straight to a public phone filled with visions of my mother lying ill, calling for me . . .

My father answered the phone. 'Is that you?' he asked suspiciously, in Neapolitan.

'Who else would it be?' I said impatiently. I asked if my mother was all right.

She was fine, said my father, just worried sick about me.

I breathed a sigh of relief. That was OK, I was used to *that*.

But then my father delivered his bombshell. Reverting to Italian – a sure sign that my mother was listening – he told me that my mother had been to church yesterday and had heard the banns called for me and Anne Sullivan. *Anne Sullivan?* I was silent for so long that my father asked if I was still there. Sarcastically he asked if I could remember Anne and, to be truthful, I hardly could. My violin teacher's daughter, the one I had taken on that fateful trip to Brighton. *Had* I asked her to marry me? I honestly couldn't remember. Maybe in the panic of getting back so late I had said, 'Don't worry, I'll make an honest woman of you,' or something of the sort. But it seemed a million years ago, in a different life.

'Are you going to marry her or not?' asked my father.

I took a deep breath and said: 'I can't, Papa. I'm engaged to someone else.'

What did I do next? I did what any well-brought-up young Catholic boy would do: I asked a prostitute for advice. I was sitting in the Osborne Hotel, nursing my third Scotch and wondering what the hell I was going to do. Was I going to marry Anne Sullivan? I could hardly remember her face – although I could remember her habit of humming under her breath, which had become irritating on the Brighton jaunt before we had left Croydon. Was I about to be condemned to a lifetime of humming? And what about Rose? If I was honest, I didn't really want to marry anyone. I was only nine-teen – I wanted to escape, to live a little, to go racing with my friends.

Then someone said, 'Penny for your thoughts, handsome.' It was a woman, thirtyish, quite good-looking, but I realised at once what she was. I told myself that here, at least, was a woman who wouldn't expect me to marry her. She introduced herself as Minnie. I bought her a drink and one thing led to another. I won't say more. Later, sitting in Enzo's MG, which I had borrowed a few days earlier to take Rose to Portobello, I told Minnie the whole story. She pocketed her money and gave me her advice: 'Run away. Run like hell, as fast as you can.'

I had never heard anything so wonderful in all my life. 'What, now?' I asked stupidly.

'Drive straight back to London,' she said, 'and don't marry either of them.' With that, she opened the car door and jumped out, waving cheerfully. It was not until I was well past Newcastle that I saw she had left her shoes, red and high-heeled, in the car.

Back in London, I extricated myself from my 'engagement' to Anne. Her mother was furious. She told me I was a cad and a bounder and, as a final insult, *not even that good on the violin*. I made it up with my parents and moved in with another racing friend, Piers Hastings. I received a tear-stained letter from Rose telling me I'd ruined her life. I felt guilty for several weeks until Enzo returned from Edinburgh to say that she was now engaged to a nice Jewish medical student.

Poor old Piers. I've been thinking a lot about him recently. He was nothing like Enzo. Piers was your typical upper-class Englishman: weak-chinned, stammering, not very bright. But he was a devil on the track. He knew no fear, taking corners on two wheels, getting so far into your slipstream that you could practically see his face on your back seat. That was his only fault as a driver: he was too reckless – sometimes you have to be able to see the danger to avoid it and Piers simply never thought about it. Thinking wasn't his strong point.

Piers had a friend called Michael Sanderson, who was also very rich. Sanderson had one of the first cine-cameras and he had the idea that he would like to make a film of us racing. Then he got more ambitious and said he wanted to film some stunts. What he wanted was for one of us to lie down in the road and the other to drive over him. 'Great fun, what?'

I'll never forget that day. Very early one morning, we drove over to Croydon airport – Sanderson thought one of the runways would be more suitable than a city street. It was winter and I remember there was frost on the ground. Sanderson had a hip-flask of whisky and we all had a sip – no rules about drink-driving in those days. Sanderson fussed with the camera, talking about angles and lenses, but Enzo seemed to understand its workings better than he did.

'Right, chaps,' Sanderson said at last. 'Who's going to drive and who's going to be run over?'

Piers and I looked at each other. For a moment, it felt almost as if we were in a duel and Enzo and Sanderson, standing slightly behind, were our seconds. We both knew it had to be the better driver who did the stunt. There was such a long silence that Sanderson started to go on about losing the light. Then Piers said, 'You do it, Ces.'

I had recently got a job racing the new Fiat Ballila and I was driving it that day, a beautiful car, bright red, shaped like a bullet. I took off my gloves – I never drive in gloves, as you know – and got into the car. Enzo followed to give me some last-minute instructions. I could see that he was nervous too. A few hundred yards away, Sanderson was showing Piers where to lie down. I could see his cashmere scarf fluttering in the breeze. I asked Enzo to tell Piers to take off the scarf.

Enzo walked over to Piers and I started the engine. The

Ballila roared its beautiful gusty roar. Sanderson raised his arm and I put my foot on the accelerator. I got up speed quickly and took the corner without braking. I had just one glimpse of Piers's face, pale but oddly calm, before I banked the car on two wheels and drove over him. And that is how I always see him in my dreams, lying there in the road, looking up at me. I can see his eyes briefly before I drive on, over him. In my dreams, he does not get up again.

Afterwards, as we were smoking and drinking whisky from Sanderson's flask, Sanderson kept saying, 'You've got guts, Cesare. I'd never have had the nerve to do that.' Even Enzo seemed impressed. But I always knew that Piers had been the brave one.

Once I took Piers to visit my parents. We drove through the little Clerkenwell streets in a white Lagonda, our silk scarves flying behind us. People came out of their houses to see us go by. No doubt we looked ridiculous. My mother cooked us a huge Italian meal and Piers was extremely polite to her. Too polite? I wondered afterwards. Like an explorer visiting a strange new tribe and not wanting to upset their primitive sensibilities? All I know is that my mother liked him. Years later, when she heard of his death, she wrote to his family saying how sorry she was. They never wrote back, of course.

Was Rosaria at that lunch? I don't know. She was around a lot at that time as Auntie Clara was having another of her bad spells and she and my mother took turns to look after her. Like me, Rosaria left school at sixteen: she was quite clever, though, I'll give her that, got a scholarship to the grammar school. She had a job as a seamstress in a local factory. I used to see her sometimes with the other girls, their hair tied up in scarves, giggling as I went past. I didn't have much to do with her. She'll say it was because I was a snob and maybe that's true. It's just that I was so much concerned with other things: cars, drink, parties, girls. What? Rosaria was a girl? Well, I suppose so, in a way.

I didn't see much of Salvatore either. He had gone to the local secondary school – unlike Rosaria he was not clever, and I think he had a hard time there, without me to protect him. He just sort of dreamt his way through life. I always remember seeing him wandering home from school, satchel dragging on the ground, stopping to talk to all the local dogs and cats. Salvatore loved animals. He used to spend hours with Papa's old horse – the one that used to pull his trap – in the brewery stables, talking nonsense and giving it sugar lumps. I could never understand what he saw in it. The incident with Nicholls had put me off horses for life.

When Salvatore left school, with no school certificate, of course, he had no idea of what he wanted to do with his life. Eventually, my father took him into one of his shops and I think he liked it well enough. My father used to say he'd never make a cobbler, he was too vague and inattentive to learn, but he had a nice, shy way with him and I think he was popular with the customers. By this time I was too busy crashing cars and going out with girls to see much of Salvatore but we always got on well when we met. On Salvatore's eighteenth birthday, I took him to Brooklands and drove him round the track. He loved it, whooping as if he was in a fairground. But afterwards, when we met some friends of mine in the clubhouse, he wouldn't say a word. When we got home he said that my friends were very clever. 'Of course they're not,' I said. 'They're just a bunch of good chaps.'

'Cleverer than me,' said Salvatore.

But suddenly Rosaria and Salvatore had a new passion: Mussolini. By this time, the Fascists were in power in Italy. My father was devastated. 'Do you know who this is?' he shouted at me once, pointing to a picture of Mussolini. 'Matteotti's murderer!' But to most London Italians Mussolini was a hero. And I know you'll find this hard to believe, but it wasn't just the Italians. Many British people admired Mussolini. Churchill even called him 'one of the most wonderful men of our time'. In prison we used to quote this to the guards to annoy them. At the time, though, I was concerned with my own affairs. I didn't think much about Mussolini; that came later.

I will always remember one Sunday lunch at my mother's house. I hadn't been home for a while and my mother made a big fuss of me and cooked a huge lunch – pasta followed by roast beef, green beans and grilled aubergines. When we had finished, Rosaria came in. She seemed very excited and looked prettier than usual. She said she had been at the *fascio*, teaching the children to sing 'Giovinezza', the Fascist anthem. My mother looked interested and began asking questions when, suddenly, something happened that I had never seen before. My father exploded with rage. 'Mussolini! That clown!' he shouted. 'Do you know what he's doing in Italy? He's even put Gramsci in jail. He'll finish Italy for good.

Him and his blackshirt goons!' He spoke in Italian, so there was no chance that we wouldn't understand.

Uncle Antonio laughed – he had no time for politics of any sort – and Auntie Clara looked frightened, as she always did when voices were raised. My mother asked me what I thought but I said nothing. I had no views on Mussolini and, besides, I had something else on my mind. I had come to tell my parents that I was going to marry Joyce.

I know, I know, Sophie. Why haven't I told you about Joyce before? Well, it isn't an episode that I'm particularly proud of and I suppose I didn't want you to know that I had any life before your grandmother. To tell you the truth, I can hardly remember Joyce. She was Piers' sister: pretty in a chinless, blonde kind of way. She was fun – that was the main thing about Joyce. Whatever we did, she would say, 'Isn't this fun? Oh, what fun. Oh, the fun of it. I *am* having a lovely time.' And I liked that. Life seemed to be getting rather serious all of a sudden and it was nice being with someone who thought everything was a tremendous joke. But, of course, that was not the real reason. I married her because she was pregnant. When she told me, my heart sank, but there was no question that I wouldn't do the decent thing. She was pretty, upper class and Piers's sister. It could have been worse.

My parents were shocked. They tried to make the best of it, though. She was obviously 'a lady', pretty and vivacious too, just not what they had hoped for me, which, in my mother's case, was a Tuscan heiress. Joyce smoked and wore trousers and didn't know how to cook. She called me Chessie and couldn't get her debutante's tongue round the simplest Italian word. But they tried to like her, for my sake.

We were married at Chelsea register office. Piers was best man. The only other guests were Enzo, my parents and Joyce's parents, Colonel and Mrs Hastings. I'll never forget the look on Mrs Hastings' face when she heard my mother speak for the first time. My parents had dressed up for the occasion; my mother was wearing a good fur coat and her family jewellery. The Hastings were probably quite relieved at her respectable appearance but, my God, when she spoke . . . Despite those evenings spent with the English paper, neither of my parents ever really learnt English. My father could read and write English fairly well but they both had thick, music-hall-Italian accents to the end of their days. By now, my father was a fairly rich man, but when he opened his mouth the Hastings looked at each other in horror. What was this family into which their daughter was marrying?

The Hastings weren't bad people. They tried to be pleasant to my parents, although I gritted my teeth when I heard the condescension in their voices. They liked me – I think I was better than a lot of Joyce's boyfriends. I was Piers's friend and I, at least, sounded like a gentleman. And Joyce was having my child.

Except she wasn't. To this day, I don't know if she had a miscarriage or if she had never been pregnant. All I know is, a month after the wedding Joyce told me she had 'lost the baby'. I was shocked. I wanted to comfort her, to take her to doctors, but she told me she didn't want to talk about it. To all intents and purposes, life carried on as before. We moved into a flat in North Kensington. I continued to race and test-drive cars and in the evenings we went dancing. Joyce loved to dance.

We were staying with Joyce's parents when war was declared. Piers was there too, with his girlfriend Betty. I remember Colonel Hastings turning to him as he switched off the wireless: 'Well, my boy,' he asked, 'what are your plans?'

'Join the RAF,' replied Piers promptly.

We had all recently become obsessed with flying. Enzo had already got his pilot's licence and would sometimes take us up in an old First World War biplane.

Joyce's mother turned to me. 'What about you, Cesare?'

'Oh, me too,' I said, without missing a beat.

But that night I lay awake for hours. Would I join the RAF? It had its attractions: the uniform, the wings, posing and being fatalistic about death, drinking champagne from girls' shoes. But however much I stammered and drawled and called people 'old boy', I wasn't English. I suppose that English public school had taught me this much: you choose your side and stick to it. I was Italian. Italy wasn't in the war yet but I knew she soon would be. Should I return to Italy to fight? Believe it or not, I wanted to fight. Remember, I was a racing driver: I loved speed, I loved danger. I was never any great intellectual. I liked action, doing things. Part of me wanted to run away to Italy and join up the next day. But how could I leave my family, my home, Joyce? All night, as Joyce slept beside me, I turned things over in my mind. Then, as dawn began to break, I had an idea. I would ask Enzo. After all, we were both British Italians. Hadn't we faced the

Edinburgh bully boys together? Perhaps we could go off to war together: friends, brothers, compatriots.

The next day, I caught up with him at the track. Enzo, in filthy overalls, was lying underneath his MG. I sat on a pile of tyres. I remember taking care to keep my new trenchcoat away from the oil and grease. I sat there and told him of my predicament. What should I do? Should I try to get to Italy?

I'll always remember that Enzo didn't look at me. He stayed under the car and told me that he had applied to join the RAF but that they had turned him down and told him to join the Pioneer Corps. It was more suitable for someone of his nationality, they said. What was I going to do? Enzo asked. I told him I had no idea. I walked away without looking back. I think we both knew that the old days were over.

I walked around all day. All the old haunts: Shepherd's Bush, da Bruno's in Hammersmith, the Frattelanza Club. Eventually I ended up on my parents' doorstep. I stood there and told them I was going to try to get back to Italy. 'Does Joyce know?' asked my mother at once.

'No,' I said.

Then my parents, who had been standing together in the doorway, stood aside and I saw that Salvatore was there. I wasn't surprised – like Rosaria, Salvatore spent a lot of time with my parents. But then I saw the expression on his face. He looked awkward but also defiant, something I had never seen before. 'I've joined up,' he said.

For a moment, I was full of jealousy. Salvatore, timid little Salvatore, had had the nerve to join up while I was still hesitating. But then I understood and I knew that my cousin and I were on different sides. 'The Italian army?' I asked. Salvatore shook his head. 'But you're Italian,' I insisted. 'You're a di Napoli.'

With a curious kind of pride, Salvatore told me that he had changed his name. He was Stephen Denning now. 'I'm British,' he said.

It was the final straw. I took a step towards him – I don't know what I was going to do: I had never hit Salvatore in my life. My father put out a hand to stop me and, for a moment, I just stood there on my parents' doorstep, looking at them. It was as if, suddenly, I had become the outsider. Then I turned and began to walk away. Salvatore ran a few steps after me. I think he called my name, I don't remember. I do remember what I said to him, though: 'You're no cousin of mine,' I said. '*Stephen.*' They were the last words I ever spoke to him.

Two days later I went to see the Italian ambassador, Giuseppe Bastianini. I had met the previous ambassador, Count Dino Grandi, at the Mazzini Club on a couple of occasions. Grandi had been popular among London Italians because, unlike previous ambassadors, he actually spent time in the Italian Quarter. He was also a powerful figure in the Italian Fascist party. I didn't know Bastianini but I'd heard that he had an agreement with the British to take a group of nominated Italians back with him to Italy when war broke out.

Bastianini sat at an ornately carved desk. A huge picture of Mussolini loomed from the wall. He asked me why I wanted to return to Italy and I responded with a lot of pompous rubbish about fighting for my country – 'and Il Duce', I thought it prudent to add. Bastianini looked at me, giving nothing away. He told me that he had a ship, the *Monarch of Bermuda*, and permission to take seven hundred men to Italy. He asked why he should take me. I said that I was a racing driver, I knew about mechanics, I spoke perfect English. Bastianini looked at me for another long moment. Then he sighed and said, 'Very well, Signor di Napoli. You have a place on my ship.' I asked when we were to sail. 'You will be informed,' was all he said. He stood up to show that the interview was over.

Italy entered the war on 10 June 1940. As soon as I heard, I rushed to the embassy, only to be sent back at the door. The ambassador knew all about me, come back tomorrow, there was enough time. That night, at midnight, police burst into the flat and arrested me as I lay in bed with Joyce. As they tried to manhandle me, I hit out and asked them what the hell they were doing. At the sound of my voice, the policemen fell back in genuine confusion. 'I'm sorry, sir,' one said. 'Only doing my duty.' I went with them without protest.

Joyce came to the door, shivering in her silk nightdress. 'Don't worry, Chessie,' she called. 'I'll stand by you.' I never saw her again.

CHAPTER 3

I was taken to Brixton prison. Later I found out that this was highly unusual. Most Italian internees were taken to their local police station and then to 'collecting points' around the country. Apparently, I had been classified as 18(b) – a threat to national security – and was to be imprisoned with British Fascists. In other words, they thought I was a British traitor rather than an Italian prisoner of war. Actually, I was in good company. The cream of the British aristocracy was at Brixton prison, including Sir Barry Domville, Admiral of the Fleet in the First World War. Sir Oswald Mosley himself was there. I never saw him but my mother once saw his wife Diana. She said she looked beautiful but sad.

At Brixton I was locked in a cell for twenty-four hours. I didn't mind too much. After all, I had a lot to think about.

Then the door opened and a British officer came in. He held out his hand. 'Captain Harris,' he said briskly.

I took his hand and gripped it. Some sort of test seemed to be taking place. Harris offered me a cigarette and sat down on the only chair in the cell. I stood looking at him.

'Have a seat, old boy,' said Harris, expansively.

I sat on the bed. Harris grinned at me, showing all his teeth. He asked me how they were treating me, I said, 'All right.' Then he asked if there was anything I needed, and I said, 'No.'

Then, suddenly, he said: 'Now, look here, Cesare, you seem like a decent bloke. You tell us the truth and we can help you. Do you know why you're here?'

'I'm Italian,' I said.

Harris laughed heartily as if this was a wonderful joke. 'Italian, are you? I'll tell you something, old boy, I've never met an Italian who talks like you.'

I said nothing. I had no idea what he was getting at. Harris leant forward and his manner became less friendly. He told me they knew I'd seen Bastianini. Who had sent me? Was it Mosley? Was I working for the BUF? I said, with perfect truth, that I had never met Oswald Mosley. I wasn't a member of the

BUF. I had gone to see the ambassador because I wanted to go back to Italy to fight. 'Against the British,' I added helpfully.

Harris laughed nastily. 'Come off it, old boy. An Italian who talks like you and is married to a rich Englishwoman? Who are you working for? Is it Grandi? We know you've met him too.'

That was the start of it. For over a week I was kept alone in the cell apart from these visits from Harris. Sometimes he would come in the night and shine a light in my face. Who was I working for? Why had I gone to see Bastianini? Why was I pretending to be Italian? My answer was always the same: 'I am Italian. Bugger off and let me sleep.'

Sometimes Harris would ask about my school. Was it a rugger school or a soccer school? Was I a 'varsity man'? Sometimes, bizarrely, he would try to catch me out with my English: try to get me to say lounge instead of drawing room, to say mirror instead of looking-glass. I just laughed. My accent was now as much a part of me as my black hair and brown eyes. There was no chance that I would suddenly slip and talk like a lovable old ice-cream seller, which seemed to be what he wanted.

Eventually I understood. They thought I was some sort

of impostor – either an Englishman passing himself off as an Italian or an Italian pretending to be an Englishman, but in any case, a likely spy. I understood something else too. I realised that Harris had probably been to a minor English public school, just as I had. He, too, was trying to be posher than he was. He just couldn't understand how an Italian had the damned cheek to be playing the same game.

After about ten days of this, the authorities finally became convinced that I was, after all, an Italian. Perhaps it was seeing my father when he came to visit and hearing his accent. Here, at last, was the broken English they longed for. Perhaps it was just that they couldn't link me to any of the British Fascists. I had an Italian passport – perhaps I really was a dirty Eyetie. Eventually Harris washed his hands of me and I was sent to Warth Mills in Bury in Lancashire, with the other Italian internees.

How to describe Warth Mills? Well, to me it looked like hell, pure and simple. It was a disused cotton mill, a huge place still full of rusting machinery. I arrived in the evening and the building loomed up in the twilight, rows of broken windows reflecting the last of the sun. I had been taken there with a group of other London internees, some of them just schoolchildren, and we all stared in horror. Inside it was worse. The walls ran with oil and grease; in several places the glass in the roof was broken, letting in the freezing air. The abandoned machinery made sinister shapes in the half-light. Next to me a young boy, sixteen or so, began to cry.

All around, in the gloom, stood small groups of Italians, miserable and subdued. Afterwards I heard that there were over two thousand internees in Warth Mills, but the vastness of the place made it seem fewer. There were straw palliasses on the floor for us to sleep on; otherwise there was no furniture. The stench in the air told its own story about the sanitary arrangements. The boy was still crying. I patted his arm. 'Cheer up, *amico*. Wait until you see the third-class accommodation.' The boy gulped and smiled. He looked very young. I asked him his name.

'Giovanni Volpi,' he said.

I must have spoken quite loudly because, at the sound of my voice, one of the men nearby glanced at me. He was standing with a group who, even in this place, looked elegant and aloof. I recognised some of the faces: Bruno Baldasare, the well-known architect, and Ernesto Ferri, the catering millionaire. The man who had glanced at me I also knew slightly, Luigi Zazzi, a wealthy Italian with an interest in motor racing. He came over. 'Cesare!' he said. 'I'm sorry to see you here.'

I shrugged. 'Where else would I be?'

'On a ship home to Italy, I presumed.' Luigi looked at me slyly and I had the feeling he knew about my visit to the embassy.

'I missed the boat,' I said. Later, I found out that the *Monarch of Bermuda* had eventually set sail with some six hundred Italians on board.

Luigi laughed, throwing his head back. He was a tall man with an actor's talent for gestures. He put his arm round me. 'Come and meet the boys,' he said.

The 'boys' welcomed me cordially, as if I had just stepped into a West End club rather than a makeshift prison. Bruno Baldasare was a big man, ugly-attractive, with piercing black eyes. I knew he was a prominent Fascist, heavily involved with the *fasci*. Ernesto Ferri was small and thin. Despite his expensive clothes he looked more like the Italian peasant he had been than the tycoon he was. With them were two other men: Stefano Cavalli, a pianist, and another whose occupation was never mentioned. He lounged, completely at ease, gazing round the room with a strange, inward smile. I introduced myself and he smiled without speaking. Eventually, I asked him his name and he gave it with a shrug, as if it didn't mean that much to him: 'Fausto Marini.'

I asked Bruno, who seemed to be the leader, what happened next. That depended, said Bruno, on whether I was classified as a dangerous character. If I was, I was destined for Canada. If not, the Isle of Man. I asked Fausto if he considered himself dangerous. 'Extremely,' was his reply.

Cara mia, I will never forget that night. Although it was June, it was freezing in the mill. Many of the old men suffered and some of the younger men, Bruno included, gave them their coats to put round them. Selfishly, I wrapped my cashmere coat round me and thought of my parents, wondering if I'd ever see them again. I was sure that I'd be classified as dangerous and sent to Canada. I didn't once think of Joyce. Next to me, Fausto lay staring at the broken glass in the ceiling, smiling to himself.

In the morning we were fed, for the first time in twenty-four hours, and herded into groups. Many fathers and sons had been arrested together and now, it seemed, they were to be separated. All around me tough, hard-faced men were weeping and begging to be allowed to stay with their relatives. In my group, one man pleaded to have his eighty-year-old father with him. This was eventually allowed. I often wondered afterwards what happened to them.

As predicted, Bruno, Luigi, Fausto and I were in the same group. Ernesto was not. Bruno smiled when I queried this. Ernesto was too good a friend to the British. Didn't they all eat at his restaurants? Stefano was also in our group, as, to my amazement, was Giovanni. I protested to Bruno, 'He's only a baby. How can he be a dangerous character?'

Bruno shrugged: 'Who knows? Look at the old man over there. He can hardly stand but he's still considered dangerous enough to be locked up.'

Eventually, my group was marched out to the waiting truck. Bruno asked the guard where we were going. The guard smiled nastily. 'On a nice sea-cruise.' We were to set sail for Canada. On the *Arandora Star*.

It sounds stupid to say it now, but from the first moment I saw the *Arandora Star*, I had a terrible sense of foreboding. You never know how huge a ship is until you stand beside it. We stood on that deck in Liverpool and looked up at it in silence. A crude swastika was painted on the ship's hull. Ridiculous, I know, but that was the moment when I realised I was on Hitler's side. This was not some game with the local *fasci*, singing 'Giovinezza' and then going home for tea. I was a Fascist, a prisoner of war, a desperate character. I don't know when I have ever felt more desolate.

I turned to Fausto and joked that I was no sailor. 'Planes I like, but boats are another thing.' Fausto smiled grimly and told me he had just finished his national service in Italy – a year in the navy. 'What was it like?' I asked.

'Terrible,' said Fausto.

Giovanni was nearby, literally shaking with fear. I put my arm round him and, to lighten things up, asked Fausto if he had any tips for the inexperienced. 'Just one,' he said. 'If the boat sinks – jump off. Don't wait for the lifeboats.' Even Giovanni laughed.

Fausto and I were assigned a cabin on A deck, the lowest of all. In general, the German prisoners had the highest cabins and the Italians the lowest. Despite Bruno's words about dangerous characters, many of the Italians were old and looked as if they wouldn't last the journey. Giovanni, who was to share with Bruno, was one of the youngest on board. I was glad he was with Bruno – I felt certain he would look after him.

I wasn't so sure about Fausto. In our cabin, he just lay down on his bunk as if he was on a Caribbean cruise. I felt miserable: the motion of the ship made me feel sick, and worse than that was not knowing what would come next. I had always lived such a pampered life: what was I doing here, shut in this tiny cabin, being transported to the other side of the world? I will admit that I was close to tears. But I didn't want to show any weakness in front of Fausto. So I lay down too, trying not to think about the cramped, windowless cabin. I've always hated being in enclosed spaces. Eventually I asked Fausto how well he knew Bruno. 'Hardly at all,' said Fausto.

'He's important in the Fascist party,' I said.

'Evidently,' replied Fausto. There seemed nothing else to say.

That night I slept fitfully, dreaming about Brooklands, motor racing, flying in Enzo's plane. It must have been shortly after dawn when I was woken by a huge explosion. Still half asleep, I thought I was in London during an air raid. Sitting up, I found the cabin in total darkness and Fausto saying, in a curiously calm voice, 'Come on. Time to jump off.'

I staggered to my feet. The ship was lurching violently and, in the pitch black, it was almost impossible to keep my balance. 'We've been hit,' said Fausto. 'Let's go.'

Outside, the narrow corridor was in chaos. As the ship listed, people were flung to the ground and, in the darkness, others were scrambling over their bodies. All around me, I could hear Italian voices raised in prayer or curses. No English ones.

Fausto pushed his way through the crowds and I followed him, even hanging on to his coat at one point. I had no idea where I was, just that I was stumbling forward in complete darkness. I felt sure I was about to die and began frantically to say an act of confession. Suddenly Fausto seemed to be floating above my head. It took me a few seconds to realise that he was climbing a ladder. I launched myself after his disappearing legs. As I clutched the ladder, a body fell heavily on me from above. I clawed it away and went on climbing. I still see it sometimes in my nightmares, that body, falling past me into nothingness.

We seemed to climb for ever, while the ship lurched and

swayed. I kept my eyes fixed on Fausto's shoes – leather, handmade, I still remember them – and clung on desperately. Then, suddenly, my face was wet and we were on deck. By this time, the ship was almost vertical in the water. I could hear a German shouting orders and an Italian yelling: 'Cut the ropes! Cut the ropes!' He had a Neapolitan accent and I wondered if it was someone I knew. A particularly violent lurch threw me to the floor and I realised I'd lost Fausto. Frantically, I called his name but my voice was lost in the confusion. Then, miraculously, he was beside me. He was shouting at me to take off my coat. I just stared stupidly, so Fausto wrenched it from my shoulders. 'Now,' said Fausto, 'it's time to jump.' I reached for him, meaning to hang on to him again, to stop him jumping, to save myself, I don't know what. But Fausto just smiled – I remember his teeth, very white in the darkness – took a step backwards and jumped. Not knowing what else to do, I followed him.

It felt as if I was falling down the length of my life: Clerkenwell, Nicholls squaring up to me in the street, Auntie Clara sobbing in the night, Joyce's voice when she told me she was pregnant, the first time I flew in a plane, my mother's face when she kissed me goodbye through the bars in

Brixton. It was like those dreams where you fall and know that you will die when you land. When I hit the water, I went down and down. This, I felt sure, was what dying was like. Then, suddenly, I surfaced, gasping and choking. I swam a few desperate, floundering strokes and caught hold of a piece of driftwood. There, hanging on with my fingernails, I saw the *Arandora Star* go down.

It was a terrible sight. Such a little time for such a huge ship to sink. The awful screams of those who were left on board. I heard afterwards that both her captain and a German naval captain had gone down with her, saluting as the waves met over their heads, but I saw nothing so heroic or so neat. There was just a sudden Godforsaken silence, broken only by the cry of the seagulls overhead. Even today I hate that sound.

I managed to heave myself up so that I was lying face down on the piece of wood – it was a door, I think. Then I just lay there. I was so exhausted, I felt as if I would never move again. I think I even slept, lying there on the water. Eventually I managed to raise my head and look around me. Nothing. When you're lying flat on the sea, you can see only a few hundred yards about you. There was not a living soul in sight. Floating beside me were a few pieces of debris: a uniform cap, what looked like a leather-bound Bible and the remains of a chair. I remember tilting my head up and looking at the sky. It was bright blue, like a holiday poster.

I tried to paddle forward with my hands and feet but the waves made this difficult. At one point, I saw a lifeboat on the horizon but although I shouted I was too far away to be heard. Then, drifting past me, like something from a dream, there was a raft with two men on it, naked except that one had a monocle screwed into his eye. They passed near enough to touch but I just stared. One of the men spoke. He was English, an officer by the sound of him. He called out, 'Land ahoy.' His voice was calm, like someone in a play, but there was no land anywhere. I stared until a wave separated us and then, face down in the icy water, I laughed until I cried.

I lost all track of time. I didn't know if hours or days passed. I felt as if I had been floating in that weird half-life for ever. Then I saw a body. It was drifting towards me, carried by a strong current – not in uniform, so it must be a prisoner of war, I thought. Young, probably Italian, judging by the thick black hair floating in the water. Thinking I could at least identify it, maybe inform the relatives one day, I reached out and grabbed the collar. The sodden weight almost capsized me but, eventually, I turned the body over. It was Giovanni.

Oh, Sophie, I will never forget that moment. That poor boy, younger than Daniele, floating in the water, dead. I suppose it was then that I grasped what someone more intelligent would have understood long ago. Now, being Italian was a matter of life or death. Giovanni was dead for no other reason than that he was Italian. Sixteen years old. I can see his face before me as if it was yesterday. That poor boy . . . that poor boy.

I was rescued later that day by a Canadian destroyer. When they lowered the rope ladder, my hands were too swollen to take hold of it. They had to send a man to hoist me up on his shoulders. Bruno, who had been picked up minutes earlier, had spent ten hours holding an old man above the water. When the old man took hold of the rope ladder, he slipped and fell, knocking out Bruno's two front teeth. Bruno told me this, through a bloody grin, as we shared a can of soup and a cigarette.

I started to tell him that I had seen Giovanni but could not continue. '*Poverino*,' said Bruno softly. He told me that he had tried to get the boy on to a lifeboat but they were all tied up and no one knew how to undo the ropes. Officers were wielding hatchets and there were people sitting on top of the boats, waiting for something to happen. Bruno told Giovanni that they had to jump and the boy obeyed him instantly. Bruno and Giovanni jumped together, holding hands. When they hit the water, Bruno swam over to Giovanni but he was already dead. He must have hit his head. There was debris everywhere.

I looked around. There didn't seem to be many survivors. Bruno said that a lot of the Italians on board had been so old that when the ship was hit, they didn't know what to do. Many had been from the mountains: they didn't know anything about ships or the sea. They had just stood on deck, waiting to die.

I told Bruno I owed my life to Fausto. 'If it hadn't been for him . . .' I began.

'You would still have had your coat,' said a voice behind me. It was Fausto. We embraced. I forgot my earlier reservations. Now Fausto Marini seemed like my best friend in the world and I hugged him fiercely, trying to hide my tears in his shoulder.

They say there were 1,564 men on board the *Arandora Star*.

Of these, over seven hundred were Italians, the rest Germans and British servicemen. Four hundred and forty-six Italians died, mostly the older men. Only young men, like Fausto, Bruno and I, had any chance at all. And the irony of it all was that now we really *were* dangerous men. How dangerous, the British still had to learn.

CHAPTER 4

Fausto and I were sent to the Isle of Man. Other *Arandora Star* survivors went to Australia or Canada. I never knew why we didn't. Bruno was going to Australia but he was ill with pneumonia and the ship sailed without him. By the time he arrived on the island, Fausto and I had been there for a month.

We were sent to Onchan. The internment camp consisted of rows of boarding houses, joined together by corridors of corrugated iron and surrounded by barbed-wire fences. A more cheerless, depressing place it would be hard to imagine. It was unbelievable to think that people had ever come here on holiday. The first person I saw at Onchan was Ernesto Ferri, who was chatting pleasantly to one of the guards. There were several catering tycoons at the camp and soon the food improved considerably. Stefano Cavalli was not there: he had been drowned on the *Arandora Star*. Bruno said he had gone back to his cabin to save his musical scores.

Onchan was my education. As I have said, previously I had been a typical London playboy – I didn't know, or care, about politics, history or philosophy. But somehow the *Arandora Star* had made me grow up. Maybe it was because I had nearly died, maybe it was seeing Giovanni's body and realising that he would never have the chance to grow up, but suddenly I was ready to become an adult. I wanted to learn and, believe me, at Onchan, there were plenty of teachers.

Who was in the camp? Sometimes it seemed as if the whole world was there. First, there were the wealthy London Italians, like Luigi Zazzi. Luigi had also escaped from the *Arandora Star*. By dint of wielding a hatchet, he had got a place on one of the few lifeboats to be released. He described how British officers had told them to row away from the ship, ignoring the old men who were still trying to climb on board. Then there were the catering people, like Ernesto Ferri. They were non-political and, by and large, on excellent terms with the guards. There were the Italian Italians, like Fausto. Usually through sheer bad luck, they had been caught in England when war broke out. They were also mostly non-political; in fact, many were Communists. There were the English Italians, older men who had sons in the British army: a lot of people despised them as traitors but I always felt sorry for them. One man had six sons in the British army. Two were killed at Arnhem. Then, finally, there was the elite group, the intellectuals – doctors, university professors, architects, writers. This group were fiercely political, pro-Italian and pro-Fascist.

When Bruno arrived, he quickly became the leader of the elite group. He was an incredible man, Bruno Baldasare, I wish you could have met him. He was tall, not handsome but with an immense presence. And he was so eloquent! To me, it seemed as if Bruno knew everything there was to know in the world. And, for some reason, Bruno took an interest in me. Remember, I left school without any qualifications, but now this man, an architect, a great craftsman, a friend of world statesmen, was talking to me as if I was his equal.

Bruno was a Roman. With his bald head, fierce eyes and hooked nose, he looked like Caesar himself. You could imagine him in his toga, facing down a rebellious senate.

'Never forget,' he told me, 'we ruled the world when the British still lived in mud huts.'

We talked and talked. Bruno told me about Mussolini. About his prowess as a horseman, fencer and athlete. About how he had drained the Pontine marshes and driven the Mafia out of Sicily – the Americans let them back later, of course. About how Mussolini was turning the Italians from a country of waiters and opera singers into a hard, warlike nation.

I will never forget one thing Bruno told me. One day he asked me if I knew what Machiavelli had said to my name-sake, Cesare Borgia. Of course, I knew nothing of the sort. 'He asked him,' said Bruno, '"Is it better to be loved or feared?" And do you know what the answer was?' I didn't. 'The answer was: "It is better to be feared." You see, Cesare,' said Bruno, 'that is what Mussolini has done. Maybe they loved us before: amusing little Eyeties with our cafés and our ice cream and our "O Sole Mio". Now they fear us.'

Fausto was the only person who didn't seem to fit easily into any group. He was an Italian Italian, in London on holiday when war broke out. He was non-political, though definitely more inclined to the left than the right, but he wasn't a collaborator. He kept himself aloof, with his inward smile and occasional ironic aside. No one knew quite what to make of him. He was an artist – he had studied in Paris before the war – but wasn't interested in taking part in any of the discussions about art and culture. In fact, apart from one caricature of Bruno, drawn on the back of a cigarette packet, I never saw him put pen to paper.

Fausto and I were always good friends. I always maintained that Fausto saved my life on the *Arandora Star*, though he denied it. 'I was only trying to save myself,' he would say. 'You insisted on tagging along.' The only thing I couldn't understand about him was that he didn't admire Bruno. They were both Romans, which was probably why they distrusted each other. As Bruno used to quote: 'Now Roman is to Roman more hateful than the foe.' I don't know where it's from. Shakespeare or someone, I suppose.

The commander of the camp was a man called Blick. The Germans liked him, possibly because his name had Germanic origins, but most of the Italians didn't. However, Blick and Bruno understood each other, respected each other. Blick made Bruno camp commandant – as a leading Fascist he had a full rank in the Italian army – and left a lot of the discipline and organisation up to him. To my amazement and delight, Bruno made me his deputy.

Periodically, the British held tribunals to find out whether Italian prisoners of war were willing to collaborate with the British authorities. Surprisingly, even the least political internees were not. After all, we were at war. For Bruno, though, this was a matter of life and death. He called a special meeting of the elite group and told us that we had to treat the request with the most disdainful answer possible. What answer was that? someone asked. 'This!' replied Bruno, snapping out his arm in the Fascist salute.

Now, it may seem extraordinary to you but I had never made this salute before. Up to this point I did not even consider myself a Fascist, but – thanks to Bruno's teaching – I had come to admire Mussolini. The idea of making this gesture in front of the British tribunal seemed to me incredibly significant, as if I was taking an irrevocable step into a new, warlike existence. I wouldn't be a soft city boy any more, I would be a soldier. I would be a Fascist. So, when Blick asked me if I was prepared to aid the British war effort, I looked him full in the face and shot my arm forward in the Fascist salute. It felt like the most thrilling moment of my life.

Otherwise, *O Dio*, it was a boring time. We talked, we played cards, sometimes one of the professional men gave a lecture. You children always ask why I won't play cards or any of those board games you like so much. The answer is, I can remember too well a time when there was nothing else to do but play those games. Unlike most Italians, I have never liked cards and I was never a great reader. I was desperately bored.

My best times were when Bruno taught me to fence. He was a great sportsman, an amateur boxer and, like Mosley, an accomplished fencer. He lectured us on the need to keep physically active and obtained permission to have fencing equipment sent from London. Soon he was organising boxing competitions and fencing tournaments. I loved fencing and I was a good pupil. Motor racing had given me fast reflexes and I loved being physically active again. I felt as if I was at last becoming a fighter.

Visiting days were high spots. Bruno was always visited by his wife, Livia, a dark, elegant woman. Fausto received letters on lilac paper from his girlfriend in Paris. Joyce never wrote. Later that year I got a letter from her solicitor, asking for a divorce. My parents came, though. Families of enemy aliens had to get special permission to visit the Isle of Man.

The first time I saw my parents, walking along the steep hill path that led to the camp, barbed wire on all sides of them, they looked so small and defenceless that I almost cried. For the first time in my life I felt ashamed. My parents had given me everything and how had I repaid them? I had wasted the expensive education they had given me, alienated all their neighbours, broken up the family. I was about to get divorced without even providing a grandchild. Even at birth I had tried to kill my mother. Yet never, not once, did they reproach me.

I sometimes wondered why my parents hadn't been interned, when so many Italians their age had been. Later I learnt that they had been called in for questioning but my mother's British neighbours had risen up in outrage. In a body, they went to the police station exclaiming that my mother was a saint. Hadn't she nursed their children back to health, cared for their grandparents, given them food, money, medicine? If Mamma Laura was not set free, there would be trouble. My parents were released the next day.

The first time she saw me after the *Arandora Star*, my mother flung her arms round me and wept. 'Thank God, you're alive. I prayed to all the saints. Thank God they've preserved you. Even your father prayed to St Christopher. It's a miracle.' It was very embarrassing. To change the subject, I asked about the family. Clara was suffering badly with her nerves: the air raids terrified her but she wouldn't go to the shelter; Antonio had had to put reinforcements over their bed. Rosaria was working for a Jewish clothing company as a seamstress. They were very good to her. Her previous place had sacked her for being an Italian. Yes, there was a lot of anti-Italian feeling about. Italian shops attacked, some set on fire. Everywhere you saw notices in Italian shops: 'The proprietors have sons serving in the British army.' 'Their sons,' said my mother, 'who tried to kill my son.' Useless to remind her that it was the Germans who bombed the *Arandora Star*.

I asked about Enzo. My mother said he had a reserved occupation as a motor mechanic. He worked at Croydon aerodrome. Apparently, one day as he was going into the aircraft hangar he had thought: This plane is going to Italy to bomb my grandparents, so he had refused to fly. He had nearly been sent to prison but, eventually, was moved into another job. He was still refusing to work on planes that were going to Italy. Good old Enzo. I was proud of him: we were comrades after all.

Bruno said we should pity those who hadn't the courage

to be good Italians. The inference was clear. We, who had refused to collaborate, were good Italians. But sometimes, on long afternoons staring out of the window at the dreadful, grey sea, I found myself thinking that a really good Italian should be out there – fighting. Bruno told me not to reproach myself. I had tried to get away to Italy, hadn't I? Hadn't I nearly died already for my country? But I wanted some action. As you know, I'm no intellectual and sometimes I found all the talk and political debate stultifying and depressing. I was only twenty-eight. I missed the thrill of motor racing. I missed the danger. I wanted to fight.

Some internees went to work in the fields or for local labourers. But we 'political' prisoners refused to work. We spent our time trying to be as soldierly as possible. We held parades and always referred to each other by military rank. Fausto refused to have anything to do with us. He said he'd had enough of playing soldiers during his military service.

One man, an engineer, made a makeshift radio and we used to gather round it in secret to hear Mussolini speak. Yes, I know he sounds ridiculous now but so does Churchill, and words can't describe how wonderful his speeches sounded then. It was like hearing Mark Antony declaiming from the balcony. He spoke about the glory of ancient Rome, about the power of the Italian people, about how we would make the world listen to our voice. 'It is better to live one day as a lion,' he said, 'than a hundred days as a sheep.' When he had finished we would stand together and give the Fascist salute. '*A noi!*'

Other prisoners found different outlets. One man, a Sicilian called Chiappa, used to escape regularly to sleep with local girls. Having spent the night with one, he would turn up again in the morning and bang on the gates, saying he was too tired to climb back over the wall. 'Put me in solitary,' he used to shout. 'I need a rest.' Other men had more discreet liaisons with local girls and I think that at least one of these relationships ended in marriage after the war.

God, I missed women. You know now that I was no monk before the war and I loved the company of women. Now, in camp, I dreamt about Joyce, Rose, Minnie, even Anne Sullivan. Weird, disturbing dreams. Once I dreamt I was rowing Anne home in a boat when it started to sink. The waves lapped over us in a hypnotic, even sensual way, making me long to fall asleep, to drown, but Anne kept shouting, 'You've got to marry me! You've got to marry me!' I woke up sweating.

I missed women but, as Bruno's deputy, I could hardly climb over walls or make assignations with local girls. We had our dignity to consider. So Bruno arranged for me to write to a German woman prisoner of war. For a while this went quite well. She was interesting, a countess, and I began to look forward to her letters. But then I had the unlucky idea of asking her to send me a photograph. *Dio mio.* All I can say is that she had been photographed with her dog and, forgive me, I knew which one I'd rather sleep with. I never wrote again.

Of course, some people tried to escape. One man was even found in a fishing boat, ten miles out to sea. But there was nowhere to escape to. And, besides, where would we go? Even Bruno, with all his phenomenal strength, could hardly row back to Italy.

I must have been at Onchan for nearly two years when my father came to tell me that Salvatore had been killed. He came on his own – my mother was comforting Auntie Clara. I didn't know what to say. I remember my father had brought me some cigarettes and he spent the time building them into a tower, as if that was the sole purpose of his visit. After he had left, I just sat there, staring at the neat pile of blue and white boxes.

I could not stop thinking about Salvatore's death. Night after night I lay awake, thinking about him as a child, following me around, begging for a turn on my go-kart, asking me to beat up the bullies for him. I couldn't stop thinking that if I'd been with him, to protect him, he wouldn't have died. Ridiculous, really. Salvatore died miles away, ironically only a few miles from Naples where his father had been born. He'd been fighting for the British, my enemies. Logically, I should have rejoiced. But I didn't, of course. I missed him. My stupid, shy, giggling cousin. I couldn't believe I'd never hear his laugh again.

I wrote to Auntie Clara and Uncle Antonio, saying how sorry I was about Salvatore. Rosaria answered. She said they were proud he'd died for Britain. And that, Sophie, is why I can never forgive her. For that piece of mindless, jingoistic spite. He was her *brother*.

I didn't tell anyone at the camp about Salvatore. I don't know why. I suppose I was a bit ashamed of having a cousin in the British army – he'd even been registered as a di Napoli rather than under his ridiculous new name. But, more than that, I think I was scared of showing any weakness in the camp. Like any environment where men are locked up together, it could be a tough place. If you showed weakness, you were finished. You went under. So I kept the news to myself and outwardly carried on as normal: fencing with Bruno, listening to the debates – 'Vegetarianism: a cure or a poison?' – talking to Fausto, trying to teach myself German.

But I do think that my depression over Salvatore contributed to what happened next. Certainly, if I hadn't been upset about my cousin's death, I don't think I would have accepted Father Cristofoli's invitation to come to his room 'to talk'. And that was when the trouble started.

There were a few priests in the camp – there were two on board the *Arandora Star* – but it was this Cristofoli who really stood out, Father Pasquale Cristofoli. You may have heard of him – these days, he's quite a media personality. But in those days he was just another priest.

I'm not much of a Catholic – God knows, my mother tried her best but I always hated going to church and refused point-blank to be an altar boy. It always seemed so servile somehow, balancing the book on your forehead so that the priest could read, wearing that stupid white frock. After the flag-suit fiasco, I even refused to take part in the Easter procession. But some of the men in camp were religious. It stood to reason, really. People are always more religious in wartime and, besides, there wasn't much else to do. There was a mass every morning, celebrated by one of the priests in a former games room. I was always amazed to see how many people trooped out of the room after the service. And, among this devout group, Father Cristofoli was definitely a star.

He was a good-looking man, tall, grey-haired, more like an actor than a priest. He was intelligent and witty too – you would often see him at the centre of a group of men, laughing and gesticulating. Like most of the priests, Cristofoli was not opposed to Mussolini – he said that Il Duce had put the crucifix back in Italian classrooms – so he got on well even with Bruno's elite Fascist group. The guards liked him and he was allowed special privileges, such as having a gramophone in his room.

Even so, I was surprised when Cristofoli came up to me one evening as I was trying half-heartedly to learn some German verbs. He spoke to me in his deep actor's voice and asked how I was. I replied that I was fine, thank you, Father. Cristofoli looked at me intently and said he had a feeling that something had been bothering me lately. I was surprised. Not one of my friends had noticed the change in me but here was a man who had only spoken to me a few times and he had spotted that something was wrong. I muttered something about having a lot on my mind. He put his hand on my shoulder and asked if I would like to talk about it.

Well, I'm sure you know what's coming next. But you have to remember that things were different then. I had no idea what was going to happen. Cristofoli was a *priest*. I trusted him absolutely, even though I didn't consider myself a religious man. And, I suppose, I wanted someone to talk to. I was lonely, missing Salvatore, missing my family. I agreed to go to his room the next evening.

Cristofoli's room was nothing like a prison cell. There were soft sheets on his bed, the gramophone, books along the window ledge, even a jam jar of flowers. Cristofoli told me that the flowers were a present from one of the guards – 'I was able to give him a little advice about a family matter. Not a Catholic, of course.' Then he asked if I liked music. I said, truthfully, that I did. He put on a record of violin sonatas.

I told you I had learnt the violin. I wasn't very good – as Anne Sullivan's mother pointed out – because I never prac-tised enough but, like my father, I loved music. And this music! I can't tell you how beautiful it was. When it finished,

I sat in silence for a moment, unwilling to break the spell. Eventually I asked who was playing. Cristofoli told me that it was Yehudi Menuhin, the Jewish prodigy. I said it was beautiful. 'Not as beautiful as you,' said Cristofoli, and then he leant forward and kissed me on the lips.

Sophie, I can't tell you how shocked I felt. Nowadays, maybe it would mean nothing. Things like this go on all the time. But then I didn't even have a word to describe what had happened. I was appalled, aghast, rigid with horror. Then Cristofoli moved closer, put his hand on my leg, and I came back to life. I pushed him away violently, making him fall to the floor, flung a revolting Neapolitan swear word at him, and rushed out of the room.

At first, I didn't tell anyone what had happened. I suppose I was ashamed. Maybe, in some way, I had encouraged his advances. I should never have gone to his room and listened to music with him. I felt I'd been a fool.

Then, a few days later, at one of our meetings, Bruno started to talk about 'sexual deviancy'. As he was company leader and I was his deputy, we were allowed half an hour a day for 'staff meetings'. We met in what was called the 'mess room', which had once been a boarding-house dining room. Although all the original furniture had been taken away, you could imagine exactly what sort of meals used to be eaten there. You could almost smell the stewed meat and overcooked cabbage. Even so, I liked these times. I enjoyed being with Bruno and talking as if we were soldiers rather than prisoners.

On this occasion Bruno was striding round the room, talking about the need to train the young men in the camp as fighters, keeping them fit, of course, but also morally healthy. We couldn't afford any deviancy. I'd been staring out of the window, watching the prisoners exercise, but now I looked up. 'What do you mean, "deviancy"?' I asked.

'You know,' said Bruno, 'hysteria, neurotic behaviour, homosexuality.'

'Is a homosexual always a deviant?' I asked.

Bruno looked at me oddly. 'Of course.'

'Even if he's a priest?' I asked.

Bruno stopped his pacing and turned to look at me. 'What do you mean?'

So I told him.

That evening, we held a company meeting in the mess room. All the Italian prisoners in our wing were there: the old men complaining about being dragged from their card games, the young men eager for any distraction, Fausto, smiling slightly and standing at the back of the room, Luigi Zazzi, eyes bright with interest. Cristofoli was not there. I wondered if someone had warned him beforehand.

Bruno stood on a chair and called for silence. '*Compadriy*, we have called this meeting because it has come to my ears that a cancer has grown up among us.' He paused impressively. 'And that cancer is . . . homosexuality.' Another pause. Someone laughed and turned it into a cough. I remember seeing Fausto looking at me quizzically. Bruno continued. He was not a prejudiced man, he said. In peacetime, he would be the first to leave each to their own. But this was not peacetime. He raised his voice to a controlled shout worthy of Il Duce. 'We are not civilians,' he bellowed. 'This is a camp and we are soldiers. In military terms this behaviour is *punishable by death*.' It was a magnificent performance.

Now there was complete silence in the room. Bruno went on in a quieter voice. He was not, he said, suggesting that we kill these people even if, in Roman times, they would have been sewn into a sack and thrown into the sea. He smiled to show this was a joke. I always remember that Fausto cut in here and asked Bruno what he proposed to do, 'given that sacks are not readily available'. Bruno looked at him and I thought I saw something pass between the two Romans. Not hatred, not dislike, but a kind of contemptuous understanding.

'I intend to stamp it out,' Bruno answered. 'We must demand that any known homosexuals are moved to another camp, or a separate wing.'

Someone asked how Bruno would know who was homosexual and who was not. Bruno said that anyone to whom approaches were made should see him in private. When he had a list of names, he would act. 'How?' asked Fausto.

'I'll make an announcement,' said Bruno grandly. He got down from his chair. People began to file out.

I don't know who went to see Bruno. But one man came to me. A boy, really, barely eighteen, called Angelo Bonetti. I didn't know him well but I felt sorry for him – as I felt sorry for all the young men in the camp. Bonetti had been about to start university and now he was locked up in a camp with a lot of men twice his age. He had been born in England so could easily have taken British nationality. But he was a good Italian, and I respected him for that. He reminded me a bit of Giovanni.

Bonetti came to see me and, haltingly, told me the story. How Cristofoli had always been kind to him, talking to him and giving him books. How he knew that his mother would be pleased that he had a priest as a friend. How Cristofoli asked him to come to his room and listen to music. How he had kissed him and told him he was beautiful. Bonetti told me that he had run away, revolted, but something in his face made me think there had been more to it than that. Either Bonetti had been tempted or he felt sinful somehow to have rejected a priest – or not rejected him. In any event, this boy was clearly upset. I reported the incident to Bruno.

Bruno said that we had to act immediately. All in all, ten people had come to him with tales of homosexual advances and Bruno had made a list of 'known homosexuals' in the camp. There were three, apart from Cristofoli. Two Italians and an Austrian Jew. I had never liked the Austrian because he had made it known that he despised Italians. Also, he had slovenly table manners – for some reason he would only eat once a day so he saved his breakfast and lunch in a little bag and ate everything at the evening meal. It was revolting to see him gobbling up the congealed mess of porridge and potato. I went out of my way not to sit near him.

I did know one of the Italians, though. He was a gentle soul called Santini. He was best known in the camp for trying to put on plays and musicals, usually deeply unsuitable things for his audience. He once asked me if I was interested in being in a production of *Charley's Aunt. Mamma mia!* I said no immediately. I hate the theatre at the best of times, especially anything that involves men dressing as women. It reminded me of my school and those ridiculous Gilbert and Sullivan things they used to put on. Travesties of opera with the classics masters dressed as three little girls or some such rubbish. But Santini meant no harm. I couldn't help wondering if Bruno would have counted Santini's approach to me as deviancy.

Bruno's first move was to go to Blick and ask for these men to be removed. Blick refused. He said that the named men were model prisoners. So Bruno resorted to plan B. It was all carefully organised. The first bell of the day rang at seven o'clock. We prisoners were supposed to be up, dressed and ready for inspection at half past. At half past seven the guards unlocked the doors at the ends of the corridors. We were then supposed to march down into the kitchens and be counted – as P.G. Wodehouse said, prisoners of war are always being counted – before breakfast. But that day, as the guards unlocked the doors we grabbed them and pushed them into the empty cells. Then we marched smartly into the mess room and barricaded ourselves in.

In minutes Blick had arrived with an armed guard. Bruno pushed a message under the door demanding the removal of the four men from the camp. There was a silence as Blick, I suppose, considered his options. Then there was an almighty crash as he and his men tried to storm the room. Our barricade was overturned and one of the guards forced himself in. Bruno and one other man – Luigi, I think – threw themselves on to him and he fell to the floor, bleeding from the head. For all our talk, the sight of blood was a shock. We could hear Blick shouting outside and the guard was pulled away. Bruno shouted at us to replace the barricade and for a few minutes we rushed to push chairs and tables against the door. Now there was silence outside.

The stand-off continued for twenty-four hours. I'm sorry to say that, for me, they were the best hours I spent at Onchan. We were hysterical, drunk with the excitement of actually doing something. We sang Fascist songs and jeered at the guards out of the window. '*Barboncini!*' we shouted. 'Blick's poodles!' Almost all of the company was there – Fausto, sitting silently at one of the folding tables, Luigi Zazzi, standing on a chair and doing an impersonation of Blick, frothing at the mouth and denouncing all Eyeties. The old men had brought their cards and just carried on as normal, playing their endless games of *scopa*. Bruno sat calmly at a table and discussed tactics. I sat next to him feeling that, at last, I was in a war.

It must have been a long twenty-four hours for Blick. He didn't want to contact England and tell them he had a riot on his hands, among the *Italian* prisoners, no less. He didn't want to give in to our demands but what else could he do? Besides, he knew that many of his own men sympathised with us. As one of the guards said to Bruno later, 'You only did what every soldier wants to do.' By the end of the day, Blick had agreed to remove the four men. Now the chase was on to find the ringleaders.

It wasn't hard, after all. Blick must have known that Bruno was behind it and I was his deputy. But he needed more evidence. For the next few days the whisper went round that anyone who gave the names of the ringleaders would be set free. For a few days the silence held – *omerta*, the Sicilian,

Chiappa, called it – and then, on the fourth day, Bruno and I found ourselves under armed guard.

In the end it was simple. A man called Ugo Greco had been having a lot of trouble with his wife. He was convinced she was having an affair; he would read her letters over and over trying to catch her out and, when she came to visit, would stare at her like an inquisitor, as if he could stare the truth out of her. I told him that if she wasn't having an affair his behaviour was enough to drive her to one. Anyway, it didn't take Blick long to find this out and he set to work on poor old Greco. Wouldn't he like to go home, just to check that everything was satisfactory *on the domestic front*? Surely his wife would be pleased to see him. It was difficult for a young woman with her husband in prison. Wouldn't he like to be with her to protect her? Of course Greco cracked and Bruno and I found ourselves up on a charge and heading to good old Chelsea Barracks.

We sailed for Liverpool on a cold November morning. We travelled under armed escort, with four guards apiece. I always remember one of the camp guards, a man called Lewis, brought his whole family to the docks to watch the dangerous Fascists setting sail. It was one of the proudest moments of my life. Certainly, in his leather trenchcoat, Bruno looked capable of anything. Later on, when I saw the *Godfather* films, Al Pacino's face, so dark and dangerous, reminded me of Bruno. He looked like a man who could order hundreds of deaths and not move a muscle. I did my best to live up to him.

So I left the Isle of Man branded a dangerous criminal and I was delighted. In all honesty Blick could not have done anything else. And Greco? Did they set him free? Of course not. If there's one thing the British hate, it's a telltale.

CHAPTER 5

Can you imagine it, Sophie? Your little old grandfather, a dangerous criminal, surrounded by armed guards? At Liverpool we were handed over to two military policemen. Bruno gave the guards the Fascist salute and received a crisp salute back. The MPs looked extremely nervous. They escorted us to the station where we had a closed carriage on the London train. As it pulled out of Liverpool, I looked out of the window and was shocked. On the Isle of Man we had been fairly sheltered from the war. Now I saw the empty craters where houses had been, boarded-up windows, everything grey, defeated and hopeless. I wondered what on earth London looked like now. I sat there in silence, staring out of the window, until one of the MPs called my name: 'Cesare di Napoli? From Clerkenwell?'

I looked at him in amazement. He was a heavily built man of about my own age, one of those soldiers who look uneasy in uniform, the material straining at his waist, the sleeves slightly too short and too tight. Then he smiled and it came back to me: Clerkenwell, the taste of pavement as I struggled on the ground, Rosaria's cry of 'Cesare! Stop fighting or I'll tell Auntie Laura,' the horse galloping wildly through the cobbled streets. 'Nicholls,' I said.

Nicholls laughed delightedly. He seemed gentler than he had as a child. Strangely enough, the army seemed to have taken the aggression out of him. He asked me what I was doing there, gesturing at the locked carriage, Bruno, the trenchcoats, his companion's gun. He laughed when I replied that I was a dangerous character – Bruno smiled too. Nicholls replied that I always had been dangerous. He turned to his companion and told him I had once beaten him up when we were children. I said truthfully that I had been no match for Nicholls, but he protested, seriously, 'No, you were a good fighter, not like that cousin of yours. What's he doing, by the way?' I told him that Salvatore was dead, killed in Italy. I noticed that Bruno looked up sharply but said nothing. 'I'm sorry,' said Nicholls. We lapsed back into silence for the rest of the journey.

An armoured car met us at Euston. Nobody spoke. Nicholls seemed oddly preoccupied. I was happy just to look out of the window. Perhaps it was because the sun had come out but London looked a lot better than Liverpool, as if it would take more than a few bombs to defeat it. There were craters and missing houses here too, but the railings had been taken away from the parks and the grass looked green and inviting. After months and months of grey sea, it felt wonderful just to be in a city.

At Green Park, Nicholls suddenly spoke to the driver and the car stopped. He turned to me, looking very serious, and I wondered what was coming. To my surprise, he asked me how long I had been in prison. 'About two years,' I said. Then Nicholls said something I will never forget: 'How long since you had a woman?'

I stared at him. Suddenly I thought of Joyce in her silk nightdress. 'Almost two years,' I repeated.

Nicholls leant forward. 'There's a place near here. Really good. Clean. High-class. Meet us back here in two hours.'

I couldn't believe my ears. Nicholls, a British military policeman, was giving two prisoners time off to go to a brothel! I turned to Bruno and saw that he was laughing.

Nicholls, still very serious, kept telling me what a high-class place it was and how clean the girls were. I asked Bruno what he wanted to do – after all, he was a married man. In answer, Bruno turned to Nicholls. 'Thank you,' he said. 'We'll try to be finished in two hours.'

Again, I won't go into details. The girls were certainly clean and quite classy. In fact, they could have been a great deal worse and I would still have thought them perfect. Mine was called Louise and, what with one thing and another, the two hours were nearly up when Bruno knocked on our door. I didn't want to go. It had been wonderful just to be with a woman again, to hear her laugh, feel her skin, her hair . . . But Bruno was dragging me away. I said goodbye to Louise. Somehow it didn't seem right to kiss her so, ridiculously, I shook her hand. She patted my cheek and said, 'Have a good war, handsome.' I thought of Minnie and the high-heeled shoes on the back seat of the car. I pulled on my coat and followed Bruno out of the room. As we ran down the stairs, Bruno said that his girl had told him the establishment was very popular with the British military. Apparently, even at that moment, a four-star general was in one of the upstairs rooms.

I burst out laughing. Here we were, two dangerous criminals who had been making love with prostitutes a few feet away from a British general. It had certainly been a good day for me, the day I had the fight with Nicholls.

You want to know why we didn't try to escape? I think we both knew that there was no chance and, anyway, where would we go? London was as familiar to me as my own face but I was no longer welcome there. It is a strange thing to be an enemy alien in one's own city. And we could hardly get back to Italy. Besides, it would have meant big trouble for Nicholls, and I, for one, felt seriously in his debt. So we ran back to the waiting armoured car. Nicholls held open the door for us. 'Nicholls,' I said, 'I will never forget this.'

Chelsea was much more like a prison than the Isle of Man but I liked it better. For one thing, it was the officers' prison and it felt good to be called by my rank – as deputy camp leader I had a courtesy rank – and treated with a bit of respect. And, as I say, I was happy to be back in London, even though I used to lie awake at night listening to the silence when the doodlebug engine cut out, wondering if I was going to die in prison. My next-door neighbour was a German officer who used to shout 'Heil Hitler' as the bombs fell. Perhaps I was just happy to be treated like a proper prisoner rather than one-of-those-amusing-Eyeties. Also, my parents could visit more often. They brought clothes and food, and news of the Italian Quarter. Rosaria was still working for the Jewish clothing company; apparently she was exchanging letters with some soldier. Auntie Clara had never got over Salvatore's death: she went to mass every day and talked about him as if he was still alive. Did I remember Marco Fantani? His whole family had been killed in an air raid – direct hit. Enzo's brother Luca had been killed in Egypt.

It was my mother who told me about Piers' death. She had read about it in a newspaper. It affected me very much. I kept thinking about the day when we had done the stunt driving for Sanderson; I could see Piers, reckless, high-spirited, his scarf flapping in the wind. Then I saw his face looking up at me as I drove over him. It was almost as if I had killed him. I wrote to his parents – they did not reply – and tried to imagine how they would be feeling. The colonel would think it was unmanly to cry and Mrs Hastings would be brave, sitting very upright on her chair and talking brightly about 'what he would have wanted'. I couldn't imagine how Joyce would be behaving. We were divorced now and it was hard to remember that I had ever been married to her.

Enzo came to see me too. As soon as I saw him in the visitors' room, a book about cars on his lap, all our old friendship came flooding back. I didn't blame Enzo for not being interned, as I blamed Salvatore and all the other anglicised Italians. Enzo had no interest in politics but he did not want to fight against his mother country and I respected him for that. And, in a way, it was soothing to sit with him and talk about cars. I was still too much in awe of Bruno to have this kind of conversation with him. Besides, he knew nothing about mechanics. I realised that after the war, as soon as I sat in a car with him.

I was in Chelsea Barracks when I heard that Italy had surrendered. It felt like the end of everything, all our glorious dreams of a resurrected Rome. What was worse was that it was such a *little* ending, a shabby, pathetic ending. Later, when I heard of Mussolini's death, I felt the same thing. If Mussolini, like Piers, had been shot down in battle, I could have grieved. As it was, I felt only shock and disgust. I felt hatred for the partisans and their vindictive bloodlust. It always makes me angry to hear Italians talk as if Italy had

had no army. To listen to Italians today you would think that every man, woman and child in Italy was in the resistance. Listen, if we'd had that many people in the resistance, we would have driven the Germans out in a week. No, Italy had an army. Like all armies, it was full of people who didn't particularly want to fight but who did so because they had no choice. They were no more or less brave than any other soldiers. They fought without thinking about it because their country was at war. But because Italy lost, no one can even admit to having fired a shot in anger. And, to cap it all, the Italians don't even have the dignity of playing the villains. The Germans cornered that market, with their dashing uniforms and duelling scars. No, we were the stooges: amusing, chaotic, lovable, cowardly. Well, it's fitting, I suppose, for the country that invented the Punch and Judy show.

With Italy now on the same side as the British, I couldn't see any reason to refuse to co-operate. The prison commandant, Captain Lister, asked me to do some translating for him and I agreed. He and I grew to understand each other, even became friends in a way. He was a young man, earnest, bespectacled – it would be hard to imagine anyone less like a soldier. Before the war, he had been a keen classics scholar and he used to talk to me about Virgil and Catullus. I had no idea what he was talking about, of course, but it was pleasant to have a civilised conversation. Lister told me about his girlfriend and how they had been about to get married before the war but he had thought it wasn't fair on her so she had gone to her mother's family in Cornwall. I had my doubts about the wisdom of that but I kept my mouth shut. It was one skill I'd learnt in prison.

There was an Italian naval captain at Chelsea. He was a diver, one of those men who used to ride on their bombs – they were called 'little pigs' – and attach them to submarines. This man, Novelli he was called, had lost a leg and had to go to Roehampton hospital for treatment. Lister asked me to go with him to translate what the doctors said. He was a brave man, Captain Novelli, always cheerful and good-humoured, joking with the nurses, asking them if he'd be able to dance better with his artificial leg. I could see that all the medical staff admired him and, somehow, this made me feel better about Italy. And about myself.

In 1944, Italian prisoners of war began to be released. I knew, though, that it would be a long time before it was my turn, 'dangerous Fascist' that I was. However, I was surprised to get a letter from Fausto telling me that many men on the Isle of Man were opting to remain in prison rather than disown Italy. All the authorities required was a vague promise to help the British war effort but many internees, Fausto among them, had refused. 'If patriotism is the last resort of the scoundrel,' he wrote, 'then it is time for me to resort to it.'

However, with Italy out of the war, things did relax a little. I spent a lot of time doing translations and improving my written Italian. I read the books my parents brought – and the technical manuals Enzo sent – and played chess with Lister. But, my God, what a terrible, boring life. I have never forgotten looking at my watch and being shocked to realise that only a minute had passed since I'd last looked. Your mother asks me why I don't slow down in my old age. I tell her, 'To slow down is to start to die.'

I was in Chelsea when the war ended. I remember sitting with Bruno and listening to crowds cheering outside. We were silent. There was nothing to say. Mussolini was dead. Whichever side we had ended up on, Italy had lost the war. Bruno was released a few days later. He came to my cell, holding the Home Office letter, and I knew at once. I congratulated him. He said there was nothing to celebrate: Italy had lost the war. 'You're going home to your family,' I reminded him.

His face softened. 'There is that.' He came over and put his hands on my shoulders. 'And as soon as you get out, we'll have a party. At the Hungaria. We'll forget all this shit and just have a party. All right?'

I nodded and smiled. I hated to see him go.

After Bruno had been released, Lister wanted to let me go, too, but the Home Office refused. Apparently they still considered me a major security threat. In fact, years later when I saw my Home Office files they had recommended immediate deportation to Italy. God, I wish they had deported me! Instead I stayed in prison. Lister did his best: he gave me free run of the place – I wasn't locked in my cell any more. In fact, I spent most of my time in his office, helping to translate letters from the Italian government, talking and playing chess.

One evening, when we were in his office together, Lister asked me why I couldn't give them what they wanted: renounce Fascism and Mussolini. The war was over, he said, even Bruno had been released – if I said that I'd been wrong, and that I was sorry, I could be home tomorrow. I told him I couldn't do it.

Why not? The war was over. Fascism had failed. Mussolini had failed. In my heart I knew that I had never had any great intellectual commitment to Fascism. Even the most political prisoners had been released. I was only thirty-two. Why couldn't I just do what Lister said, go home and start my life again?

Perhaps it was because it was all I had left. I had lost all my possessions, my home, my wife. The only thing I had left was a belief in a cause that was well and truly dead. But I wasn't going to renounce it. I had chosen my side and I was going to stick to it. Not giving in now was all that kept me going. I wanted to be a good Italian even if I was the last good Italian in the world.

It was my mother who finally broke me. The next visiting day Lister took my parents aside and talked to them in his office. When they came out, my mother said, 'Why don't you do what he says, Cesarini? Write that letter and then you can come home. I miss you.' It was the only time she ever asked me to do anything for her.

Lister rejected my first draft as not conciliatory enough.

Eventually, he dictated it: 'My enthusiasm for Fascism was merely youthful foolishness. I was carried away by the power of Mussolini's rhetoric. I respectfully point out that, in those days, Churchill himself was a supporter of Mussolini. I deeply regret my actions since that time. I hereby renounce any support for Fascism or Mussolini.' So few words . . . so few words to betray everything I had believed in.

I was released on a Sunday. I found out later that this was unusual – perhaps Lister thought the Home Office would change their minds if he kept me there until Monday. My parents didn't know I was coming so I caught a bus back to Clerkenwell on my own. It felt incredible to do such an ordinary everyday thing: getting on the bus, giving my money to the conductor – I remember being shocked that she was a woman – watching London go by out of the window. When I got off, I stood at the bottom of Farringdon Road. Everything looked exactly the same. The shops selling olive oil and pasta – some boarded up – the children playing in the street, the old women coming home from mass. It was all the same, but I felt a hundred years older.

Then I saw my parents. They must have been to mass because my mother was carrying her missal with its ivory cover and trailing ribbons. For a moment I just stood there, gazing at them. My father's hair was white in the sunlight, and he held my mother's arm as they crossed the road. My mother looked tiny, smart in her black coat, her veil fluttering from her hand. Sophie, *cara mia*, for a second I wondered what would happen if I turned away and never went back. After all, what was left for me here? Then they saw me and my mother called my name. I began to run towards them.

What happened next? I went home and my mother started washing my shirts again. Auntie Clara came round and asked if I was going out to play with Salvatore. I thought about going to Italy. Fausto had already gone back and he wrote me long letters saying, with typical Fausto logic, that everything was awful and I should go and live there. It was tempting. A new life, a new country. Italy was being rebuilt, I could be part of that. Perhaps, after all, I could be a proper Italian. But then Enzo got me a job with Fiat, setting up their first franchises in England.

But what really made me stay in England was that I met your grandmother. At the age of thirty-two, I fell in love. It happened, literally, out of the blue, at Croydon aerodrome.

Enzo had invited me there to fly with him. I almost didn't go. Although I would never have admitted it to Enzo, I was scared. Ever since Piers' death, I had been haunted by dreams of falling to Earth in a burning plane. That morning, it was all I could do to get to Croydon without breaking out in a cold sweat.

When I got to Croydon, Enzo was already there with his girlfriend Joanie and another girl. She was young, about twenty, with curly dark hair tied up in a scarf. Joanie introduced her: 'This is my friend Sylvia.'

How do you know when you've fallen in love? I don't know the answer for anyone else but as soon as I saw Sylvia I felt as if I'd come home. Until that moment, I'd never felt at home anywhere. I didn't want to stay in England, where I had been born, but I was reluctant to go to Italy, the land I professed to love. Now, suddenly, it didn't matter any more. My fears vanished as if they had never been. I flew with Enzo, laughing as the plane tilted and swooped. Then, when Enzo took the girls up, I stood and watched them climb into the bright blue sky and realised that I was happy, properly happy, for what felt like the first time in my life.

We were married three months later. My parents were

delighted, of course. When my father first saw Sylvia, he said, 'At last I have seen you with a beautiful woman.' Bloody cheek. I had had lots of beautiful girlfriends. But I knew what he meant. There was something about Sylvia that put all the others in the shade. She, at last, was the real thing.

My mother was in seventh heaven. Sylvia came from a good family but she wasn't a hard-faced aristocrat like Joyce. She was pretty and 'respectable' and she loved me. My mother, for her part, took Sylvia to her heart and, in a funny way, I think she loved her more than she had ever loved me. Perhaps she had wanted a daughter all along. At any rate, she set about teaching Sylvia to cook Italian food and to look after me as she thought her boy should be looked after. Perhaps it was lucky that Sylvia never quite turned herself into the kind of wife my mother had in mind. True, she cooks wonderful Italian food – my God, all this rubbish these days about Italian food! All those stupid chefs, none of them Italian, splashing wine into *sugo* and tasting it without washing the spoon afterwards. My mother would have had a fit! Sylvia cooks like a true Italian but she has never been the little-wife-indoors, catering to the master. She is my friend, my companion. That's what matters. That's why I can't do without her.

My mother's joy was complete when Emma was born, a year later. At last she was a grandmother. She doted on Emma and Louisa. She always said that boys are nothing but trouble, and I couldn't agree more. I'm so glad she lived to see you, her first great-grandchild. And, you know, you remind me of her. I'm not sure why. Perhaps it's because I have a feeling that if you fell in love with a penniless Neapolitan cobbler you'd marry him, no matter what your family thought.

My father died five years before you were born. Auntie Clara, who had become keen on spiritualism, said she'd been visited by his ghost, a calming, slightly vague presence at the foot of her bed. My mother was furious: *she* was his wife! How dare Giuseppe visit another woman – in her bedroom too! When she died, I remember thinking, Well, now she can have it out with him.

I'll never forget my father's last words. We were all there: my mother, Clara, Antonio, Sylvia and me. Papa was weak but seemed serene, calm as ever. My mother was holding his hand but suddenly he reached out and spoke hoarsely in another language. It was a few seconds before I realised he was speaking Neapolitan. Antonio stepped forward and took his other hand. I knew enough Neapolitan just to make out Papa's words. 'We made it, Tadone,' he said. Then he just smiled and shut his eyes. He died a few hours later.

Antonio died only a year later. As I said, the brothers were very close. Clara, as you know, lived to be nearly a hundred, still seeing ghosts and wondering when Salvatore was coming home for tea. Rosaria? She married her soldier boyfriend, a *cafoun* called Reg Cooper. After we were married, Sylvia wanted me to call on Rosaria, to try to make up. I agreed but barely ten minutes after we arrived at their house this Cooper started to lecture me about Italy. He'd been in Naples during the war and considered that this made him an expert. He had been in the army of occupation in *my* country and thought that this gave him the right to tell me where Italy was going wrong. I stormed out of the house, saying I would never go back. And I never have.

What happened to the others? Well, Bruno and I stayed close for a while. He was best man at my wedding and I was godfather to his daughter, Italia, born a year after the war ended. But then Bruno left Livia for another woman, years younger than him. I had no reason to feel let down, but I did. I remembered how Livia had visited Bruno in prison and how I had envied him for having such a loyal wife. In the end, stupidly, I said something of the sort to Bruno and he never forgave me. When he died we were barely speaking.

Luigi Zazzi and I went into business together. Though the business failed, we stayed friends. He was a strange man, Luigi, vain and arrogant, but he was also kind. He lent me the money to start my second business venture – the one that eventually made me my money – and I have never forgotten that. He married a pretty Irish girl called Kitty but, like Bruno, was hardly the most faithful husband. Kitty put up with a lot but divorced him when he started an affair with her sister. Sometimes Luigi turned up on our doorstep, always with a new car and a new girl. When he died, he was living in France with a woman half his age. His children still send cards at Christmas.

Ernesto Ferri went from strength to strength. He even ended up opening a hotel on the wharf in Liverpool from which the *Arandora Star* had set sail. I'm sorry to tell you that the hotel is called Ferri Across the Mersey.

Angelo Bonetti went back to university and became a scientist. Very well known and respected now, I believe. He married and had four children, which, no doubt, Bruno would consider justified our actions during the riot. I'm not so sure. As you know, Cristofoli left the priesthood and wrote countless articles about coming out and being gay for God. I wonder what he's doing now. I'm sure he's thriving.

Fausto and I kept in contact for a while. He got married, although not to the girl with the lilac notepaper, and settled in Rome. He used to write, asking me to go and stay, but somehow I never did. We lost touch. When he appeared out of the blue that day, it was as if he had come back from the dead. For a second, we were on board the *Arandora Star* again. I almost expected him to say, 'It's time to jump.' I can see him now, standing on the deck, grinning in the darkness. Whatever he said, I know he saved my life.

Well, he's dead now. They're almost all dead. It's a terrible thing to survive your friends. I suppose that's why I'm telling you this. It's frightening to realise suddenly that soon there will be no one left who remembers the *Arandora Star*, Onchan, Warth Mills, the chestnut-sellers in Clerkenwell. Soon we will be nothing but a memory, a few pages in a history book, a few minutes in some patronising documentary with accordion music in the background.

Only Enzo is left. He still rings me every Sunday and we talk about Italy's chances in the World Cup or Ferrari's recent run of bad luck. Funnily enough, only the other day he mentioned the war, which we hardly ever do. He asked me if I despised him for not fighting for Italy, for not being a 'good Italian'. Who was I to despise him? I asked. I'm not judge and jury. We all did what we thought right at the time.

I no longer know what I think. It all seemed so simple then. Good Italians, bad Italians. Fight for Italy, support Mussolini, stamp out homosexuality. Had we any idea how much more complicated it all was? *Il mondo e paese*, my father used to say. The world is a village. As usual, he was right. In the long run, there was not much difference between me and Piers, between Salvatore and Enzo, between Bruno and Reg Cooper, the great Italian expert.

I'm not ashamed, whatever your journalist friend might think of me, but I am sorry. I'm sorry I caused my parents so much heartache. I'm sorry I treated Rose and Anne and all the rest so badly. I'm sorry I spoke so harshly to Salvatore that last time. I'm sorry I didn't have the sense to run to the hills and join the resistance as soon as war broke out. But I did what I thought was right. I'm just no longer sure that I know exactly what that is.

When I walk down the street in Canterbury I see the

Italian flag everywhere: on clothes, on bags, on shop windows, on motorbikes, on cars. 'Are you Italian?' I ask a young man wearing an 'Italia' T-shirt. He looks at me as if I'm mad. Perhaps I am. Italy has become a fashion statement. Now it's cool to be Italian. If I were to tell the young man that people once spat at me in the street for being a 'dirty Italian', he wouldn't believe me. I used to hate films that showed how lovely and warm-hearted the Italians were – like the stupid film, *Moonstruck*, with that girl Cher, who used to be married to the Italian. I despised Pavarotti, with his handkerchief and his simpering at Princess Diana. I preferred the *Godfather* films for all their violence. Better Don Corleone than Toppolino, any day. But now I'm not so sure.

It will be up to you to sort it out. I have great faith in your generation. You and Daniele and Alfredo and Antonio. You'll have to work out what it means to be Italian and British at the same time. Perhaps it doesn't mean anything. But then I think of my father and I know it means something. To this day, I don't know why he came to England, but he came. He sold ice cream, mended shoes and ignored the insults. He worked like a slave and became a rich man, but every time he spoke, someone, somewhere despised him. I can still see

Colonel Hastings's face when my father couldn't pronounce 'Tottenham Court Road'. I was not half the man my father was but I was acceptable because I pronounced golf 'goff' and talked about looking glasses not mirrors. I was so acceptable that the Home Office thought I must be a spy rather than just an Italian.

I chose Italy, but maybe you won't have to choose. That's what I hope, anyway. Perhaps it is no bad thing that Italy no longer means dirty immigrants or even fearsome Fascist hordes. Perhaps it's a better thing to be the country of a thousand logos. Perhaps, after all, it is better to be loved than feared.

LONDON, 1910

Giuseppe stood stock-still in the centre of Victoria station. He had been travelling for so long that he seemed, literally, to have run out of steam. Train to Rome. Another train – endless journey on wooden third-class seat, surrounded by families with hot, unhappy children – to Paris. Walk to Calais as he wanted to save the last of his money. Boat to Newhaven, standing all the way but then, by this time, he felt too excited to sit. Now this last train into Victoria. And a full stop.

Seen from the train, London seemed endlessly grey. Grey river reflecting grey sky, line upon unbelievable line of grey houses; smoke, dust and fog rising around him in an almost tangible cloud. For some reason, this did not make him miss the blue skies of his homeland but, rather, added to his rising sense of excitement. London was so magnificently grim that it was almost exhilarating. There was so much of it, and all so horrible. Not a bird, a tree or even a woman's bright dress to be seen. It was as if he had walked into a sepia photograph.

Standing in the centre of the station, Giuseppe pulled a worn leather wallet from his pocket. Inside there was a picture of the Madonna of Pompeii, given to him by his mother, a silver St Christopher medal from the nuns at the orphanage and the picture taken by a street photographer in Naples. It showed Giuseppe and his brother Antonio, uncomfortable in sailor suits, standing in front of an open doorway. Giuseppe raised the St Christopher to his lips. He wasn't a religious man but it seemed the right thing to do. Patron saint of travellers, pray for me.

Also in the wallet was the last of the money given to him by Don Vittorio. If St Christopher seemed a shadowy presence, Don Vittorio was a much stronger force. Giuseppe could hear his voice quite clearly, and see his gloved hand holding out the folded notes. 'Take this, my son. It's not much but it should be enough. Remember me.'

Remember me.

'Giuseppe!'

Marco Fantani, his friend from Naples, was coming across the platform like an angel of mercy. Everything about Marco looked familiar – his blue overalls, his black beret, his brown Neapolitan face split in a delighted grin of welcome. 'Amico! You made it.'

They embraced.

'Marco! How did you know when to meet me?'

'My father had some friends coming on the same boat.'

Marco took Giuseppe's bag and linked his arm with his own. This gesture, so natural to them both, caused several English passers-by to draw away from them, but neither man noticed.

'You're here. At last.'

'I can hardly believe it. It seems so . . . so strange.'

'I know, amico.' Marco steered Giuseppe deftly out of the station and down a bewildering succession of streets. 'But you will get used to it. This is England. You have come to make your fortune.'

PART THREE

CHAPTER 1

August, 1998

When Louisa comes back to take over with Cesare, I go back to London. It's quite a relief to get back to my old life, although I know I'll miss Cesare and our strange afternoons together by the coffee machine in the hospital. But I want to go back to my flat. The summer holidays have started and I want to get my life in order. Also, I can hardly look at Louisa without remembering that she was named after a prostitute.

I had collected my car from Gatwick during the week, so now I drive straight home. As soon as I realised that Cesare was going to tell me the whole story about his life, the war and the riot, I asked if I could tape him. It made me feel like Guido with his traitorous bag; it made me think of Watergate and policemen taping false confessions; but I think Cesare was quite pleased with the idea. Now, as I inch through the traffic outside Canterbury, I put the tape into the machine.

'. . . pushing a handcart of ice cream through the streets . . .'

'. . . she made me a suit from two flags . . .'

'Is it better to be loved or feared?'

As I come off the motorway and drive through Catford, Cesare has nearly finished his story. His voice sounds huge in my small, non-Italian car. All our family have loud voices – it's one of my only gifts as a teacher that I can call my class in from break without raising mine – but Cesare sounds as if he is declaiming, like poor Pavarotti with his despised handkerchief.

'So few words. So few words to betray everything I had believed in.'

So, now I know. Cesare claimed to have followed Mussolini but it seems to me that all he wanted was an identity. To be a *lavoratore italiano all'estero* and not a dirty foreigner. For a while, with his silk scarves and public-school stutter, he almost assumed a new identity, that of an English gentleman. But then the war came and everything was polarised. He had to choose between England and Italy. I remember what Antonio said: that the first generation of immigrants doesn't assimilate, the second tries too hard, and the third gets the balance right. But where did I fit in? Was I Robertino's English 'Sophie Richmond' or Antonio's passionate Italian lover?

In all the time I was at Canterbury, I didn't once speak to Antonio. One evening, I went for a stroll to the cathedral to clear my head after a day under the fluorescent lights of the hospital. When I got back, Cesare said, 'Oh, Antonio rang.'

Instantly, all the emotions of Rome came flooding back. 'What did he say?' I asked breathlessly.

'Oh, nothing much. Are you going to cook supper now? At my age, it's not healthy to eat too late.'

All evening, as I sliced onions, braised meat and poured wine, I waited for Antonio to call back. But he never did.

Guido rang, though. He called one afternoon and asked for Cesare. 'I'm afraid he's out.' In fact he was asleep. 'Can I take a message?'

'Is that you, Sophie?'

'Yes.'

'What are you doing there?'

'I'm staying with Cesare while my grandmother's in hospital.'

'What about school?' Curiously, Guido is the only person to have asked this question.

'They're OK about it.' Not strictly true: Jane, the head of department, took care to point out that the last week of term was a most inconvenient time to be away – 'There's lots of planning to do, Sophie.' How that woman loves planning! In the war, she would have been one of those servicewomen who pushed the flags about on maps, looking important.

'When are you back in London?'

'I'm not sure. Maybe next week.'

'I'll call you. I may have found out something about the riot. I think you'll be interested.'

I'm not sure how I feel about seeing Guido again. I had hoped that we could forget our one-night stand and be friends, but there's something urgent, almost needy, about his voice that disturbs me. On the other hand he, at least, has rung me.

It's evening when I get back to my flat, but still light. From the common I can hear shouts, blasts from sound systems and the faint, far-off call of an ice-cream van. Oh! Oh! Antonio with your ice-cream cart, where the hell are you?

When I get into the flat, wading through piles of post and fending off a frantic Tybalt (a neighbour has fed him while I was away but he acts as if he is starving), the phone is ringing. I snatch it up with a wild excitement that I don't want to acknowledge, even to myself.

'Sophie?' It's Guido.

'Guido. Hi.'

'Hi, Sophie. You know I said I think I may be on to something about the riot? Well, I've found this priest, Pasquale Cristofoli, and he says he knows all about it. Sounds an extraordinary bloke. Lives in Brighton. Anyway, I thought . . . Would you like to come with me to see him?'

For a moment I don't say anything. As clearly as if it is in the next room, I can hear the violin music and a man's voice, very low and amused, saying, 'Not as beautiful as you.'

'Sophie?'

'Yes.'

'Do you want to come?'

I look out of the window. People are drifting home from the park now, carrying picnic rugs and frisbees. I can still hear the ice-cream van, much nearer now. Robertino once described Brighton as 'the ugliest beach on earth'.

'Yes, I'd like to come,' I say.

I'm sensible enough to insist on driving my own car to Brighton. That way, at least I'll avoid Guido driving me home and coming in for coffee. Also, I don't want to be trapped in a car with him, making small-talk and remembering that we once shared a shower together.

It's a hot day and Brighton is packed. Pasquale Cristofoli lives in Kemp Town and I edge along Madeira Drive past a rally of Mini Coopers and crowds of sweating tourists carrying terrifying grinning toys won in arcades. I park by a derelict children's ride showing a giant apple dissected by a rotting railway line. The surrounding beach almost lives up to Robertino's description ('A beach without sand is not a beach. *Basta. Finito!*') but, looking up, I see rows of creamy Regency terraces and blue, barley-sugar railings. A wave of unfamiliar patriotism sweeps over me. 'It may not have sand,' I say silently to Robertino, 'but did the Prince Regent live in Ostia Lido?'

Pasquale lives in a tiny terraced house near Brighton

College. As I knock on the door, which is painted lilac, I see Guido's car parked nearby. It has a sticker in the window saying, 'A dog is for life, not just for Christmas.'

'Sophia!'

The door is opened by a tall, grey-haired man wearing a pink shirt and beautifully cut cream trousers. He is also wearing a green Harrods apron. There is a wonderful smell of cooking in the air and, for a dizzying second, I am back in Viale Vaticano, blinking in the sunlight.

'Sophia. Cesare's granddaughter. Let me look at you.' He puts both hands on my shoulders and looks at me intently – which, considering we have only just met, should seem like a gross invasion of my personal space, but somehow it doesn't. Perhaps enough of the priest remains to make Pasquale's body language seem non-threatening, even benevolent.

'So, you are beautiful too. That is how it should be.' Even after all these years he still has a slight Italian accent.

I follow Pasquale into a tiny sitting room, with red walls and hundreds of framed photographs. Guido is perched on a green leather chair, balancing a plate on his knee and looking acutely uncomfortable.

'Sophie.' He gets up, looking desperately for somewhere to put his plate.

'Hi, Guido.' I don't move towards him and, after a few seconds' hovering, he sits down again.

'Sophia, can I get you a drink?' Pasquale is at my elbow, smiling with great charm. Like Cesare, he's a good-looking man for his age.

'Could I have a glass of water, please?'

'No wine? How about a tiny glass of chilled white?'

'OK,' I say ungraciously, wondering if he has the power to turn the former into the latter.

I sit next to Guido and accept a glass of delicious wine and a selection of prawn-type things in crumbly pastry. I'm wondering if we'll have to sit through all the pre-dinner drinks and snacks, not to mention what smells so good in the adjoining room, before we get on to the subject of the riot, when Guido snaps on his tape recorder and says: 'So, you say you know about the riot.'

Pasquale looks at me and smiles. 'Yes, the riot,' he says softly. 'What do you know about the riot?'

'We know there was a violent riot at Onchan Camp, which was hushed up by the British authorities,' says Guido, sounding as if he is reading from a prepared script. 'We know a guard was injured and that the two ringleaders, Cesare di Napoli and Bruno Baldasare, were sent to Chelsea Barracks under armed escort. That's all.'

'It's quite a lot,' says Pasquale admiringly. A sleek Persian cat slides into the room and makes a neat leap on to his lap. The James Bond villain look is now complete.

'Cesare,' says Pasquale slowly. He looks at me. 'How is he, these days?'

'He's OK,' I say. 'Lives in Canterbury.'

'Is he still married?' This seems an odd question, given Cesare's age, but I reply, 'Yes, he and my grandmother have been married for over fifty years.'

Pasquale smiles, stroking the cat, which arches its back in ecstasy. 'Fifty years. So he is happy. Good.'

'Were you friends with Cesare?' I ask.

Pasquale laughs. 'Friends? No. I was not in his circle. He associated with men like Baldasare and Luigi Zazzi.'

'Fascists,' says Guido flatly. It is not a question.

'Now, young man,' says Pasquale mildly, 'that is not a term to bandy around so freely. Like homosexual, it is not a category that is so easily identified.'

I look around the room, at the framed prints of 1930s Brighton, at the cluster of white candles in the fireplace, at the bowls of shiny sweets like precious jewels, and think, This is a room that is fairly easily categorised. Straight men do not have candles. Unless they are priests, that is.

'We know Cesare di Napoli was a Fascist,' says Guido. I turn to look at him; he avoids my gaze.

'Well, then, you know wrong,' says Pasquale calmly. 'He was no Fascist. He was a young man who loved his country. Or who loved what he imagined was his country.'

'Mr Cristofoli,' says Guido slowly, 'what happened in the riot?'

Pasquale gets up, tipping the cat gently to the floor. He goes to the mantelpiece and reaches down a photograph in a classy silver frame, which he hands to me. It shows a handsome, middle-aged man in sunglasses. 'My partner, Ramón,' says Pasquale. 'I didn't come out until I was nearly fifty. All those wasted years. Not that I consider the priesthood wasted, though. I would love more than anything to continue as a priest. I still perform spiritual ceremonies for friends – I married a couple last week, on the beach at midnight. It was very beautiful.' Guido shifts awkwardly.

Pasquale continues smoothly, 'When I was in the prisoner of war camp, I repressed my true feelings, but sometimes they came to the fore. Sometimes, surrounded by all those handsome young men, I could not restrain myself. Your grandfather was very handsome, Sophia.'

'You made a pass at Cesare?' asks Guido.

Pasquale looks at me. 'I think Sophia already knows.'

I nod. 'I do.' In my own ears, remembering the midnight ceremony, it sounds oddly like a vow.

Guido stares at me.

'You knew?'

'Yes. Cesare told me.'

'Did he tell you that I made a pass at him?' asks Pasquale.

'Yes.'

'And that afterwards Baldasare demanded that the "known homosexuals"' – he puts delicate quotation marks around the words – 'be moved to another camp?'

'Yes.'

Pasquale shrugs. 'Then that is the truth. The commandant refused at first, so Baldasare started a riot, a guard was injured and we were moved.'

'How did you feel about that?' I ask.

He looks at me and, for the first time, he seems an old man: above his jauntily tied cravat, his skin seems thin and stretched. 'I didn't resent them,' he says. 'They felt threatened. They thought they were protecting the youngsters in camp.'

'But they were homophobic.' My voice comes out too loud in the small room.

'Homophobic, Fascist,' says Pasquale, 'you young people are very keen on these labels.' He looks at me. 'Your grandfather was a good man, Sophia. Don't let anyone . . .' his eyes flick towards Guido ' . . . tell you otherwise. He looked after the young men in camp. He tried to help them, to listen to them, to help them adjust to life in prison. They say he saw a young man killed on the *Arandora Star* and it affected him greatly. He was even polite to me, up to a point. He was a good, ordinary man, in difficult times. Shall we eat?'

Later, as we are leaving, I ask, 'Pasquale, do you consider yourself Italian?'

He smiles. In the dark hall, the actorly good looks have returned. 'Of course,' he says. 'That is one label I can never lose.'

I say a hasty goodbye to Guido and he does not press me to stay. He looks stunned, as if Pasquale's revelations have destroyed the whole narrative. 'I'll be in touch,' he says, as I head off towards my car. I wave at him cheerfully as I stride away. For myself, I feel a tremendous sense of relief. Cesare's story had allowed me to acquit him of being a fervent Fascist and anti-Semite but Pasquale's has acquitted him of being a bad person. *A good, ordinary man, in difficult times.* How Cesare would have hated that. But I disagree. It is better to be loved than feared.

It is dark when I reach the flat. Not bothering to put on the hall light, I bound upstairs, two at a time.

'Sophie,' says a voice in the darkness.

I jump, reach for my rape alarm, which, of course, is buried in the depths of my bag, and swear loudly. It is Antonio. 'What the fuck do you think you're doing?'

'Waiting to see you.'

'You nearly gave me a heart attack.'

'Sorry,' says Antonio, in a typically uncontrite voice.

I upend my bag and eventually find my keys. We go into the flat. I am still shaking but somehow I don't want Antonio to know this. I feel ridiculously guilty, as if I've been caught with another man. Tybalt rushes up to me and I pick him up, burying my face in his fur.

'Any chance of some coffee?' asks Antonio.

I look at him. Antonio, I want to say, you can't just turn up after not calling me for a week, lurk outside my flat and demand coffee. Who the hell do you think you are? What the hell do you think you're doing? Then I see that his face is pale with black circles under his eyes. His shirt is crumpled and he has a rather wild look about him, like someone who has been sleeping rough. The relief over Cesare, which has sustained me all the way back from Brighton, makes me want to be kind to him.

'I'm sorry,' says Antonio again, 'it's just . . . I've been having a hard time. Melissa's definitely taking the kids to America. Simonetta's really upset. And then . . . I didn't know if you wanted me to ring you.'

'I'll make you some coffee,' I say.

We go into the sitting room. It's early evening but still light outside. I can hear children playing in the street. It's like Italy, where the children never sleep and the parents look hollow-eyed from exhaustion.

Antonio follows me into the kitchen. 'Very tidy,' he says.

'Don't,' I say.

'Don't what?'

'Say "like mother, like daughter".'

'I wouldn't dream of it.' Antonio whistles under his breath while he examines my spice rack. 'But Auntie Emma *is* very tidy, isn't she?'

I throw a tea towel at him. The thought of my mother makes me twitchy.

'Can we have a proper drink?' asks Antonio. 'It's been a hell of a day.'

I look doubtfully into the fridge. I haven't been shopping since I got back from Cesare's and all I have is a bottle of sweet white wine given to me by a pupil's parent and a lemon liqueur brought back years ago from Sorrento.

'Bloody hell,' says Antonio rudely. 'I'll have the liqueur. It's probably more alcoholic.'

'I haven't been shopping,' I say. I'm damned if I'm going to apologise.

'No,' says Antonio. 'Where *have* you been anyway? I've been trying to ring all day.'

I say nothing. I don't want to tell Antonio about Pasquale Cristofoli and I especially don't want to tell him that I've spent the day with Guido. The cassette containing Cesare's story is on my desk in the sitting room. I find that I don't want to tell Antonio about that either. Perhaps I don't want to talk about the family. Perhaps I want to concentrate on our relationship, whatever it is. Perhaps I simply don't trust Antonio not to turn Cesare's life story into an hour-long Radio 4 special, narrated by himself.

'Out,' I say shortly, handing Antonio his glass.

We sit on my tiny balcony and drink the lemon liqueur, which is disgusting, somehow managing to be sweet and acidic at the same time. The heavy beat of music comes from the flats opposite. With a jolt I realise it's Saturday night.

'So,' says Antonio, 'how was Cesare?'

'OK,' I say, casting an involuntary glance at my desk where the innocuous-looking black cassette sits on top of a pile of papers.

'Thank God Sylvia's going to be all right,' says Antonio. 'I can't imagine Cesare coping on his own.'

'No,' I agree. Looking after Cesare, as I know from first-hand experience, is a full-time job.

'It's funny, isn't it? All our lives it's been Cesare this and Cesare that. It's easy to forget how important Sylvia is.'

'Typical comment on women's roles in general.'

Antonio shrugs an impatient shoulder. 'All I'm saying is

that Sylvia could survive without Cesare but Cesare could never survive without Sylvia.'

'They love each other,' I say, remembering that Sylvia's first thought, on regaining consciousness, was for Cesare. Thinking also of Pasquale and Ramón, living in Brighton with their cat and their carefully chosen antiques. Thinking, despite myself, of Antonio and me, and the heat of the midday sun in the graveyard and the feel of his body on mine.

'Yes, they do,' says Antonio. We sit in silence for a while. It's almost dark now and the street lamps are lit. Antonio stands up, looking very tall suddenly on my ridiculous balcony. 'I'd better go,' he says.

'Don't,' I say.

Antonio looks at me. It's too dark suddenly to see his face. I stand up and go to stand in front of him, not touching him but so close that I can feel his sharp intake of breath. For a second we just stand there, not speaking, but then Antonio grabs me, desperately, urgently, like a drowning man. He tilts my head back and kisses me fiercely. I can't break away but then, of course, I don't want to.

*

Much later, I ask Antonio, 'Is this incest?'

Antonio grins. 'Vice is nice but incest is best'

We are lying, entangled, on the bed. The rest of the world seems very far away. The buses passing outside sound like messengers from another planet. 'No, seriously,' I say, 'are we allowed to do this?'

'Allowed? By whom? We're cousins, second cousins, it's perfectly legal.'

'Just think what Cesare would say.'

Antonio lights a cigarette. 'He'd say, "I always knew this would happen."' Cesare is, indeed, the champion of hindsight.

'He'd be horrified,' I say.

'Then let's not tell him.'

'What are we going to do?' I ask idly. At this moment, nothing seems very urgent.

'Let's go for a picnic,' says Antonio, handing me the cigarette. 'You can meet my children.'

CHAPTER 2

I had met them before, of course. I remember countless family gatherings: Simonetta in a staggeringly elaborate christening gown, made by Aunt Rosaria, and in an only slightly less elaborate first-communion dress, from the same source; Marco, aged three, falling in Cesare's garden and cutting his head open (Cesare yelling for an ambulance, Sylvia calmly bandaging the cut); Simonetta singing 'Nella Vecchia Fattoria' for Cesare; Marco crying because Daniel wouldn't lend him his baseball cap. When I last saw them, they were about six and four.

Tom and I were at the zoo. It was one of those panicky gestures of togetherness that come towards the end of a relationship. It was a sunny afternoon, why not go to the zoo? Look at us, we can still have fun! As we were walking

past the monkey house, defiantly eating ice creams and pretending to have a good time, we met Antonio. He was sitting
glumly on a bench surrounded by the detritus of a family
day out: picnic bag, crisps wrappers, abandoned cuddly toys.
Simonetta was solemnly filling in one of those quizzes that
they give children to pretend that a day at the zoo is educa-
tional, and Marco was crying.

'Hi, Antonio,' I said. 'Bit of a cliché this, isn't it?' Looking
back, this was pushing it a bit; Antonio and Melissa had
only just got divorced, it was a bit early to make jokes about
single fathers and days out. Fortunately Antonio gave no sign
of having heard.

'Hi, Sophie,' he said. 'Hi.' He nodded at Tom whom he had
met but obviously didn't remember.

'What's up, Marco?' I squatted down next to him.

'My balloon's popped.' Marco held out a piece of soggy
orange plastic. 'It was a special tiger balloon.'

'I said I'd get him another,' said Antonio, rather defensively.

'But this was a special one,' Marco sobbed. 'My special
balloon. I loved it.'

If I have one talent, it's an ability to turn soggy bits of
plastic into tiny but perfectly formed balloons. I took the

popped balloon, sucked it unattractively and produced a miniature tiger balloon. Marco was entranced and stopped crying immediately. I only hope I can work the same magic this time.

I prepare for the picnic like a military exercise. Antonio has said that he will bring the food but I bring chilled white wine, a selection of juices for the children (nothing fizzy or artificial), some balloons (the old tricks are the best) and a cricket set. I imagine us playing cricket as the shadows lengthen over Richmond Park, passers-by watching us indulgently and thinking that we're a family.

The first thing that goes wrong is that it's *freezing*. Although it's early August, there's a biting wind and the promise of rain later. Both children, when we meet by the East Gate, are wrapped in anoraks, scarves and hats. I leave the cricket set in the car.

And they've grown so much that they hardly seem to be children any more. Simonetta is eight but she could be about thirteen, with her long black hair in a complicated plait and her trendy blue jeans. Marco is six, solemn and dark with Antonio's frizzy hair squashed down under a woolly hat, which he refuses to take off. He glares at me angrily, not seeming to remember our bonding moment over the tiger balloon.

'Well, here we all are,' says Antonio unnecessarily. In a desperate attempt to be optimistic, he's wearing only an Italy T-shirt and is visibly shivering. 'Let's walk, shall we? It's going to clear up soon.'

It doesn't. The day gets colder and colder. Antonio and I walk together, talking brightly. The children trail behind us. At least this part of my fantasy is coming true – we look all too much like a proper family. Soon the rain comes and Antonio slaps his arms against his sides in an attempt to get back some circulation. 'I know,' he says brightly. 'Let's forget the picnic. We'll go to the café. Have a hot drink. What do you think?' Silently, we follow him.

The café is packed but at least it's warm. We queue with all the other quarrelling families and eventually buy coffee for Antonio and me and chips for the children. Marco has hot chocolate but Simonetta refuses with a shudder. We find a corner of a table and I wipe it fussily with a paper napkin. It's all I can do to stop myself stacking the dirty plates of the previous occupants. I'm longing for a cigarette and I know Antonio is too. Instead I take a gulp of grey, lukewarm coffee.

'So, Simonetta,' I ask, 'what's your favourite band?'

Simonetta looks at me coldly. 'Are you going out with my dad?' she asks.

I'm tempted to ask where they are in the charts. Antonio and I exchange glances. 'No,' I say. 'I'm your cousin, remember? You saw me at Max's sixteenth birthday party.'

'I remember,' says Simonetta, without enthusiasm, taking a single chip and blowing on it fastidiously. 'I just wondered why you were here.'

'Simonetta!' says Antonio.

'It's OK,' I say. I look round at the dreary café with its steamed-up windows and smell of frying onions. 'We just thought it would be fun,' I say.

'I'm sorry,' says Antonio. It's later the same day. Antonio has dropped off the children at Melissa's and come back to my flat. The rain is thundering against the windows and we're drinking the wine I brought for the picnic.

'It's OK,' I say. 'I enjoyed it.'

'No, you didn't.'

'No, I didn't.'

'It was a terrible idea.' Antonio slumps back against the

sofa. The rain has made his hair curly and he keeps pushing it irritably off his forehead.

'No, it wasn't,' I say quickly. For some reason, this is terribly important to me. 'It wasn't a terrible idea. We had a good time later, didn't we? Playing "let's shoot the squirrel"?'

Walking back to the cars, I redeemed myself in Marco's eyes by remembering a game we used to play on school trips. Two points if you shoot a squirrel, three for a dog, four for a deer and five for a child in a pushchair. Marco had joined in enthusiastically, peering through the sights of an imaginary revolver and taking careful aim at a family with three children who were trying to encourage the squirrels to eat from their hands. Antonio, displaying a humourless father side I had never seen before, told us to stop.

Now, perhaps at the memory of the game, Antonio groans. 'It's so difficult,' he says at last. 'I only see the children for a few hours a week. How can anyone be a father in that time? And when they go to America I'll see them even less. It's hopeless.'

'At least you've got children,' I say.

Antonio looks up. 'Did you ever? Would you . . .?'

'No,' I say shortly. 'Let's have another drink.'

288

'No.' Antonio stands up. Unsmiling, he pulls me towards him. 'Let's go to bed.'

Much later, I go to the kitchen to make coffee and feed Tybalt. I'm wearing an old white shirt with frayed cuffs. The kitchen floor is cold under my bare feet. Antonio stands in the doorway, wrapped in one of my black towels and looking like a slightly gone-to-seed gladiator. 'You're beautiful,' he says.

'So you like a woman in the kitchen?' I say, not wanting to think about what he has said.

'I like you,' he says. 'Isn't that enough?'

We drink our coffee in the darkened sitting room. The windows are open and the room is full of the smell of wet trees. The only light comes from the street lights outside. Antonio gets up and goes to the window. Suddenly, he says, 'You've got a visitor.'

'Who can it be at this hour?' I wonder, but even as I say it I have an uneasy feeling that it's not good news. I look out of the window and catch a glimpse of bright red hair. Oh, please, God, no.

When the doorbell rings I briefly consider not answering,

but what would be the use? Guido can see the open window, can probably see a half-naked Antonio standing there. And anyway, how can I explain to Antonio why I'm not answering the door? I press the button to open it without even waiting for the entryphone. I feel deeply apprehensive.

Guido comes running up the stairs, I can hear his voice floating upwards. 'Sophie! I met the camp commandant, Blick. Mad as a hatter but he confirms Pasquale's story. About the riot . . .'

I say nothing, there's no point, the pancetta is so disastrously certain to hit the fire. Guido reaches the top of the stairs. He is wearing a yellow windcheater and his hair is dark with rain. By this time, Antonio is standing beside me at the door, still dressed only in my black bath towel. I see Guido look at Antonio, then at me with my bare legs, then, wildly, back down the stairs, as if he thinks he may have come to the wrong flat.

'Well,' says Antonio, 'quite the little bloodhound, aren't we?'

As a conciliatory opener it lacks a certain something.

'Sophie?' says Guido uncertainly.

'Come in,' I say. Not a great idea, but what else can I do?

We file silently along the corridor and into the sitting room. Antonio sits down arrogantly, legs apart, a bad move for a man in a towel. Guido stands by the balcony window, fiddling nervously with his car keys.

'Coffee?' I ask brightly. Nobody answers.

'Well,' says Antonio, 'what have you *ferreted out* about Cesare?'

'I came to tell Sophie,' says Guido quietly, but his face has started to blend seamlessly into his hair.

'You can tell me,' says Antonio. 'Keep it all in the family.'

'You're certainly doing that,' replies Guido.

Antonio is on his feet. 'What's that supposed to mean?'

'You know what it means.'

'Guido,' I say, 'you'd better go.'

Guido looks at me. I can't read the expression on his face but he looks shocked, too shocked surely for the situation, embarrassing as it is. After all, Antonio is my second cousin, not my brother. 'How could you?' he says.

I find myself beginning to get angry. 'It's nothing to do with you,' I say. 'You'd better go.'

'It's a game to you, isn't it?' says Guido. 'Sleep with me, sleep with him – your bloody cousin, for Christ's sake!

Does anything mean anything to you? Me? Him? Even your grandfather?'

Involuntarily I glance at the cassette, which is still on my desk. I'm almost surprised it hasn't started to bleep loudly to draw attention to itself. Guido follows my glance and doesn't see the punch Antonio throws at him. Taken by surprise, he staggers. Antonio advances, still holding on to the towel with one hand. Perhaps this impedes him for when Guido, incredibly quickly, gets his balance back and swings his fist hard into Antonio's face, he goes down like a ninepin. For a minute, Guido and I stare down at Antonio's prone body. Then I say again, 'I think you'd better leave.'

'Sophie? I'm sorry . . .'

'Just go.' I kneel down beside Antonio.

CHAPTER 3

'Where is he?' Antonio asks thickly.

'Gone,' I say.

Antonio sits up slowly. The side of his face is red and puffy. He'll have a black eye tomorrow but I think it's better not to mention that now. The towel has fallen away and his nakedness makes him vulnerable. I pat his arm, rather awkwardly. 'You should put some raw steak on that eye,' I say. 'Or ice or something.' I'm not much cop at first aid. At school, all we're allowed to suggest is a brisk walk round the playground.

'No,' says Antonio. 'Get me a drink.'

I pour the last of the picnic wine. The cold morning in Richmond Park seems days away. Simonetta, Marco, Antonio, Guido. How long is it since I was in Pasquale Cristofoli's sitting room, surrounded by candles and photographs? Antonio goes into the bedroom to get dressed. Mindlessly, I begin to tidy up. I pick up Cesare's cassette and put it carefully in a drawer.

'For Christ's sake!' Antonio has come back, fully dressed and in a terrible temper. 'Are you tidying again?'

I say nothing, just pass him a glass of wine. Next to the wine, on the table, is the packet of balloons. Somehow I don't think we'll be needing them now.

Antonio takes a gulp of wine, winces, and says, 'It must be serious, then, you and Guido della Carbonara.'

I stare at him. 'What do you mean?'

'He comes in here, sees me with you and goes raving mad. How much clearer do you want it? Does he have to turn it into one of his bloody awful books for you?'

I sigh. 'Look, Antonio, there's nothing between me and Guido. We had a fling once, that's all. I don't know what today was about. Maybe you just wound him up.'

'Me?' Antonio touches his swollen cheek. 'He comes on like Rocky Marciano and I wound *him* up?'

'Well, you did hit him first.'

'Jesus. I might have known you'd take his side.'

This is all going wrong. I stand up and go out on to the balcony. The people opposite are having a party, I can still hear the steady thump-thump of their music. Suddenly I feel very tired.

'I'd better go,' says Antonio, from inside the room.

I start to say, no, don't go, let's talk about it, but when I look at him he doesn't look like my cousin, or my lover, but like a stranger. A grey-haired, stocky stranger, a little drunk, with the beginnings of a black eye.

But when he's at the door, I ask, despite myself, 'When will I see you?'

Antonio shrugs. 'At Cesare's eighty-fifth, I suppose. Why don't you ask Guido along? I'm sure he'd love to meet the rest of the family.'

'I'm sorry,' Guido says again.

'It's OK,' I say. 'He hit you first.' We're sitting on a bench on Clapham Common. Guido's frighteningly huge Alsatian is running in huge circles round us. It's a very hot day. Guido is wearing a black baseball cap pulled down low over his eyes. It makes him look vaguely sinister, like a hitman trying to stay incognito. I sit beside him, drinking Coke and trying to get my legs brown. I see Guido look down at them and quickly look away again.

'I was just so shocked,' says Guido at last.

'Why?' I ask.

'You and him. I just . . . I never dreamt . . .'

I take a swig of Coke. When Guido rang to ask me to meet him so he could 'explain', I suggested Clapham Common as it seemed less intimate than going for a meal or even a drink. 'That's fine,' said Guido. 'I can bring Rocky.' Of course, his dog *would* be called Rocky. But now it seems almost worse to be sitting together in the sun, like a couple, with our drinks and our massive dog, while all around us families are having picnics. I think back to the miserable outing with Antonio's children two days ago. Why couldn't we have had the sun then? Why did Guido have to come in with his red hair and his eagerness and his stupid obsession with Italy and spoil everything?

'It's not illegal,' I say nastily.

'I know,' says Guido. 'It's just . . . Antonio Cooper.'

'What about him?'

'He's such a – such an arse. With his stupid radio programmes, sneering at everyone. He thinks he's so clever. He's not even a proper Italian.'

'He's a quarter Italian. Like me.'

'Going on and on about being Italian,' Guido seems not to have heard me, 'when he can't even speak the language. He doesn't even care about your grandfather. Probably just wants to turn it into another of his crappy books. *Mussolini and Me* by Antonio fucking Cooper.'

'You met Blick,' I say, hoping to change the subject.

'Yes.' Guido strokes Rocky, who slobbers unpleasantly. I feel I have much more in common with Pasquale and his neat Persian cat. 'I found out his address from the MoD. He lives in a retirement home in Kent. Ironically very near Cesare. Anyway, he didn't want to talk at first. Apparently the whole episode was hushed up. I told him we'd seen Cristofoli and it all came out. How there was a full-scale riot. Quite violent. A guard was hurt and they conceded to the prisoners' demands.'

'Why?'

'Well, look at it from their point of view. They were helpless. They didn't want to publicise the situation in case things got nasty in the other camps. There was a lot of sympathy from the British military – they didn't like homosexuals either. I've been researching it and apparently similar riots took place in British prisoner-of-war camps in Germany.'

'All homophobes together,' I say, thinking of Pasquale's gentle mockery of the term.

'I suppose so. But you have to think what attitudes were like then.'

'That doesn't make it right'

'No.' Guido sounds undecided. He obviously thinks that an anti-gay riot is more understandable than an anti-Semitic one.

'So Pasquale was telling the truth?'

'Apparently so.' Guido looks awkward. He pushes his hat back and rubs his eyes as if they're hurting him. 'Look, Sophie,' he says, 'you said your grandfather had already told you about the riot. I was thinking, is there anything else he told you? Anything that I might use in the book? You know, setting the record straight and all that.'

I think of the cassette, now safely locked inside my desk. I think of Cesare's birth certificate and Giuseppe's medal. I think of Fausto on board the *Arandora Star*, Giovanni's body in the water, Bruno teaching Cesare to fence, Nicholls offering the best welcome-home present he knew, Luigi Zazzi lending Cesare the money to start his business.

'No,' I say, 'there's nothing else.'

'Don't you want people to know the truth?' Guido persists.

I remember, as a child, sitting through endless Good Friday masses, lots of chanting and the statues covered with purple robes. The only bright spot was the gospel reading, which was normally done as a kind of play, with three readers. The bit I remember best is when Pontius Pilate – a great hero of Cesare's – says, 'Truth. What is that?' Now, I feel a great sense of kinship with the cynical old Roman prefect. *Truth. What is that?*

'I know the truth,' I say. 'That's enough for me.'

Guido is silent for a moment, staring at the children playing on the bleached grass. Rocky whines and looks at him expectantly. Guido ignores him. Then, he says, 'Is it serious, you and Antonio?'

It's my turn to be silent. What can I say? We have sex, we go on picnics together, we sat at Sylvia's bedside, I think about him all the time. It feels serious to me but what does he feel? He has never said he loves me, but if he did, would thunderbolts rain down from heaven? How serious is it allowed to be? I don't know. I don't know.

'I don't know,' I say. 'Look, what's it got to do with you?'

'I'm in love with you,' says Guido, in an odd, strained voice. 'I assumed you knew.'

CLERKENWELL, 1945

'*The Italian dictator Benito Mussolini has been killed by partisans in Milan. His companion Clara Petacci was killed alongside him when partisans dragged them from their car . . .*'

Giuseppe reached out and turned off the wireless. He had never liked Mussolini, had quarrelled with his wife and son about the man many times, but now, when it came to it, he did not feel like celebrating. He held no brief for the partisans, who, he would learn later, danced around the dead bodies of Mussolini and his mistress, jeering and spitting. Later the bodies were hoisted into the air by their heels. It was said that Clara did not even have a run in her stockings.

Well, perhaps this would mean that Cesare would come home soon. At least with him at Chelsea Barracks, Giuseppe and Laura could visit him. At least, unlike many of their friends, they had not lost their son. Giuseppe thought of the Fantani family, Marco, who had welcomed him to England and found him his first job, killed when a bomb landed on their house. He thought of his brother Antonio with his son dead in Italy, just a few miles from where they had been born. He thought of Lusardi's, the Italian tailors in Newport Street, which had a sign in the window saying, 'The proprietors of this shop are British subjects and have lost two sons serving in the British army!' At least he still had his son, affectionate and bloody-minded as ever, imprisoned in London and still swearing allegiance to that clown now swinging in the air.

Giuseppe put on his coat and went out into the garden. Since the war, most of the gardens in Clerkenwell had been given over to vegetables and Laura had made sure that they grew the herbs she needed for her cooking. Some people also kept chickens but Laura considered them insanitary. Of course, being an aristocrat, Laura did not do the gardening herself. Rather, she directed operations, but Giuseppe didn't mind that. Perhaps it's because I'm a peasant at heart, he thought, as he dug his spade into the London clay, but I'm happiest doing work like this.

Cesare hated gardening. Nature bored him – he had once scandalised a Sunday-school teacher by declaring, 'Of course God makes good trees. What do you expect?' – and he thought the only purpose of a garden was as a place to sit, drink wine and eat. One thing was certain, Cesare was no peasant.

For the first time in many years Giuseppe thought about Naples: about the heat and the noise and the smell of the sea; about his mother singing to him; about the orphanage and the bell ringing for evening prayers; about Montagna and the stench of tanning leather; about Don Vittorio and the dog cart and the gloved hand reaching out to him.

Remember me.

Giuseppe stopped digging. Laura was at mass. These days, she went to mass every morning. Giuseppe did not accompany her. It was enough for him to go on Sundays and even then he stood at the back by the holy water and the hymn books. Like a lot of Italian men, he believed that sitting down in church was for women and children. He could not remember ever kneeling in church. After mass Laura would probably call in on Clara. Poor Clara had taken Salvatore's death very badly and would sit for hours crying over his photograph. Or else, distressingly, she would say that she had to cook Salvatore's dinner, he was due home from school soon and he did like his frittata alla Romana. Laura was good with her, talked gently about what had happened and, unlike many people, didn't assume that she knew what Clara was feeling.

So Laura would be at least another hour. Giuseppe took off his boots ('Your shoes, Giuseppe! On my good carpet!') and went into the sitting room. Laura had made him construct a safe behind one of the bricks in the fireplace. 'What will happen to my jewels if the Germans come?' As always, Giuseppe had done as he was told, but in the little safe he had put not only Laura's precious Florentine jewellery but also a small sheaf of papers belonging to himself. His birth certificate, his parents' death certificates, a picture of himself with Antonio, taken by a street photographer in Naples, and a handwritten letter beginning: 'My dear son, though I have no right to call you that . . .'

Giuseppe sat down with the letter on his lap. He didn't read it; he knew it by heart. What would Cesare think if he knew that his grandfather was a Don, a capo, *a man who knew the* amici gli amici? *Giuseppe had an uneasy feeling that he would be delighted. He knew now, of course, where Don Vittorio's volcanic personality, which had bypassed him, had made its mark. And Antonio? What would he think? Giuseppe loved his brother almost more than anyone else in the world. Hadn't they sworn always to stay together? He was not going to allow this knowledge to come between them.*

Giuseppe thought of Naples. 'The old days' they always called them, 'the old country'. Always with an implication that old was better, that the past was better than the present.

Holding Don Vittorio's letter in his hands, he felt as if he was actually touching that past. The Don had given him the chance of a future. Giuseppe had come to England, made his money, given his son a good education (an education that had, indirectly, led him to detention in Chelsea Barracks). Did the old days still matter? Should he tell Cesare the truth about his grandfather? Or should he forget the past and put Naples behind him?

Giuseppe sat for so long that he began to worry that Laura would be back from church, taking off her hat and fussing about putting on the sugo for lunch. Quickly he got up and lit a fire in the grate.

He waited until the flames were high enough, then threw Don Vittorio's letter on the fire. Some secrets just aren't worth keeping.

CHAPTER 4

The cast list for Cesare's eighty-fifth birthday party is almost the same as for his seventieth. My father is away on a golfing holiday and Alfredo and Max haven't arrived yet, but there are three new guests in the shape of Joanne's other children, Elena (aged twelve), Mario (aged ten) and Gabriel (aged five). And instead of the walled garden and the white linen, Cesare has decided in favour of an Italian restaurant in Canterbury, all bumpy plaster walls and checked tablecloths, which is, of course, owned by a friend of his.

Even so, the family, including Louisa's rather louche boyfriend Darius and Daniel's silent wife Rebecca, makes enough of a crowd for other diners to be looking around nervously and hoping that we aren't about to start singing. Carmine, Cesare's friend, is all smiles as he ushers us to a private room upstairs. He refrains from kissing Cesare's hand – but only just.

I arrive early and walk with Cesare and Sylvia to the restaurant. Except for a slight droop to the left side of her face and a tendency to forget words like 'teapot', Sylvia seems completely recovered. It's a beautiful evening and the birds are flying low in the cathedral grounds. When we reach the restaurant, Antonio is already there. I haven't spoken to him since the day he left my flat with a nasty quip about Guido and the beginnings of a black eye. Today, when he takes off his dark glasses, all you can see is a slight bruise. He is wearing a dark suit and looks even more sombre than he did at Fausto's funeral. I'm reminded of Fausto himself, standing formal and somehow magical, like a man in a painting by Magritte, at Cesare's other birthday party. Antonio is sitting sideways in his chair, smoking and talking to Joanne. When he sees us, he stands up and comes to greet us, embracing Cesare and kissing my cheek. His lips feel cold and he smells of cigarettes.

There isn't a table plan but I find myself between Darius and Daniel and opposite Antonio. Daniel ignores me as usual and Darius looks bored. I take a gulp of wine and prepare myself for a long night. Cesare is complaining that there's an empty seat next to him. 'What's the matter with you all? Are you scared of the old man? Elena – come and sit next to your *bis-zio*.'

Elena looks scared – as well she might: Cesare's smile would terrify the wolf in *Little Red Riding Hood* – but before she can answer, a distraction occurs. Carmine opens the double doors with a theatrical flourish and Alfredo and Max come in, supporting between them – Aunt Rosaria.

Cesare gets to his feet and, for a terrible moment, I think he's going to tell her to get out, that he doesn't want to see her, that he hasn't forgiven her for cramping his style with the Clerkenwell street urchins or for marrying the bastard. Instead he moves, rather slowly, towards her. 'Rosaria! How are you?'

'Still alive,' says Rosaria tartly. She is breathing heavily.

Cesare takes her arm. 'Come and sit by me.'

Alfredo and Joanne exchange a relieved glance, though neither looks as relieved as Elena.

Getting through the ordering is as tedious as it always is in a group meal. Cesare translates all the Italian for us ('Spaghetti is very long, thin pasta') and Gabriel says loudly that he wants chips. Antonio is still smoking, though my mother, who is sitting next to him, keeps waving away the smoke with exaggerated hand movements. I catch his eye only once, when Rosaria says that she heard him on the radio: 'Very rude you were, to that poor writer fellow. They won't ask you again unless you learn to be more polite . . .'

Then, when the vast, tasselled menus are cleared away, Carmine approaches with the champagne. Even Gabriel is allowed a sip ('Yuk, disgusting') and Cesare rises to his feet. He looks at Rosaria. 'Absent friends,' he says at last.

Rosaria's lips move and I think that she's going to risk Cesare's wrath and invoke the name of the bastard himself. But then she raises her glass to Cesare. 'Salvatore,' she says.

'Salvatore,' repeats Cesare softly.

It is only afterwards, among the crumpled Amaretti papers, that trouble starts. Max, aged sixteen, who was only a baby at that other party fifteen years ago, has been drinking heavily, unnoticed by his parents who are so relieved at pulling off the Aunt Rosaria coup that they're oblivious to everything. Suddenly he stops picking pieces out of the candle in front of him and says loudly, 'Uncle Cesare? Were you a Fascist?'

There is a silence, broken only by Darius's half-stifled laugh. Cesare looks at Max through half-lowered lids: suddenly he looks dangerous again, a Roman emperor sitting among the ruins of an imperial banquet. But, when he speaks, it is in a curiously gentle voice: 'Yes, Max, I was a Fascist.'

Max takes a deep breath and sways slightly in his seat. 'But how could you? How could you support Mussolini? He was like Hitler. He was worse than Hitler. He invented Fascism. We did it at school.'

I look at Max and think a thousand different things. First, admiration: I would never have dared take on Cesare at sixteen. Second, I agree with him: I could never admire Mussolini, he did invent Fascism (I remember my own A-level notes: 'Fascism: the authoritarian nationalistic movement led by Benito Mussolini in Italy, 1922–43') and did terrible things in its name. But third, and most strongly, I feel that Max doesn't understand. He doesn't understand what it was like for Cesare.

'No Max,' I say. 'He wasn't a Fascist. He supported Mussolini because he gave the Italians in England an identity.' Antonio looks up at me quickly. 'When Uncle Cesare was a child, people laughed at Italians, called them dirty and stupid. Mussolini made the English see the Italians as fighters. People to fear. And it wasn't just the Italians. A lot of people admired Mussolini then.' I steal a look at Aunt Rosaria but her face gives nothing away. 'Even Churchill called Mussolini "one of the most wonderful men of our time". It was a different time. We can't look back and judge them.'

Everyone is looking at me now: Cesare with a faint smile; my mother with embarrassment because she thinks I'm causing a scene; Antonio with a scowl of dawning understanding; Darius with amusement; Max with resentment.

'But the Jews,' says Max, 'the concentration camps.'

'Anti-Semitism wasn't part of Mussolini's thinking,' I say, 'not at first, anyway. And Cesare wasn't anti-Semitic. The only people he was against were . . . priests.'

'Priests!' says my mother in shock.

But Cesare is laughing, 'You're right, *cara mia*. It was all the fault of the priest. Just one priest, you understand. Nothing against your beloved Father O'Hara, Emma. Just one priest. I hope he's forgiven us.'

I'm about to tell Cesare that he has indeed, with extraordinary grace, forgiven them but at this point Max causes a distraction by lurching to his feet and rushing out to the loo.

'I don't really care any more,' says Cesare grandly, pulling on his cigar and cradling his brandy in his other hand. 'I'm just a poor old man now. Waiting for death.' The idea seems to cheer him up no end and he leans over the table to Daniel. 'Daniele! Did you get it?'

Daniel looks embarrassed. 'Yes,' he mumbles.

'Well, show me, then.'

Scarlet in the face, Daniel whispers to Rebecca who pulls out of her bag a large, flat parcel. Silently Daniel hands it to Cesare. It is a large, silk Italian tricolour.

Cesare is delighted. He holds it up for everyone to see. Looking at it, I think that he was right: the Italian flag has become a fashion statement. Just looking at the bright bands of red, white and green makes me think of holidays, wine and designer sportswear.

'What's it for?' asks Elena boldly.

Cesare grins. 'Why, to go on my coffin, *carina*.'

Elena shrugs. 'Oh.'

But my mother squeals in distaste. 'Daddy! How morbid! Daniel, how could you?' She looks pale with shock.

'I asked him to,' Cesare says serenely.

Aunt Rosaria reaches out and fingers the silk flag. I can see Cesare wanting to push her hand away. For most of the meal, Rosaria and Cesare have talked pleasantly enough about the old days, the Italian procession and the impossibility of finding a good minestrone in restaurants; but now, looking at Cesare at eighty-five, I see him momentarily transformed into a bullying Clerkenwell schoolboy. 'Why d'you want the Italian flag?' she asks. 'Isn't the English flag good enough for you?'

There is an audible hiss as everyone around the table draws a sharp breath. Even Darius, dreamily stubbing out his cigarette in his tiramisu, is aware of the heresy that Rosaria has just uttered. I'm almost cowering, imagining the roar of rage as Cesare explains exactly why England is not, and never will be, good enough for him.

But instead Cesare smiles. 'It's not a question of not being good enough, Rosaria,' he says sweetly. 'It would be pretending to be something I'm not. I'm an Italian. I must live and die an Italian.'

'Oh, me too,' says Rosaria, noisily slurping her port. 'I'm Italian too. I was born there, remember.'

Now I really am surprised. Rosaria, who sold her birthright for an English surname, who married the bastard, who sometimes sounds like Alf Garnett on speed, considers herself an Italian. I look across at Antonio. He grins, his teeth very white in his dark face.

'You consider yourself Italian?' Cesare is saying faintly.

'Of course,' says Aunt Rosaria. 'What else would I be?'

What indeed?

This seems to be the signal for the party to break up a bit. Gabriel is asleep on a velvet banquette, Louisa gets up and goes round the table to talk to Sylvia, Darius stares out of the window, Daniel and Rebecca are whispering together, Cesare and Rosaria are suddenly deep in conversation.

'Hi.' Antonio has moved into Darius's empty chair next to me.

'Hi,' I say.

'You knew about the riot,' he says.

'Yes.'

'How?'

'Cesare told me. When I was staying with him.'

'What else did he tell you?'

'Lots of things. About the war, his life, the *Arandora Star*, his friends.'

'I hope you took notes,' says Antonio. I say nothing. I'm still not going to tell him about the tape.

Antonio pushes away Darius's ashy plate. I find myself staring at the black hairs on his wrist. 'Sophie,' he says, 'we have to talk.'

'OK,' I say. 'Talk.'

He stares at me and I can't read the expression on his face but suddenly it all seems far too intense for a family birthday party. I feel as if we're about to burst into flames, as the hot coals did at Cesare's last party, fifteen years ago. I stare back at him, saying nothing.

'Sophie!' my mother calls from the end of the table. 'I want to talk to you.'

'Sorry,' I say, getting up and mumbling something about the loo. I almost run out of the room and begin to descend the hundreds of stairs to it. Past the main restaurant where a man at the electric organ is singing 'Torna a Surriento', past the mysterious doors marked 'Private', until I reach the safety of the doors marked 'Signor' and 'Signora'.

'Sophie!'

I look round. Antonio has followed me, running so fast down the steep stairs that it looks as if he'll fall through the velvet curtain at the bottom.

'Sophie,' he says, 'we must talk.'

'What about?'

'What about? About what's going on with us. Are you still seeing Guido della Ravioli? Do you give a fuck about either of us?'

As he speaks, he gets closer and closer to me. I put up a hand, I suppose to ward him off, but he grabs it and pushes me back towards the curtain. I put up my other hand and find myself pulling him against me. Oh, Christ, I think, it's happening again. Antonio pushes me back through the curtain into a little cubbyhole full of coats. I flail backwards through the fur and the tweed and think of Lucy going through the wardrobe into Narnia. Antonio's lips are on mine and I am pressing against him greedily. Part of me says: Stop! What are you doing? In the middle of a family party you're about to screw your cousin in a cloakroom. But another, louder part of me says: More, more, more.

'I love you,' Antonio says into my neck.

'I love you too,' I say. I'm literally pulling his shirt off him and he has his hand up my skirt. 'We can't,' I say weakly.

'No, we can't,' agrees Antonio, pulling my tights down. I know that nothing can stop us now. Nothing, that is, except the sudden pulling across of the curtain and the sight of Cesare and Sylvia staring at us and my mother falling in a dead faint at our feet.

CHAPTER 5

It's two weeks later and I'm driving slowly through the wet Surrey countryside to visit my mother. Summer is nearly over and I have to go back to school tomorrow. In some ways, teachers are like children: you never escape that beginning-of-term feeling. Sometimes the kids say to me, 'What are you going to be when you grow up, Miss?' and I have to think, I really have to think, before I remember that I *am* grown-up, that this is what I do.

Last night, Antonio asked me if I was happy with my life.

'I don't know. Not particularly. Are you?'

'No,' he said. 'I'm fed up with journalism. Writing stupid articles that no one wants to read. But what else can I do?' I tell him that any adult male Catholic can become Pope.

My mother is diabetic. She has suspected for some time

but, typically, refused to see a doctor. That was what she had wanted to talk to me about before I rushed from the table and down the steps into mortal sin. Then she felt ill and, 'not wanting to be a nuisance', had decided to leave quietly, not even asking Carmine to get her coat. Worried, her parents accompanied her downstairs. I can imagine their descent: Cesare torn between worry and not wanting to miss the party, Sylvia walking carefully in her unaccustomed high heels, my mother stoical and white. Then the curtain pulled back and the Babylonian scene before them. Even two weeks later, I go hot and cold at the memory.

At first Cesare and Sylvia were too busy staring open-mouthed at me and Antonio to notice their daughter's collapse. Antonio, with great presence of mind, shouted, 'Emma!' while pulling his trousers up.

'Mum!' I squeaked, pulling down my skirt. In all my life, I have hardly ever known her to be ill: silent suffering was more her forte. Now she lay motionless at the foot of the stairs, looking oddly peaceful.

'Emma!' Sylvia took her hand. Cesare still said nothing: he was leaning against the wall and almost looking his age. Antonio called an ambulance on his mobile phone (a piece of pretentiousness that would otherwise have earned him Cesare's strongest censure). I went with my mother in the ambulance, holding her hand as she lay, looking curiously peaceful among the tubes and monitors.

At the all-too-familiar hospital, the doctors did all sorts of tests. Cesare and Sylvia turned up with Daniel, but when they heard that she was in no danger they went home. Antonio and I stayed. 'Someone must be here to take her home,' I said. I felt terribly guilty, not just about being found in flagrante but about all the times in my childhood when I hadn't loved my mother enough. We always seemed to be in the middle of some undeclared war – there was none of the easy affection between us that she shared with Daniel. I remembered the time she had come after me to Rome to try to get me to give up Robertino. I remembered sitting with her in the Piazza Navona, by the ornate fountain whose bronze figures, Roman legend has it, are averting their faces from the ugliness of the buildings opposite. We were sitting, exhausted by the heat and the arguments, watching the tourists paddle in the fountain. Finally the temptation was too much for me and I took off my espadrilles and bathed my feet in the cool green water.

'Don't do that,' said my mother, automatically.

'Why not?' I asked, with equal promptness. 'Does it embarrass you?'

'Yes,' said my mother. 'And there's nothing wrong with that. Being embarrassed is a sign of growing up.'

At the time, I had thought that this was rubbish. Home-counties, tight-lipped rubbish, typical of my mother. I was in Rome and I was in love and I could paddle in any fountain I liked, thank you very much. But now, having been caught by my mother in a far more embarrassing scene, I thought she might have a point. What is embarrassment if it isn't concern for other people's feelings? The same concern that stopped Cesare telling Guido about the riot because he thought he was gay. The same concern that made Laura turn up at Cesare's first wedding in her fur coat and best jewellery. In the past, I hadn't cared about my mother's feelings at all. I was her only daughter and I was throwing away all her hopes for my future. No wonder she had wept over every tourist attraction in Rome. Now, I vowed, as I sat in what seemed like the same waiting room as before, surrounded by what seemed like the same magazines, things would be different. I would take my mother's feelings into account. I would take *her* into account.

But where to start? I wonder, as I turn into the gravel drive at the ranch-style house in Surrey. What can I do to usher in this new era of mature mother-daughter relations? Bring her flowers every week? My mother would certainly complain about the mess caused by all those petals dropping wantonly over her clean surfaces. Take her up to town and go to the theatre together? I can't imagine my mother sitting through *The Tempest* or, worse still, any musical that involves people prancing around dressed as animals. We had a cat once but my mother was almost indecently pleased when it died. Animals, like flowers, just cause unnecessary mess. I'm sure I acquired Tybalt in defiance of her (effortlessly combining her twin dislikes of Shakespeare and cats), but in many other respects, I reflect glumly, I'm exactly like her. My jars, like my mother's, are neatly labelled. I, too, throw away drooping house plants because they look untidy.

I drive past the lawn, neatly mown in stripes. My father is out there, forcing nature to be even tidier, and I wave to him as I get out of the car. 'Hallo, darling.' He comes over, after carefully laying his trowel on the piece of green sacking laid out for the purpose.

'Hi, Dad. How's Mum?'

323

'Oh, much better today. She's thinking of doing the ironing.'

'My God. Won't the excitement be too much for her?'

When I was younger, I hated this house. I hated the smug half-circle of identical houses with their company cars parked neatly in the driveways. I hated the 'country-style' kitchen with its dried flowers and tricky pine corners. Real country kitchens, I used to say, have cats sleeping on the Aga, not wipe-clean surfaces and shiny double ovens. I hated the pretend open fire (in a smoke-free zone) and the useless poker set in front of it. I hated the bookshelves filled with matching hardback books – 'Bought by the yard,' I used to sneer.

In those days, my mother used to defend the house. At least, she used to say maddeningly, 'Well, it suits me. When you have your own house you can decorate it to suit you.' But over the last two weeks I've discovered that my mother, too, is fed up with the view of other people's Volvos. She has her heart set on a little flat in London, somewhere with a balcony so that she can watch the red buses going by. My father will miss his golf but he will – as usual – do as he's told. Only Daniel is moaning on about 'my home!' and 'all the good times we had there'. Name five, I tell him.

My mother is in the sitting room reading a library book. The television is resolutely off. If I were in her position, ordered to take things easy for a month, I'd be indulging in orgies of *Richard and Judy*, but my mother sees daytime TV as decadent.

'Hi,' I say, kissing her. 'I've brought you some olives.'

She loves olives. She says they remind her of Italy and perhaps they do (I'm prepared to allow her that). I've brought her Greek olives today, from the deli opposite my flat, and she digs greedily into the greasy paper carton. She offers them to me but I shake my head. 'I thought you liked olives,' she says.

'I do, but I feel a bit . . . you know . . . today.'

'You're working too hard,' says my mother automatically, although she must know that I've been doing nothing for two weeks but lie in the sun and have sex with Antonio.

'Have you thought any more about moving?' I ask, sitting down in an uncomfortable winged chair.

'I've been looking at some details. I wondered about Brixton but somebody told me it was full of . . .'

'Full of what, Mum?' I ask, hoping to catch her out in some indefensible racism.

'Wine bars. Too trendy for me. And Streatham isn't on the Tube, though it does have the park and the ice rink.'

'Ice rink? Since when have you liked ice skating?'

'Oh, I used to love it when I was young,' says my mother brightly, licking olive oil off her fingers. 'I thought I might take it up again – but then I thought maybe Clerkenwell.'

'*Clerkenwell?*'

'Yes, you know, near the City. You won't remember it but it's where my *nonno* and *nonna* used to live. I remember Nonna taking me to the Italian church – she used to walk all the way, very upright with her stick and funny hat with a pin through it. Anyway, it's very trendy now, Clerkenwell.'

I get up and look out of the French windows into the garden. Dad is raking the grass and, when he sees me, he does a big pantomime wave, pretending to overbalance. This used to make me laugh as a child but now, for some reason, it makes me sad. Clerkenwell, I'm thinking. Somehow it never occurred to me that my mother would have memories of the Italian Quarter. I had almost forgotten that she was part of the family but she's Cesare's daughter, Laura's grand-daughter. She can say '*nonna*' without being embarrassed.

'Dad'll miss the garden,' I say at last.

'He'll get over it,' says my mother. 'It's just a place where he can get away from me, the garden. In London, there'll be lots more places for him to hide in.'

Over these last weeks, I feel as if I've got to know my mother all over again. I remember her as sharp but restrained, always hinting at something but covering it with a layer of cool good taste. I can never really remember her raising her voice: her weapons were the fingertips pressed to the forehead and the tactical migraine. 'Don't start, Sophie,' I remember her saying to me. Perhaps that was why our relationship always seemed so stultified – it never had a chance to start. Now I know that she can be cutting and cruel and often very funny, and I like her much better for it. On the first day when I took her home from hospital and settled her in her flounced beige bed with a glass of fruit juice (for the sugar) by her side, she looked up at me and said slyly, 'You and Antonio. Who would have thought it?'

I muttered something, deeply embarrassed.

'Of course, I always knew he liked you but I didn't think you liked him. I never knew why. I think he's gorgeous.'

If it's true that Antonio has always fancied me (and he says it is) I certainly didn't fancy him when we were young. He was too fresh-faced and eager to please, crawling to Cesare about Italy. I prefer the older, more battered version. Perhaps I've always preferred older men and it's just that now I'm 'older' myself.

Now my mother says suddenly, 'Are you seeing Antonio tonight?'

'Yes,' I say.

'That's every night this week. Why don't you just move in together?'

'We're thinking about it.'

My mother stares past me and says dreamily, 'You young people do too much thinking. Why don't you just get on and do it?'

'I don't remember you being so much in favour of direct action when you came all the way to Rome to drag me away from Robertino.'

'That was different. He was years older than you. And a libertine.'

'Libertine. That's a good Victorian word.'

'I suppose I was jealous of you,' says my mother. 'You were in Italy, doing the whole Italian thing. I never had the nerve.

I wanted to go and live in Italy before going to college, but Daddy wouldn't let me.'

'Why not?'

'I don't know. I think he didn't really want any of us to know too much about Italy. He wanted us to be pro-Italy but his Italy, not the real one. That's why he never taught us Italian. He didn't even want us to speak Italian. That's why he never admits how fluent you are.'

'Why did you do what he said?' I ask.

Mum sighs and takes another olive. 'Oh, I don't know, Sophie. We were too good, too obedient, Louisa and me. Louisa rebelled a bit, but only to the extent of going to music college and not Oxford. I never really had a career. Oh, I know I trained to be a teacher but I was really just waiting to marry Simon and have children.'

'Are you glad you had children?' I ask my mother.

'Of course.' Mum looks shocked. 'Of course I'm glad I had you and Daniel. I'm just saying that I wish I'd done a bit of living first. That's why I think you should just go out there now and do what you want. Marry Antonio, live with him, whatever. Just go for it.'

*

I'm meeting Antonio in Clerkenwell. He has to visit the offices of the *Guardian* (he writes a spoof column in the persona of an Old Labour-style trade unionist called Alf Pickett) and it seems convenient. But I also have another motive. Ever since I heard Cesare's story, I've wanted to see Clerkenwell for myself. To see the streets where my great-grandfather once sold ice cream, pushing his decorated cart like a little gondola.

Although I've lived in London for eight years, I've never been to Clerkenwell, except once, as a student, to a rather druggy party there. But now, walking along Farringdon Road, I'm not sure what I'm expecting to see. The streets are full of wine bars and people in pinstriped suits talking on mobile phones. There are Italian restaurants and delicatessens but, then, there are in any part of London. At random, I turn off into a side street and find myself looking into the window of Terroni's, the famous Italian delicatessen. The window is full of salamis sporting little Italian flags, and inside there are shelves and shelves of bottles, like a magician's store. I decide to buy Mum some genuine Clerkenwell olives. I go in, hearing the doorbell ring with old-fashioned jollity.

There are two men in the shop, both elderly and

Italian-looking. A pretty dark-haired girl is serving them. They all stop talking when I go in. 'A quarter of stuffed olives, please,' I say.

The two men stare at me in a very Italian way and, suddenly, I'm excited, as if I've stepped into the past. The girl weighs my olives on a grocer's scale and, on impulse, I turn to the men and say, in Italian: 'Have you lived in Clerkenwell long?' They stare at me. 'My grandfather was born in Clerkenwell.' I beam. 'Has the area changed much? I mean, it used to be the Italian Quarter . . .' My voice trails away.

The tallest man backs away a little. 'I don't know what you're talking about,' he says, 'I don't speak Spanish.'

I look helplessly at the girl behind the counter, who is holding out my olives. 'I'm from Liverpool,' she says, with a shrug.

I meet Antonio in one of the wine bars. He's sitting moodily under a sign that says 'No Smoking'. As soon as he sees me, he jumps up. 'Let's go somewhere else. This place is giving me a headache. And they keep putting fruit in my beer . . .'

We go to a small dark pub off Saffron Hill. Inside, it's tiny, with battered leather chairs and one depressed-looking barman reading the *Sporting Life*. I try, and fail, to imagine Cesare coming in here with his posh friend Piers to shock the locals with their silk scarves and racing slang. Cesare never has been much of a pub-goer.

Funnily enough, though, Cesare and I were in a pub the only time we spoke of my relationship with Antonio. It was about a week after my mother's collapse and I had driven him over to see her. On the way back he had asked, uncharacteristically, to be taken to a pub. 'Emma never has any proper drink in the house. Did you hear her offer me a herbal tea? *A herbal tea.*' His voice rose incredulously.

So we stopped in a modern pub outside Weybridge, all chrome and smoked glass. Cesare liked it. He hates anything old-fashioned and, to him, this looked like the height of modernity. I ordered mineral water, and he had a double whisky.

He drank it quickly and put the glass down with a bang. 'So,' he said, 'you and Antonio.' It was as if he was continuing a conversation we had been having but, in fact, neither of us had mentioned Antonio since the night in the restaurant. Antonio had sent my mother flowers but had prudently kept out of Cesare's way.

Cesare was looking at me intently. To avoid his gaze, I

started fiddling with my drink mat, spinning it round and round on the chrome tabletop. Finally, Cesare said, 'It's a bit close to home.'

'We're only second cousins,' I said quickly.

'Even so. Cousins. There's a blood tie.' He laughed shortly. 'God knows, being in love with my cousin was one problem I didn't have.'

'But you've made it up now, haven't you, you and Aunt Rosaria?'

He gave a noncommittal grunt. Then he asked, 'Do you love him?'

'Yes.'

Cesare picked up his drink and swallowed the last bit of melted ice. 'Well, mind you look after him. He's a sensitive boy, Antonio.'

'*Antonio*? Sensitive?'

'Yes. Like his great-grandmother, Auntie Clara. He loves you, I know, he always has. Just don't hurt him. Do you want another drink?'

Now Antonio lights a cigarette and offers me one. I say, 'No, thanks.'

'Are you giving up?'

'Maybe.'

'How was your mum?'

'OK. Still talking about coming to live in London. I can't believe it! After all those years in that awful house.'

'Maybe she thought it was a nice place for you and Daniel to grow up. Like Melissa thinks about America.'

'Have you heard any more about that?' I ask.

Antonio shrugs. 'She seems to be having second thoughts. Maybe she's realised that it's not all like you see on TV and she won't necessarily get a loft apartment in Manhattan and an assortment of beautiful friends in a wine bar.'

'Sounds a bit like Clerkenwell,' I say.

Antonio laughs. 'What do you think of the Italian Quarter?'

I tell him about the men in Terroni's. 'I just wanted to see a bit of how it was in the old days.'

'You should see it during the Easter procession. Statues and bunting and old ladies in veils. I covered it once for a local paper.'

'I'd like to see it.'

'Well, we'll go next year, shall we? Do you want to eat? I'm starving. Let's find an authentic Spanish restaurant.'

'Let's go for a walk first.'

We pass estate agents displaying pictures of trendy apartments at astronomical prices – my mother could never afford to live here. Maybe Antonio's right, and real Italian life *is* still here, waiting underground ready to emerge with a burst of Ave Marias at Easter. But it's certainly nowhere in sight this evening. There are a few restaurants with people sitting outside pretending it's still summer, but mostly it's office blocks and converted warehouses bristling with entryphones and 'Sold' signs. And maybe there isn't a real Italian Quarter any more. Maybe Italians are so well assimilated that they don't need a separate identity. Then I think back to when I was at primary school and a teacher is asking me, 'Does your grandfather have his own restaurant?' At the time I didn't realise what she was saying – I was only dimly ashamed of Cesare for doing something boring with cars instead of something exciting with ice cream – but now I understand: Italians are waiters but some go as far as owning their own restaurants. And all the fashion statements in the world won't change that.

We walk as far as Queen Anne's Square before I can tell Antonio what I've been waiting to tell him all day. I'm pregnant. I did a test this morning but I was almost sure already. I'm having a baby.

'Are you certain?' asks Antonio, after a moment's silence.

'Yes,' I say, and then suddenly, without warning, I start to cry.

Antonio immediately takes me in his arms. 'Don't cry, Sophie. It's wonderful news. Amazing. We'll get married. Move to Rome. Do anything you like. I love you. It'll be fantastic, you'll see.'

But, of course, it's not as simple as that. Because my day in the park with Guido didn't end with my receiving his declaration of love with cool, kindly dignity, but with our going back to my flat, talking through the long afternoon about war, Italy and Fascism, drinking gallons of red wine and, eventually, having sex on the sofa, under the horrified eyes of Tybalt and Rocky. I know that it was once compared to hundreds of times with Antonio, but what if the baby turns out to have bright red hair and a liking for Alsatians?

And it's more complicated even than that because, when I flew back to England in a daze after Robertino dumped me I was – of course – pregnant. At the time, compared to the trauma of losing Robertino, the abortion didn't seem like such a big deal. I sleepwalked through it, telling no one. It's only in recent years that it's come back to haunt me, like one of the apparitions in *Macbeth*. The sight of Robertino's sons at Fausto's funeral was like a wound to the heart. O Sacred Heart. So I cry and cry and Antonio holds me and says he loves me. And that is the thing I cling to. I love Antonio. I've come through this whole weird summer, delving into my family's past, with that truth intact. I love Antonio.

Eventually we walk on. It's getting a bit cold and I put my jacket on. My fingers close on something smooth and cold in the pocket. Cesare's father's medal. Giuseppe's St Christopher. I wonder what he thought, all those years ago, when he set out for England. Was he sure he'd find success and happiness? Did he wonder what life would be like for his children and grandchildren? Could he have imagined a world where his great-granddaughter would be pregnant and not know who was the father? I wonder why I don't feel worse and realise that it is because somewhere, deep down, I think that it will be *all right*, even if I have to tell Antonio. I take a deep, shuddering sigh.

Antonio puts his arm round me. 'Cheer up. It'll be a lovely baby. Just think of all the Italian blood it'll have.'

And that, at least, is true.